Write Me a Love Story

Also by Ravinder Singh

The Belated Bachelor Party

E-Singles

A Kiss in the Air
My Mother's Boyfriend
My Ex
An Unfinished Melody
The U-Turn
Love & Lies
The Runaway Groom
Love Bites

Write Me a Love Story

RAVINDER SINGH

HarperCollins *Publishers* India

First published in India by
HarperCollins *Publishers* in 2021
A-75, Sector 57, Noida, Uttar Pradesh 201301, India
www.harpercollins.co.in

2 4 6 8 10 9 7 5 3 1

P-ISBN: 978-93-5422-320-4
E-ISBN: 978-93-5422-326-6

Typeset in 11/14.7 Sabon LT Std at
Manipal Technologies Limited, Manipal

Printed and bound at
Thomson Press (India) Ltd

To Mom. For everything.

1

'Come on, guys! He'll be here any minute now.'

Maaya's tone was authoritative as she took charge of the situation. She had already explained everything to the team a week ago and yet, it seemed to her that not everyone had understood the gravity of the situation. It was so frustrating!

After all, *his* arrival in their office was a big deal. She had put in a lot of groundwork over the last six months to make it possible. And now that the D-day was here, the damn projector in the meeting room was still not working, and the editor she'd chosen to attend the meeting was yet to arrive.

'And ... what's that? The tuna sandwiches, coconut cookies and banana bread are being served on *plastic* plates!? *Oh God!*'

After all, she had made it a point to order the snacks of his choice from *his* favourite confectionary, and this is what Kaka, the office cafeteria guy, had done with them.

Seeing the scrumptious snacks she had especially ordered from a high-end confectionary in South Bombay placed haphazardly on the chipped plates meant for the daily use by the office staff, Maaya's blood boiled.

When are these guys going to become smart enough to differentiate between a special occasion and everyday affairs?

Thankfully, just as she turned towards the door, she saw Kaka passing by the meeting room. She immediately pushed open the glass door and called for him.

'Kaka, please take this back and use the white Opalware crockery.' Maaya was crystal clear as she gave him the instructions.

Sensing the anger and the urgency in her tone, Kaka immediately flung into action. He rushed into the meeting room and picked up the plates of snacks on the table, apologetically leaving the room with them.

'And please bring everything along with coffee once the meeting starts, and not before,' Maaya said to his retreating back.

She then picked up the intercom and made a two-second-and-three-word-long call. 'Romance Room. Now!'

To an outsider this might have sounded strange, but not to the people who worked at PaperInk, a publishing house which had named its meeting rooms after the genres it published.

In less than two minutes, the IT guy came running into the room. Maaya glared at him and then immediately shifted her gaze to the projector installed overhead. The man understood exactly what that look meant. In no time, he was busy fixing the machine.

Half a dozen people stood around the giant table in the Romance Room, admiring Maaya's ability to put things right so quickly. She commanded that place. And why not? After all, she had earned her position as the editor-in-chief of PaperInk. From the security guard at the entrance gate to the CEO in the corner office, people had come and gone in the publishing house's decade-long existence, while Maaya had been its only constant. She had almost single-handedly fuelled the rise of the fastest-growing publishing house in the country.

PaperInk had begun as a vanity-publishing outfit, a place for debut authors who had been rejected by other publishers to self-publish their books. Gradually, over the years, it shifted its focus and transformed into a well-known traditional publishing house, thereby commanding more respect in the publishing world. To its credit – and a fact that was a source of pride for its employees – many of its successful authors were first-time writers. The company meant a great deal to Maaya, and she often felt it was a pity that she didn't own it; that after all this, she was only an employee there.

She took immense pride in calling PaperInk her first home. It was where she would spend most of her day; one reason why she did everything possible to get the budget for the renovation of the premises approved, so that it could be redone as per her taste. At forty-three, she was doing very well for herself and, of course, for her employer.

The IT guy asked Maaya for her laptop. He had to connect it to the projector.

Maaya pushed it towards him and got up from her chair. She pulled out her mobile from the pocket of her red jumpsuit and pressed on the last dialled number. Holding the phone to her ear, she moved towards the door.

Outside the Romance Room was her tastefully designed office on the seventeenth floor of the Infinity Tower in the Bandra Kurla Complex.

The place looked breathtakingly creative. It was unlike any other office. Instead of the usual sense of order and drab efficiency of most workspaces, the interiors of PaperInk radiated joy and fun. There were no cubicles; instead long, dark teak tables, which rested on black cast iron frames, filled the space. Their surfaces were rough, giving an impression of being handmade by woodworkers who had chiseled them well but forgotten to smoothen them. The entire effect was rustic and charming.

Up above them, black cast-iron panels ran across the entire length and breadth of the extra high ceiling. And from them hung scores of thick jute ropes, all ending in LED filament bulbs. Suspended above the teak wooden workstations, the fashionable bulbs gave the whole place a retro vibe – a testament to the urban chic look that Maaya had had in mind.

Beyond the hanging lights was the exposed red brick wall which ran across the length of that space. While the other three sides of the office were glass façades, giving the employees a stunning view of the Mumbai skyline, it was this red brick wall that really defined the space. It was the creativity nest for PaperInk's employees.

The left side of this wall was covered with a ten-foot wide floor to ceiling bookshelf, lined with hundreds of books. On the other end, the red bricks were covered with a big blackboard, on which, with coloured chalks, people had doodled their creative ideas, like book titles and cover design concepts. And in the centre of the wall, between the blackboard and the shelves, several cover designs of new releases were pinned up on a cushioned-board.

The dull-grey tiled floor completed the rugged, rustic look of the space. On the wooden tables, book dummies, printed covers, books and manuscript cluttered the numerous workstations. And then there were the usual laptops and personal belongings of the people who worked at PaperInk.

As Maaya stared at her sanctuary of creativity, she frowned. Her call hadn't been answered, and the full ring had died its natural death.

Where the hell is she? Maaya thought and sighed in disappointment. Slipping her phone back into her pocket, she returned to the Romance Room and took her seat.

She began to go over the plan with the representatives from the sales and marketing teams again. This was a big presentation, and she needed to know exactly what they were going to say. The CEO himself was only a call away, waiting in his corner office. Maaya would call the CEO once *he* arrived.

About a few hundred metres away from Infinity Tower, in the parking lot, a German-made luxury sedan circled the perimeter, trying to find a vacant spot. But it was already 11:00 a.m. – too late for anyone to find a parking space in Mumbai's busy corporate sector. After spending more than five minutes circling the space in vain, the sedan also acquired a companion – an Indian-manufactured hatchback.

And then, in a sheer stroke of good luck, a car pulled out of its spot three lanes ahead of them, moving towards the exit gate.

'Bingo!' cried the sedan's driver and picked up speed.

The hatchback followed suit. Inside the car, the ringing cellphone fell silent and a missed call alert chimed. 'Come on! Come on! Come on!' the hatchback's driver mumbled, changing gears.

Thirteen seconds later, on the other side of the parking lot, the sedan in front of the hatchback found out that the recently emptied spot it had made a beeline for was slightly small for it.

'Damn!' the sedan's driver said, hitting the steering wheel in frustration. But it was too early to give up. The driver looked around and wondered whether there was a chance to fit the car into the spot if the vehicle was reverse parked. But that would involve pulling ahead and then reversing the car. In a split second, the driver decided to go for it.

Just as the sedan was pulling ahead, the hatchback reached the spot. The hatchback driver noticed the sedan moving past the spot, and was overjoyed. Unfortunately, it was short-lived, because the sedan suddenly stopped moving. Its brake lights came on.

'Oh no! OH NO!' the driver in the hatchback screamed and honked.

The sedan began to roll back. But there still wasn't enough space. It moved ahead again and then rolled back again. Once again, the car proved too big for the spot. The driver realized that this was going to be tricky and he'd have to be very precise.

The hatchback driver waited in disappointment. There was nothing else to do anyway. It didn't have enough space to overtake the sedan and move on in order to find a new space.

Even after four tries, the sedan couldn't fit into the spot, but with every new attempt of going back and forth, its chances looked slightly better. The hatchback continued to wait, honking every few seconds in frustration. Time was running out.

After a few minutes more, the driver in the hatchback had had enough. The mobile phone rang yet again – it was from same number that had called twice already. There was no way the driver could miss the call for the third time. The sedan rolled forward yet again in order to try another reverse parking manoeuvre – maybe this time it would finally make it. But no one would ever find out whether that was true, because just as the sedan turned its brake lights on to begin going, the hatchback zoomed ahead and took the spot.

Immediately, there was a loud, long honk from the sedan.

'HEY!' shouted the driver. *He* rolled down the window and looked back at the car that had taken his spot.

She climbed out of the hatchback and locked her car.

The woman, who must have been in her late twenties, was wearing a light-brown kurti and white palazzos. She had a diamond-shaped face, wheatish complexion and short-length hair that covered only the nape of her neck. She looked lean and just a little taller than the average Indian woman; perhaps somewhere between 5'5" and 5'6". Her sharp facial features, he noticed, were attractive. But that moment was not about appreciating her looks.

Talking to someone on the phone, she looked like she was in a tearing rush, enough to even ignore someone shouting at her.

'HEY, YOU!' he screamed, louder this time to demand her attention. When she didn't stop or turn around, he stepped out of his car.

'I'M TALKING TO *YOU*, MISS,' he said, marching towards the woman, who was quickly walking away.

She finally stopped and turned around, abruptly finishing the call and hanging up on whoever was on the other end.

His face, she thought, looked familiar. If it wasn't for those tinted aviators he was wearing, she might have been able to remember where she'd seen him before. But she was bad at remembering faces anyway. Despite the circumstances, she did notice that he was tall, dark and breathtakingly handsome. His dense curly hair bounced as he walked. He was wearing a dark grey blazer with a pink collared T-shirt underneath. His off-white chinos stylishly ended half an inch above his brown moccasin shoes.

His brisk walk came to a sudden halt just an arm's length from her. She could smell the musky fragrance he was wearing. And the scent was refreshing.

She knew what was going to unfold. She was at fault and now she'd have to defend the indefensible. She suddenly wished that the person standing in front of her wasn't so good-looking and did not smell so nice. Had that been the case, maybe it would have been easier to throw any vague reason at him, even at the risk of inviting his wrath.

Meanwhile, the man fumed. This lady had not yet acknowledged his arrival, at least not with words. He threw his hands up and finally spoke first, confronting her.

'What was that?' he asked, his body tense.

She took her time to collect her thoughts. *I should apologize and let him know why I did this. After all, it was an emergency.*

However, just when she was about to speak, his next words changed her mind.

'Who the fuck do you think you are?' he yelled, running out of patience.

Instead of accepting her fault, she frowned and asked, 'WHAT? What did you just say to me?' She paused for a second, crossed her arms and added, 'Is that how you talk to a woman?'

'Oh!' he scoffed, smiling sarcastically. He looked up at the sky for a moment and then shifted his gaze back to her. 'The woman card! What a perfect time to play it, isn't it?' And then, to her utter horror, he clapped slowly. Three times!

Anger may insult you, but sarcasm humiliates you. It sets your mind on fire. And then the only way to douse this fire is to give it back, word for word.

'Men who don't understand chivalry often hide behind words like "Oh, you are playing the woman card",' she said and tossed back her hair. Her eyes settled on his shades.

'And that act,' he said, pointing at her parked car, 'deserves chivalry?'

She wanted to refute that, to say something – anything. But she miserably failed. How could she defend what she had done?

Instead, she tried to be dismissive.

'Well, what do you want?' she asked.

'Oh! So, you want me tell you what you already know?'

So not only you are gorgeous, you also have a way with words. His manner of speaking and the style and confidence with which he delivered his biting comments impressed her. How she hated being at the receiving end of this man's wrath, when she knew he was in the right! If only she could roll back time, she wouldn't do what she had done. What bothered her even more was that instead of accepting her mistake, she had ended up defending it.

If I change tack now, what impression will I make on him? It would only make things worse, she decided, and continued to defend herself.

'I did what I had to do. You cannot block my way and then take all the time in the world to fit in your big car, especially during rush hour!'

'Blocked your way?' he asked cynically. 'Ah! And here I was thinking that this car comes with a reverse gear.' He pointed at her hatchback.

It took her a couple of seconds to connect the dots and understand that he meant that she could have turned around and taken a detour. But when she did, she got onto a whole new tangent altogether.

'Oh, so *that's* how people with luxury cars mock smaller cars?'

He was momentarily shocked by her reply, uncertain about how she had arrived at that conclusion. And then he smiled a lazy, mocking smile.

'Un-freaking-believable!' He sighed, and then added, 'You really will do whatever it takes to win this argument. Isn't that so?'

Knowing that she had taken a route she wasn't proud of, she didn't reply. Instead, she kept staring at him. The whole situation was quite awkward but she preferred not saying anything, simply because nothing else came to her mind.

He shook his head in disbelief and chuckled. To argue any more was pointless anyway. He turned back and headed towards his car to find a new parking spot, if there was one left.

As she watched him walk away, she was filled with guilt and misery. That he had refused to indulge any further in the argument; that he had instead chosen to walk away from her; that she was completely in the wrong here – all of this made things worse, made her guilt multiply tenfold. She wanted to call out to him, to stop him and say sorry. But it was already too much of a mess and it was too late to clean it up. So she did the only thing she could. She let him walk away.

Her phone began ringing again, summoning her attention. She turned around and began running out of the parking lot. It was time for work, and this unpleasantness needed to be put on the backburner. Anyway, she would never see the man again and soon she'd forget what had happened.

2

'Hiii Abhimanyuuu!' Maaya sang in delight as soon as the person she had been waiting for so eagerly walked into the reception. 'It's such a pleasure to have you here in our office today,' she added with a bright, welcoming smile.

'Thank you!' Abhimanyu said, extending his hand and adding, 'I am so sorry for making you guys wait.'

'Oh, don't worry about that,' Maaya said, intentionally ignoring the offered handshake and grabbing his shoulders instead. She went for a cheek-to-cheek hug. Abhimanyu hadn't anticipated that and stiffened slightly, while she inhaled deeply, breathing in the scent of his musk cologne.

'Traffic?' she asked as she finally pulled back.

Abhimanyu shook his head. 'Parking,' he replied simply.

'We should have sent him my car, Maaya!'

On hearing the confident, booming voice, Maaya turned around, a smile on her face.

Peter D'Souza, the CEO of PaperInk, had walked into the reception area too, just in time to welcome the leading romance writer in the country to their office.

'Oh yes! I am so sorry! That should have occurred to me!' Maaya said to Abhimanyu, briefly shutting her eyes and tapping her head with her knuckles in an exaggerated gesture of regret.

'Oh, there was absolutely no need for that,' Abhimanyu said as he turned to shake Peter's hand. Before the door closed behind Peter, Abhimanyu got a peek at the office space stretching behind them.

'Oh boy!' He whistled softly. He was impressed despite himself.

Peter turned to look at the space too, aware that it had caught Abhimanyu's eye. 'How do you like it?' he asked.

After a beat, Abhimanyu summarized his thoughts in two words. 'Very … retro!'

Peter's chest swelled with pride. 'It's all been done by this wonderful lady right here,' he acknowledged, putting one hand on Maaya's shoulder. Abhimanyu noticed how Maaya reciprocated by placing her own hand over Peter's.

'Only after he approved it,' Maaya said.

Abhimanyu smiled to himself at this show of mutual appreciation.

'Oh! I approve a dozen things every day. Not everything turns into gold.'

The CEO gestured to both of them to follow him through the doors into PaperInk's office space. 'Come on! Let's take you inside. It's time to begin!'

On the way, while Peter tried to engage Abhimanyu in casual chit-chat, the latter's eyes were busy scanning the length and breadth of the office. It was one hell of a creative space.

As the trio approached the conference room, the team inside watched through the glass walls and got up from their chairs to welcome the author.

Outside, Abhimanyu balked at the nameplate on the door. 'What on earth …' he said, his eyes widening in surprise.

'Before you get the wrong idea, let me tell you something,' Peter began. 'You see, we have named our meeting rooms after the genres we publish.'

'Aah!' Abhimanyu sighed in relief. The words 'Romance Room' had given him a moment's pause.

'So, on your right, next to this is Thriller Room. Then there's Mythology Room, and so on,' Peter finished with a smile.

'And it would be blasphemy to take the country's leading romance writer to any other room,' Maaya said, pushing the door open for him.

'Boys and girls, may I present to you, the king of romance in India!' she announced as she walked in after him.

People cheered, clapped and welcomed Abhimanyu to PaperInk.

There was a gentle smile on his lips and a twinkle in his eyes as he looked at everyone across the table. Any other author, perhaps, would have felt a bit embarrassed at such an extensive welcome or, at the very least, would have faked embarrassment in return. But Abhimanyu was a different breed. He owned and savoured the adulation; looked right into the eyes of the person praising him. It was as if it gave him a kind of high.

He was seasoned at this, anyway. Years of interacting with his fandom, which primarily comprised young women, had instilled confidence in him. These women, while reading his books, would imagine themselves as the leading lady of his stories. Their imagination wouldn't just stop there but go even further, visualizing Abhimanyu himself as the male protagonist they were falling for. Such was his spell on them. No wonder he was called the king of romance in the world of Indian writing.

Abhimanyu waited for everyone to settle down and then, in his signature style, briefly closed his eyes and spread his hands, as if embracing the room.

Meanwhile, Maaya noticed the empty chair. A fresh notebook and a pen were kept on the table in front of it.

'Thank you, everyone,' Abhimanyu said softly and simply, a touch of humility in his voice as he accepted their compliments. Then, nodding once more with a smile, he took his chair, which was right across from the screen on which the now-functioning overhead projector flashed the words 'PaperInk welcomes Abhimanyu Razdan!' in big, colourful letters.

While Abhimanyu's attention was on the screen, Maaya whispered to Nakul, the design head who was sitting next to her, 'Where the hell is she?' She looked pointedly at the empty chair across the table.

Nakul pursed his lips, raised his eyebrows and shrugged to show that he had no clue.

Maaya was pissed, but she didn't let her face reveal that. She had more important tasks at hand.

The first couple of minutes of the meeting were spent in formally introducing each member of the team to Abhimanyu. Apart from Maaya and the CEO, others included two representatives from the marketing and publicity team, the design head, the CFO and the sales head, and a couple of members of the sales and distribution department. The only person missing at the table was an editor – the very same editor whose chair was currently empty.

After the introductions, Maaya opened her laptop and went straight into the presentation that her team had put together for Abhimanyu.

The purpose of this meeting was to finalize the offer that PaperInk had made to Abhimanyu. They were proposing a three-book contract with him. Abhimanyu's first six novels, published by the Indian division of a leading international publishing house, had all been blockbusters, but with the last one, his contract with them had come to an end.

Of course, his existing publishers wanted to sign him up for his future books, just like every other publishing house in the country. But Abhimanyu had raised his royalties. His new ask was jaw-droppingly high. No author in the Indian subcontinent had ever managed to get that kind of a deal for themselves. If Abhimanyu did get one of the publishing houses to agree, it was going to set a new benchmark for the Indian publishing industry.

Rumour had it, though, that it wasn't just the money that was a conflict of interest between Abhimanyu's current publishers and him. It was the fact that they had also acquired Rizwan Siddiqui's subsequent works.

Rizwan Siddiqui was another bestselling author who had, of late, made a name for himself with his last few books. His books were also read by the same demographic as Abhimanyu's – young adult Indians.

With his superb networking skills and a mammoth PR spend, Rizwan had recently managed to become a bigger brand than Abhimanyu. However, the quintessential factor which worked for Abhimanyu, something that made him the publishers' blue-eyed boy, was the return on investment his books brought in. The sheer volume of his sales, without too much being spent on publicity, was unprecedented. Organically, each of his titles would sell more copies than those of Rizwan. And yet it was Rizwan's titles that made it to Page 3 of the tabloids, something Abhimanyu was jealous of. Rizwan was a regular in the posh social circuit of media, politics and glamour. To stay in the news, he constantly invited the feature editors of different newspapers over for drinks or bought space for himself in their publications. That had, more or less, been his modus operandi, and had made him the brand he was today. Money was never an issue for him. He pumped as much as he wanted into the promotions of his books to boost their sales. To put it simply, he knew how to buy fame, whereas Abhimanyu was building his reputation slowly and, at the same time, earning his living from his books.

It wasn't as if Rizwan's work wasn't good; it certainly was. However, when it came to popular fiction, Abhimanyu was a class apart, which was why he envied Rizwan even more, because in spite of being ahead of him in terms of writing, not getting the same kind of easy fame and following as his rival sucked big time.

They both wrote in the same genre and yet, when it came to plot and style, their stories were very different. Abhimanyu wrote about love and Rizwan wrote steamy romances. Abhimanyu's stories were deep dives into the innocence of emotions. Rizwan's, on the other hand, would make people fantasize about their deepest desires. Abhimanyu's intimate descriptions would end at a kiss, while Rizwan's would begin with one. He would go to the extent of describing an orgasm, while Abhimanyu would leave things to his readers' imagination.

With every new title, they would both make it to the top of the bestsellers' chart, but it was Abhimanyu who would stay there for a longer duration. That always pained Rizwan. He would make up for it by organizing elite launches for himself, with Bollywood guests unveiling his books. The national media would cover these events, and public figures with verified handles on social media would talk about them. All this burned Abhimanyu from the inside, and Rizwan knew that well. Which is why, when Abhimanyu's publishers expressed an interest in getting Rizwan on board, the latter agreed readily.

The rivalry between the two authors was no secret in the Indian publishing industry. As both wrote popular romances, they were often put on the same panel discussions at literature festivals, and the audience had often witnessed their sarcastic exchanges on stage.

Once, when they were both on stage during a popular festival, discussing the sales of their books, Abhimanyu, in a veiled attack on Rizwan, had said, 'One can always buy back his copies in bulk to enter the bestsellers' list.'

Rizwan had immediately caught onto those words and thrown them back at Abhimanyu, replying, 'Is my friend here sharing his secret recipe out in the open?'

The next day, a story about the spat was splashed across the front page of a newspaper which was one of the top sponsors of the festival. Abhimanyu's and Rizwan's fans had had a busy day sparring on Twitter.

Abhimanyu now turned his attention to the presentation before him, and Maaya had just begun to walk him through it when the glass doors of the room opened. Everyone looked at the newcomer and Maaya breathed a sigh of relief. Asmita, the literary fiction editor, was finally here.

Asmita looked at the guest seated at the table – the man who they were all gathered here for. She froze.

Now that the tinted sunglasses were no longer on his face, she finally realized who he was. The ground beneath her feet shook.

Abhimanyu's eyes stared back at her, widening in surprise. *So, I have the distinct displeasure of meeting you again,* they seemed to say.

Her lips trembled and for a second, she felt like she'd lose control. And then, gathering herself, she turned to Maaya.

'Abhimanyu, this is Asmita Mullick,' Maaya introduced the latecomer. 'Three out of the seven novels she worked on last year were longlisted for literary awards.'

A bleak sound managed to escape Asmita's lips. 'Ha … hello.'

The other people in the room noticed that something awkward was going on, but it was difficult to pinpoint exactly what. Usually, Asmita was suave and sophisticated. Maybe she was just awestruck at seeing this bestselling author in their office?

Abhimanyu took his sweet time before finally smiling at her. 'Hi,' he said and then, after a tiny pause, added, '*Asmita.*'

She didn't miss the underlying sarcasm in his tone, though she was the only one in the room who could detect it. She walked across the room and took her seat. The blood pulsed in her veins, and her heart was beating so hard that she wondered how no one else could hear it.

Maaya began the presentation.

The initial slides were all about PaperInk; who they were, how they were positioned in the market, the works they had published, the volumes they had sold, the awards and recognition their titles had won till date and so on.

Abhimanyu was barely interested. None of it mattered to him. After all, he was coming from a publishing house which had way better credentials. All that he cared about was what PaperInk was planning and willing to do for *his* books. Besides, the woman sitting to his left was occupying a percentage of his brain and he was finding it hard to concentrate on the information being thrown at him. His mind was busy trying to find ways to settle scores with her, now that he clearly had the upper hand.

Asmita gazed blankly at the screen before her. In her head, she was already rehearsing an apology. She was already so grateful to Abhimanyu for not spilling the beans in front of everyone or, worse, shouting at her as soon as he saw her. By some unsaid agreement, the two had kept their poker faces and pretended as if they were meeting each other for the first time.

In the second half of the presentation, Maaya laid out the big picture – what it would be like for Abhimanyu to publish his next book with PaperInk and what they had in mind for him.

While as an independent Indian publishing house, PaperInk's growth trajectory was impressive, it was still not at par with the multinational publishing houses. Their pedigree of A-list authors was something PaperInk only aspired to. Maaya knew that if she wanted to take the company to their level, she needed big names. Abhimanyu Razdan was one. She was ambitious and had Peter's backing. She walked Abhimanyu through her grand idea of what it meant for them to publish him and what they could do for him – things that perhaps other publishers wouldn't be willing to do.

Abhimanyu was pleased to see the royal treatment he would receive at PaperInk. It also gave him a much-needed ego massage, something he would deny openly but secretly loved. Even though he had still not made up his mind to join PaperInk, the idea of being a big fish in a smaller pond was appealing to him.

Maaya spoke ambitiously and, in the end, summed up by saying, 'And at PaperInk, your first book with us will not only be the biggest book of the year, but our biggest till date.'

Abhimanyu concealed his pride with a tiny smile.

When she was done, Maaya let others in the room take turns, telling Abhimanyu about their plans and contributions to his publishing process.

Abhimanyu listened carefully as they briefed him on design, marketing and publicity, and all the other logistical details, nodding every once in a while. He took everything that was pitched to him with a pinch of salt. He was a seasoned author and had seen this industry very closely, dealing with many a fake promise. He knew the great lengths to which publishers would go to get him on board. For the time being he basked in all the attention he was receiving. And, amidst all this, he was eagerly waiting for the editor's turn. It was going to bring him sweet pleasure to watch her gather her courage and present her bit to him. He couldn't wait.

'What about the editing?' he directed the question at Maaya, knowingly avoiding Asmita as if she was inferior.

'You will have me for the plot and concept-level editing, and for the detailed copyediting there is Shalini, our commercial fiction editor. She is on a week-long leave,' Maaya answered.

Surprised that she hadn't taken Asmita's name, Abhimanyu shifted his eyes from Maaya to Asmita and then back at Maaya.

Understanding his unspoken question, Maaya said, 'Asmita handles literary fiction. She is filling in for Shalini. Should you have any questions on our editing processes, Asmita will be happy to take them.'

'Ah, I see.' *So she is a trophy editor, just here for this meeting,* Abhimanyu thought.

Asmita's hesitant eyes briefly met his before settling on the notebook placed in front of her.

Gradually, the focus shifted from the presentation on screen to the discussion around the table. Meanwhile, Kaka had finally brought in coffee, along with the snacks on the specific plates Maaya had asked for.

The familiar snacks on the table immediately caught Abhimanyu's attention. He looked up at Maaya. The joy on his face was reciprocated on that of Maaya's. The two said nothing but smiled knowingly. The realization that his preferences had been noted so carefully thrilled Abhimanyu.

Abhimanyu and Maaya had had their first meeting in his favourite confectionary shop in South Bombay. The snacks on the table right now were exactly what he had ordered back then, and he had sung the food's praises till the last crumb.

Today, Maaya had charmed him by going the extra mile. She was good at this – giving whatever she was doing a personal touch.

The last leg of conversations happened over the food and coffee.

When the discussion was over, the rest of the team left, giving Maaya, Peter and Abhimanyu the privacy they needed. It was time for Abhimanyu to give them his official answer. Two copies of the contract had already been printed. Maaya had brought them along to the meeting room in her folder.

In his previous meeting with Maaya, Abhimanyu had clearly stated the royalties and advance he wanted. 'Without this, there is no way I can make it to your publishing house.'

Hence, when Maaya had invited him for the presentation in his office, he had some idea that perhaps PaperInk was willing to respect his demands.

He discovered that he was indeed right. The figures mentioned on the contract, which Maaya had pushed his way, were exactly what he had asked for. This was enough for him to seal the deal. And yet, he wanted to take a few minutes.

'Can I use the washroom first, please?' he asked.

'Sure. It's on the other side of the office space,' Peter said, getting up from his chair and pointing in the direction of the washroom.

Abhimanyu walked out of the meeting room. On his way, he enjoyed walking down the aisle of the gorgeous office.

I'm going to love coming here.

Back in the conference room, Peter and Maaya shared a few final moments of anxiety.

'This is it. What do you think, Maaya?'

She took a few seconds and then said, 'I think we have him.'

'Really?'

She nodded thoughtfully.

On the other end of the office, Abhimanyu was about to push open the door of the men's room when the door of the ladies' room adjacent to it opened first. The person that walked out of it made him stop in his tracks.

Asmita, too, stopped suddenly. To bump into the only person she had wanted to avoid was especially bad luck. What made it even more uncomfortable was the location. Abhimanyu had the option of avoiding her and walking straight into the washroom, but he wasn't one to miss an opportunity. He intended to look into her eyes and enjoy her discomfort.

'Oh, hi there,' he said, a wicked smile on his face.

'Oh! Uh ... Hi!' Asmita stumbled on her feet and fumbled for words. A sudden shiver went down her spine. Ever since she had sat in the meeting, she had been mentally preparing herself to face Abhimanyu in private, but now that it had finally happened, she found herself hardly prepared for it. And yet, she decided to say what she had intended to earlier.

'Listen, I am ...' she paused, shut her eyes for a second and then said, '... so sorry for what I did in the parking lot.'

'Oh, you *aaare*?' Abhimanyu said, almost singing the last word. He was enjoying every bit of this, crossing his arms against his chest.

Asmita had no choice but to take it. Not only had she wronged a person, she had wronged the *wrong* person, someone whom her bosses were trying hard to woo.

'I am.' She politely nodded. Guilt reflected on her face.

Abhimanyu didn't say anything. Keeping a poker face, he looked into her eyes for a few seconds. That was his idea – to humiliate her and show her her place. When Asmita couldn't face him any more, she looked away.

'Even though I was wrong, I hope you realize that I had to rush for this meeting with you. I didn't want to be late,' she added.

'So that's the justification?' he asked.

'Certainly not. I began by saying I was wrong.'

'Then don't mention it.'

'Okay,' she said dejectedly, and then added, 'I am sorry again.'

She stood there for a few seconds. When Abhimanyu didn't say anything, she excused herself and was about to walk away when he spoke again.

Of course he isn't done with me yet, she thought.

'So, you hadn't recognized me, or did you fake that in the parking lot?'

Thankfully for Asmita, there was no one around to listen to them.

'I honestly didn't recognize you.'

That hurt his ego. Immensely! In his head, Abhimanyu was such a bestselling author that everyone at every publishing house was well aware of him. At least, he had always believed so.

'What kind of an editor doesn't recognize the author she is going to meet?'

Swallowing all her frustration, Asmita gave him a detailed answer. 'I joined PaperInk a year and a half back.

Before that, I worked with a print magazine for four years. After they shut down the publication, I moved into publishing. I am not aware of many authors. Besides, I either read non-fiction or literary fiction, which I edit. I don't read commercial fiction, the genre of the books you write. I was only filling in for Shalini, our commercial fiction editor.'

'And why *don't* you read commercial fiction, if I may ask?' This time he was genuinely curious.

'I ...' she began and then looked away for a moment to think of the right words. 'I like literary works. The language, the complexity, the art ... it's what holds my interest. It makes the genre superior for me.'

'Oh, so in your eyes, commercial fiction is what?' Abhimanyu paused for a second and then, lifting his hand, he asked, ' ... Inferior? Down-market?'

Asmita understood the tangent he was getting at. She knew she was now being unnecessarily harassed. However, in light of the recent events, she chose to answer him.

'I didn't mean that,' she said.

'But moments back you used the word "superior" for literary fiction while comparing it with the commercial genre. No?'

She noticed how he observed minute details of a conversation. That's what authors do all the time. They observe. Big and small details.

'Well, I meant, I don't have the necessary skills to appreciate commercial fiction. Indeed, there is something missing within me and not in the genre, I am sure.'

Abhimanyu appreciated how brilliantly she had spun that. Her choice of words to end the debate was remarkable.

Very smart! he said to himself. 'Fair point, Miss Asmita,' he acknowledged with a smile.

She sighed in relief. She thought she could walk away from him, but then Abhimanyu had something else as well for her.

'When was the last time you read a popular fiction novel?'

'Hmmm ... I guess ... early college?' she answered candidly, trying to regain her comfort.

'Oh, that's a long time then. I do think that you should read one now and see if you have acquired the skills to appreciate this genre.'

Asmita didn't know how to react to that. She somehow managed to fake a smile in return.

'Don't worry. I will make sure that you go through popular fiction now,' Abhimanyu added.

The veiled threat in his statement dimmed her smile. Abhimanyu didn't say anything more, nor did he say goodbye. He merely turned on his heel and, pushing open the doors to the washroom, walked inside.

A little while later, back in the Romance Room, he delivered his verdict. He was going to accept their offer, but he had one condition.

He wanted Asmita to edit his book.

3

‘What?’ Asmita’s jaw dropped.

It was the day after Abhimanyu’s office visit and Maaya had just broken the news to Asmita. The editor was shell-shocked. She stared back at her boss, speechless.

‘He wants you,’ Maaya repeated.

‘But …’ Asmita started, then paused as she struggled to articulate her thoughts. She was just so astonished.

‘How …’ she tried again, and once more, the strangeness of the situation made her fall short of words.

Something, though, finally made sense to her now. She realized what Abhimanyu had meant when he said, ‘*I will make sure that you go through popular fiction now.*’

In the end, all Asmita could manage to say was, ‘But I edit literary fiction.’

‘He knows that, Asmita,’ Maaya said, sounding a little frustrated herself. ‘And I said exactly this to him, more than once. But he insists on you and just you.’

Asmita didn't know what to say. She racked her brains to come up with a robust enough reason to pull herself out of this mess.

Maaya, too, stood at Asmita's desk in silence, trying to connect the dots in her head. Then, with a sharp, thoughtful glance at Asmita, she asked, 'Do you guys … uh … know each other from before?'

Asmita immediately shook her head. 'No. Not at all,' she said resolutely.

'Or … maybe *he* knows you?' Maaya ventured. She was as surprised as Asmita at Abhimanyu asking for a literary fiction editor for his book; a person he didn't even know from before. The whole thing was a mystery to her.

Asmita stuck out her lower lip and shrugged.

Maaya frowned, trying to recall whether there'd been anything odd about the exchange between Abhimanyu and Asmita at the meeting. All she remembered was that in comparison to the other people present in the meeting room, Asmita had actually had the least amount of interaction with Abhimanyu.

In light of the facts before her – that Asmita and Abhimanyu had no previous history, and that they'd met only during the meeting the previous day – Maaya could only come up with one solid reason behind Abhimanyu's request. Before she could voice it, Asmita spoke.

'What did he say when you told him that I am a literary fiction editor?'

She wanted to know the details of what had transpired in the meeting room after she left it. Maaya looked at her, still thinking.

'I mean, what was his reason for picking me over Shalini?' Asmita rephrased her question.

Finally, Maaya replied, 'He had a vague but straightforward answer to that.'

Asmita waited to hear her this vague and straightforward answer.

'He said, "It's a gut feeling. She will do great."'

Asmita took a deep breath to calm her nerves. She turned her face away unhappily. She suddenly understood, very well, the game this author was playing with her. And she felt like she was being reeled into a trap.

The next second she heard Maaya's voice again, more optimistic than earlier.

'I think I know why he asked for you.'

Asmita turned back to face her boss with a question in her eyes, her mind restless.

'I remember telling him that three out of the seven books you edited last year had been longlisted for the literary awards. And I remember that look on his face the second I had introduced you to him. There was something in it. I can only imagine it was because he was super impressed by your achievements. And I think that all he is now trying to do is hedge his bets at a new publishing house by asking for an editor with your credentials.'

Asmita breathed a sigh of relief – not because she believed that explanation, but because she was happy that Maaya had finally come up with a theory to explain things to herself. At least for the moment, the winds had changed their direction and Asmita's secret was safe. However, she could clearly see a bigger storm coming her way.

'A commercial fiction novel like yours has to appeal to the mass market. The books Asmita edits have a niche target audience. I really don't think she is the best person to work on our biggest print run ever,' Maaya had said to Abhimanyu in the conference room the day before, after he'd voiced his condition for signing the contract.

She had tried her best to convince Abhimanyu by scaring him into changing his mind. After all, practically speaking, this was *his* book first. For PaperInk, it was one of the many books on their list that year, but for Abhimanyu, it was the only one. He had a bigger stake and he needed it to succeed as much as his previous titles.

'It's a gut feeling. She will do great,' Abhimanyu had said, his gaze confident and unwavering as he looked at Maaya.

Clearly, he wasn't going to be swayed. Abhimanyu wasn't afraid at all. On the contrary, he seemed to be completely at ease. It didn't look like he was having any second thoughts. And there was a reason to it, which he was not going to reveal to them.

The truth was, Abhimanyu had never depended on the editors of the publishing houses that published him and he didn't intend to start now. He had a personal editor, a man who had worked on all his books till date. For him, handing over his work to the editor assigned to him by his publisher was always a formality, a way to instil a false sense of belief in them that they were doing their job and contributing towards making his book a bestseller.

He made sure to thank the editor the publishing house assigned to him, copying in their boss while praising their skills. The email he sent would be effusive and so, no one would pay any special attention to one line which was always there – 'At some places, I have overwritten the changes suggested by you.' The catch was that 'some places' was actually most places. This line would be followed by another – 'Please ensure that this is the final manuscript and no further changes are made to it.'

It was a clear message, but he felt that the charm of being known as Abhimanyu's editor and the high of being mentioned in the acknowledgements section of his book, along with the praise and appreciation in an email which also had the boss marked in – all of this outweighed the editor's need to push back on the edits and challenge Abhimanyu on why he had rejected most of the changes. So far, he'd always been right.

And Abhimanyu was going to treat Asmita just like that.

'Darling! I know; but looks like you will have to do this one,' Maaya said, arriving straight to the point.

It was the day after Maaya had told Asmita about what Abhimanyu had asked for during the meeting.

Asmita had been certain that Maaya would be able to work something out, or that she herself would find some reasonably strong argument against going along with Abhimanyu's request. However, neither of the two things had transpired.

An uncomfortable silence fell as Asmita now contemplated telling Maaya what had actually happened between Abhimanyu and her. It seemed like the only way out of this mess. But Asmita was well aware of how Maaya was known for losing her cool if things didn't go her way. And there was nothing Maaya wanted more than getting Abhimanyu on board. The odds were against Asmita. Could she actually tell her boss anything? Wasn't it too late?

Maaya filled in the silence as she continued, 'Or at least pretend to edit it.'

'What does that mean?' Asmita asked.

'I can make Shalini do the job in the backend, you know.'

'Can we really do that?' she asked, giving the idea serious thought and trying to find the loopholes that could pop up.

Maaya wasn't too happy about walking down that road, but she was determined to do whatever it took to bring Abhimanyu to PaperInk. Besides, her instinct told her that Shalini was better equipped to handle popular fiction.

'Desperate demands, desperate solutions!' she said to Asmita with a shrug.

Asmita asked herself how she felt about something like this. At the very outset, what comforted her was Maaya's support. At least her boss was batting for her side and was even willing to take what felt like an immoral route.

At the back of her mind, Asmita knew that the whole thing wouldn't mean lying only once in the beginning. If she played Abhimanyu once, she would have to play him forever. And not just her, but Shalini and Maaya as well. It seemed like this solution was going to complicate a situation that was already so complicated.

She could lie on email, but what about face-to-face meetings? How would she answer his queries, give him inputs or rebut him, should there be a need to do so? It was too much of a task to pull off this deception. Also, when she communicated with him on email, her written words would stand testimony to her lies.

No. It just wouldn't do. Asmita made up her mind. She wouldn't walk down that road. She wasn't going to give Abhimanyu yet another opportunity to humiliate her. Never!

'I am so sorry, Maaya, but I can't start something that will go on to become a series of lies,' she said, getting up from her chair and picking up her empty coffee mug to refill it.

Maaya was taken aback on seeing Asmita walk out of the discussion like that. She felt like Asmita tried to escape every time she mentioned anything to do with Abhimanyu or his demand. She called out to her now.

'Is there something going on between you two, Asmita?'

Asmita came to a sudden halt. Slowly, she turned back with a look of disbelief on her face. 'WHAT?'

'Don't get me wrong, Asmita. I asked you this yesterday and you said that you guys didn't know each other. I don't want to offend you, but I am just double-checking here. And your body language tells me that there *is* something you're hiding from me,' Maaya said without mincing words. After all, she was the boss. She ran this place. And she didn't appreciate being kept in the dark. But she didn't let her anger show. She was calm and composed as she looked at Asmita. She wasn't levelling any accusations against her, but seeking a genuine response while trying to help her out as well as the company.

Asmita opened her mouth to deny the accusation but stopped. Instead, she briefly closed her eyes and thought. *Maybe this is the right moment to tell her?* she asked herself.

She took a deep breath, then opened her eyes and looked straight at Maaya.

'Can you please join me in the cafeteria?' she asked.

Maaya realized that she had been right after all, and there was something more that Asmita was finally going to share with her.

The two women walked to the cafeteria, where, over a cup of coffee, Asmita apprised Maaya of everything that had happened in the parking lot on the morning of the meeting with Abhimanyu. She then told Maaya of her conversation with the author outside the office restrooms.

Finally, Maaya understood the real reason behind what Abhimanyu was doing.

'And here I thought that he wanted you because of all those longlisted books you had worked on,' Maaya said, her lips twisting in a sardonic smile.

Asmita couldn't meet her boss's eyes and looked down into the cup in her hands.

Maaya was quiet for a while, thinking things through. Then she asked, 'But if he doesn't like you in person, why would he want you on his project?'

'God knows,' Asmita said, rolling her eyes. 'Maybe this will make him feel as if I am at his command?'

Maaya silently acknowledged that line of thought. In the end, she told Asmita not to worry. Now that she knew exactly what had transpired between the two, she would talk to Peter about it. She was also amazed at how Abhimanyu had kept all this to himself. He had played Maaya too.

Asmita felt lighter after sharing the truth with Maaya. Now that it was out of her system, there was nothing she needed to worry about.

It turned out that she was wrong.

In the evening, before leaving the office, Asmita was called to Peter's cabin. Maaya was also present. On seeing Asmita walk in, Peter got straight to the point.

'Maaya told me about what happened between Abhimanyu and you. It's very unfortunate.'

Asmita kept quiet.

'We reached out to Abhimanyu an hour back. I have written to him, apologizing on behalf of PaperInk.'

That stung Asmita. She hated that the company had needed to apologize on her behalf, considering she had already apologized to him herself – more than once. Asmita looked at Maaya and then back at Peter, who continued.

'We have asked him how we can fix this. However, if he is reluctant to budge, I want you to take up this project. I hope you understand why we need to do this, Asmita.'

Asmita didn't say anything. Her eyes shifted from Peter to Maaya, who didn't have anything to add to what Peter had said. She did look sorry, though. But Asmita, who had been so confident about Maaya being on her side, felt blindsided by her inability to help.

'Right?' Peter's voice commanded her attention now.

Asmita looked back at him and nodded silently. *What choice do I have?*

'That will be all, then,' Peter said and began packing up his bag, effectively signalling that this conversation was over.

4.

'I'd like to apologize to you once again, Abhimanyu. On Asmita's behalf too,' Maaya said into the phone.

It was late in the evening. Maaya had noticed that there was no response to the email that Peter had sent to Abhimanyu. Peter had copied her on the mail too.

Without waiting any longer, she had picked up the phone and called Abhimanyu. While Peter had already done this on email, Maaya decided to make a verbal apology too. She was going to try one last time to fix this mess.

Who knows, it might help soothe his ego! Maaya was determined to do everything possible to get Abhimanyu's signature on that contract.

'Come on, Maaya, you don't have to do that.' Abhimanyu sounded relaxed over the call. 'And this isn't about revenge.' He chuckled. 'Please don't take it that way.'

'In that case, I fail to understand what this is really about, Abhimanyu,' Maaya said.

'Oh, it's simple. This time I want to try something new. I want a literary fiction editor to edit my work. And that's why I want to go with Asmita. After all, who better than her? Didn't you tell me that three of her books recently got longlisted for an award?'

While Maaya had initially believed this to be the reason behind his request, she knew better now. Abhimanyu's words to Asmita outside the restrooms – *I will make sure that you go through popular fiction now* – were proof that he was lying.

However, Abhimanyu had played his cards well. There was little room left for Maaya to challenge his logic. Yet, she tried again.

'But, as I told you earlier, she wouldn't be able to do justice to your book. And it is the book of the year for us.'

'I understand that, Maaya, but let her try once, na. If we don't like her work, we can go for a second round of editing by the editor of your choice. I promise you that I will deliver the first draft of the manuscript early, so that you have enough time should we need that second round.'

Abhimanyu was persistent. Maaya understood instinctively that pushing him beyond this point would mean losing his book.

'All right, Abhimanyu,' she said and sighed as she disconnected the call.

That night, Maaya went to bed wondering about how Asmita was going to take the news. More than that, she was worried about the fate of the novel. Would Asmita be able to shape this one for mass consumption instead of a niche audience? It was a huge risk for Maaya, considering that PaperInk had agreed to paying Abhimanyu a mind-boggling advance and an unprecedented royalty percentage.

The next morning, in the shower, Asmita tried to calm herself down. The words Peter had said to her the day before were echoing in her head. *If it comes to that, you will have to work for Abhimanyu.*

The idea was killing her.

She had finally made the difficult decision of what she was going to do if it indeed came to that. Just when she was about to leave her house, she had second thoughts about her decision. But as she got into the car and started the drive to the office, she successfully shoved them away.

Two hours later, Asmita was standing in Peter's room yet again. Maaya was there too, like she had been the previous evening.

As always, Peter didn't waste a minute.

'Asmita, you will have to take this up. We tried. It didn't work. Sorry!'

He looked at her face as he finished talking, waiting to hear a yes. But Asmita was silent. In shock, she turned to Maaya, as if seeking an explanation. But Maaya only shook her head, confirming Peter's words.

The thought of working for Abhimanyu sickened Asmita. She abhorred the very idea. In her heart, she was no longer apologetic about stealing his parking space, now that she had seen what he was capable of.

No. She wasn't going to give in.

'I ...' she paused and then carried on, bracing herself. '... I won't be able to do this, Peter. I'm so sorry.'

'What? What do you mean, you won't be able to do this? Asmita, we need him. And this decision is final,' Peter said.

'We understand your problem too, Asmita, and we haven't left any stone unturned, but he's not changed his mind,' Maaya added.

'Exactly. So now let's get going with this,' Peter announced, gesturing that Asmita could leave his office now.

Asmita felt completely dejected. Hopelessly, she looked at the two people in front of her. She knew that saying anything more would not accomplish anything. Unhappily, she walked out of Peter's office. She felt as if she had lost a battle without even getting to fight it. And that very realization made her feel suffocated.

Just as she returned to her desk, her colleagues asked her to join them for a coffee break. Asmita shook her head. She wanted to be alone with her thoughts. Sitting at the long worktable, she revisited the decision she had made that morning. *Should I go in and let Peter know right away?*

It wasn't that Asmita was worried about editing commercial fiction. She knew it wouldn't be a difficult task for her. Of course, she wouldn't find it interesting enough, but that apart she could do it, she knew that. In fact, if she tried, she could probably do a decent job of editing it. However, that wasn't the point. What bothered her was the manner in which she was being made to take up this job – against her will. On top of that, she knew that she was being asked to work with the very man who was trying to settle scores with her. Clearly, this was some sort of vendetta at play. It wasn't the job per se but the reasons behind it that were unacceptable to her.

Asmita also took pride in her work. She wasn't just any editor. Her intention wasn't merely to survive in the publishing industry by doing a mediocre job. She had built her reputation on the basis of the remarkable work she had done in a very short period of time. The awards and the nominations that the books she had worked on had received spoke volumes about her skills. The publishing fraternity had taken notice of this too. It was no wonder, therefore, that almost all the reputed publishing houses had at one time or the other expressed their interest in hiring her. Asmita had firmly, albeit gracefully, declined all of them.

She loved working at PaperInk. She enjoyed shaping her authors' manuscripts into books. What she didn't enjoy was being bullied into doing this. Being forced to edit Abhimanyu's manuscript felt like she was being made to hate what she loved. How could she let someone do this to her? How could *she* do this to herself? Her self-respect came above everything.

Asmita spent a disturbed afternoon at work. By the evening, she had decided on the next step and there was no doubt in her mind any more.

She first thought about speaking to Maaya, but then, on an impulse, walked into Peter's cabin instead. She was sure about what she was going to say. She had rehearsed her words a few times over by now.

'What is it, Asmita?' Peter asked as soon as he looked up at her.

'Peter, I am sorry, but I won't be able to do this.'

'Are we there again? This is non-negotiable, Asmita,' he reminded her.

'Which is why I'm here to resign.'

Peter's glance sharpened. For a few seconds, he didn't say anything. He could tell from Asmita's body language and the manner in which she spoke that she had made up her mind. He asked her to take a seat and called Maaya to his cabin.

Feeling miffed about Asmita bypassing her and speaking directly to Peter, Maaya hurried to the CEO's cabin. She didn't want to miss any conversation around Abhimanyu's book.

'What happened?' she asked, shifting her worried eyes between her boss and her subordinate.

'Maaya, please handle this,' Peter said in clipped tones as he gestured towards Asmita. 'She prefers quitting over working on Abhimanyu's novel. I don't have a problem with releasing her, but you are her boss, and this needs to be handled in the proper way.'

Maaya was stunned. She hadn't been prepared for this. Asmita was the most valuable editor she had on her team. The idea behind getting Abhimanyu on board was to build PaperInk, not destroy it. *How did it all come to this?*

'Asmita, no!' she said loudly and firmly. There was conviction in her voice.

'This is about my self-respect, Maaya,' Asmita replied in a measured tone.

'No, this is about an editing project. This is completely professional.'

'I understand that it is professional. I also understand that you and Peter cannot help me with this. That is why I'm offering to quit.'

'You are being impulsive, Asmita.'

'I have taken an entire day to think about this, Maaya. I am not being impulsive at all.'

This soft war of words went on for a while. Maaya tried every trick in the book, from warning Asmita that she was ruining her career to emotional leverage, but Asmita remained unmoved. Almost an hour later, Maaya had to give up. She had already cancelled another meeting on her schedule to handle this crisis. But finally, she realized that there was nothing to be done. Maaya felt depressed about PaperInk losing a sincere editor. The whole thing was a mess.

Asmita, on the other hand, was hurt by the fact that even in the face of losing her, neither Peter nor Maaya had considered her over Abhimanyu. She finally realized her true value in their eyes of all the hard work she had put in at PaperInk. It didn't compare to the value the highest-selling romance author brought to their table.

Apart from feeling sad and helpless about the situation, Maaya was also pissed at Asmita. *Why doesn't she understand? Why the hell she is making this about her ego? Why can't she just edit this damn thing and get done with it?*

Maaya was very clear about what she wanted. She had to take the company to the next level. It was only possible by acquiring leading authors. And if her own people, in the line of duty, weren't going to make some adjustments and compromises, she wouldn't be able to adjust with them either. The heights she wanted PaperInk to achieve was not possible if her staff had this kind of an attitude.

She could see that by offering to quit her stable job, Asmita was making a sacrifice in the name of her principles. It was time for Maaya to make her own sacrifice to defend what she stood for.

'All right, Asmita. If this is what you have decided to do, then I will let you leave us. I only hope you reconsider your decision. If not, then I will understand. Please remember that you will have to serve a month's notice period after you put in your papers.'

5

Abhimanyu was shocked to learn about the turn of events at PaperInk. Two days after she had taken the final call on the matter, Maaya had rung him up to tell him about this new development, because his signature on the contract was dependent on the fact that Asmita would edit his work. With Asmita no longer in the picture, Maaya now needed to know what Abhimanyu wanted to do next.

Needing some time to process the news, Abhimanyu told her that he would get back to her. It was one of those evenings when he was home alone, having a drink and relaxing. Now, as he hung up, he wondered if what Maaya had said was actually just their way of tricking him into withdrawing his condition.

The alternative was a difficult thought for him to digest – that Asmita had actually chosen to put in her papers instead of working on his manuscript.

How stubborn is she!

The news of Asmita's decision provoked a variety of emotions in him. On the one hand, he felt that perhaps, in the name of teaching her a lesson, he had pushed things way too far. On the other, he believed that she had had a choice and it was her ego that was making her opt for an exit over working on his book. And so he didn't need to empathize with her.

A part of his brain also felt that Maaya was making a mistake by losing a valuable colleague in order to get him on board. However, it also made him feel validated to see how important he was to them. He absolutely enjoyed and cherished that feeling.

Yet, in spite of all this, there was something about Asmita that continued to rankle him. Her bold decision of quitting PaperInk had given her the upper hand now, in this battle of ego versus self-respect.

It hurt his ego to know that an editor of her stature had declined, in such a dramatic way, to work with a bestselling author like him. And suddenly, the fact that PaperInk had chosen him over Asmita mattered less to him. She had shattered his fragile ego. For a man who had always believed that any editor would consider themselves lucky to work with him, that they would consider it the highlight of their career, this was a big blow.

Shaking his head to get rid of these thoughts, Abhimanyu told himself that he'd get over it soon and poured himself another drink. This time, it was neat.

Asmita sat cross-legged, leaning back against her bed's headrest. Her dinner plate rested in her lap. Raised voices from the chaotic and loud news debate on TV filled the bedroom. Her eyes were glued to the TV screen, but her mind had sailed far away.

What will I do now? Have I taken the right decision? Asmita's mind was churning with questions and self-doubt.

Her mother walked into her room. On seeing the untouched plate of food, she frowned. 'Arrey! Why aren't you eating, Asmita?'

Asmita started and shook her head to get rid of her thoughts as she looked at her mother and then at her plate. She nodded and tore a piece of chapatti.

'What is it, Asmita? You look worried. Why are—' Before her mother could complete her question, she suddenly felt a sharp pain shoot up her left upper arm. She froze and dropped heavily against the wall, seeking its support with her other hand.

Asmita screamed and immediately jumped out of her bed to hold her mother. She then helped her to sit on the bed.

For a few days now, her mother had been complaining about sporadic aches and pains in her arm. It now appeared to Asmita that things had turned worse.

'Mom, what is happening to you?' she asked, an arm around her mother's shoulders.

'I don't know. It's the same pain. This time it was excruciating,' her mother said. She added that this time it had been accompanied by fatigue and a cold sweat.

'Tomorrow morning we are going to the hospital,' Asmita said while gently massaging her mother's aching arm.

Breathless and weak, her mother only agreed with a slight nod.

Her mother, who had always found reasons to avoid hospital visits, agreeing to do so this easily was a sign of how bad things were. It made Asmita more worried about her mother than she'd already been.

A day later, Abhimanyu got another call from Maaya. She needed to know about his decision.

'I will sign the contract,' he said without missing a beat.

'Oh! Great!' Maaya was surprised at his response. She hadn't been expecting a yes this quickly.

'So,' she began and then paused before carrying on, 'I think our editor Shalini will do incredible work on your manuscript. She—'

'I don't care, Maaya. So don't worry about it,' Abhimanyu cut her off midway.

The next second, he realized how rude that might have sounded. So he went on, explaining himself. 'I mean, as long as the final approval on the edits remains with me. You know what I mean?'

'Oh, absolutely. That goes without saying,' Maaya replied.

Maaya smiled in relief. After all the unpleasantness of Asmita leaving them, Abhimanyu's decision to come on board was finally a happy turn of events for her, albeit very costly, in more ways than one.

'Send me the contract. I will sign it,' Abhimanyu said and hung up.

Meanwhile, things were moving quite fast in Asmita's world as well.

She had brought her mother to the hospital early that morning. At that hour of the day, it was a busy place, but thankfully, Asmita had managed to find seats for them. While they waited their turn outside the doctor's cabin, she began following up with all her contacts from publishing that she had dug up in the past sixteen hours. Most of them were senior executives from other publishing houses who had approached her before. While she'd turned them down back then, she hoped that they'd still be interested in her.

One after the other, she dropped each contact a customary hello, in order to start a conversation. Two of them responded almost immediately, and she got busy chatting with both simultaneously.

Without mentioning that she was serving her notice period at PaperInk, Asmita shared the fact that she was looking for a change. As subtly as she could, she also reminded them of the proposal they had once made to her.

It turned out that they remembered it clearly, but before she could feel happy about this, both of them expressed their disappointment and apologized for their inability to reconsider the offer they had once made to her. One of the organizations had already hired someone else for the role and the other had frozen its hiring budgets till the next financial year.

Asmita felt crushed by the outcome of the two parallel chats, and that feeling lasted till the nurse shouted her mother's name. It was time to get her mother diagnosed.

After the routine procedure of recording the patient's blood pressure, height and weight was over, the mother and the daughter were directed to the doctor's chamber.

For some reason, the pain in her mother's arm had subsided to almost nothing that morning. Asmita wondered whether the reduction in the pain was psychological, considering how much her mother abhorred hospitals.

'Are you diabetic?' the doctor asked her mother, who nodded.

'High BP?'

Once again, the older woman pursed her lips and nodded.

'Hmm ... Deep breath,' he said to her, placing the diaphragm of the stethoscope against her upper back. 'Have you hurt yourself by any chance? Tripped or fallen recently?' he asked while continuing his examination.

Asmita's mother spent some five seconds trying to recall any such event and then finally shook her head.

Once the doctor finished the examination, he told them that the pain was most likely due to a muscle spasm and that it would subside eventually. He prescribed a painkiller and a multivitamin but added that because he didn't want to take any chances, he had also recommended some tests. One of them was an angiography.

'Get this done,' he said to Asmita and then, when he saw her face grow worried, he added, 'Don't worry. It's just to rule out anything else, considering her age. More so because she is diabetic and has BP issues. But most likely everything will turn out fine.'

The two women left his chamber, breathing a sigh of relief, and then headed straight to the hospital laboratory.

6

The final signatures on the contract were inked at the dinner table of a five-star hotel in South Mumbai. Maaya had insisted upon a little celebration. It was a closed group of three – Maaya, Peter and Abhimanyu. An impeccably dressed server poured sparkling wine into the three champagne glasses just as Abhimanyu signed his name on the contract before him with a flourish.

'May this book break all our records!' Maaya said, raising a toast.

'And yours as well,' Peter said, looking at Abhimanyu.

'Amen,' Abhimanyu finished.

They clinked their glasses and took a sip of the delicious champagne.

Maaya was satisfied. She had finally achieved what she had set out to do so long ago. Her next goal was to see the first of the three novels become a blockbuster. Asmita's resignation had swiftly taken a backseat in her mind. On the forefront was a to-do list, with the press release on top of it. And Maaya would be drafting that herself. She could already see the headline – 'The King of Romance Finds Love at PaperInk'.

'So, do you have a storyline in mind?' Maaya asked, taking a bite of the golden-fried prawns with mint chutney.

Abhimanyu had anticipated this question and had the answer ready.

'Let the advance hit my bank account first.' He chuckled. Peter and Maaya joined in, laughing at his witty retort.

'I am kidding. Ah!' Abhimanyu wiped his lips with the napkin and said, 'I do. In fact, I am already on it. I hope to finish writing the first draft in a month or so.'

Maaya was surprised. 'What? In a month?'

Clearly, she hadn't expected the manuscript to be in that fast. They hadn't discussed the timeline for Abhimanyu's next novel before this, and now that she realized how close he was to finishing it, Maaya felt herself grow more excited. Her next goal turned out to be closer than she had thought it would be.

'That's great!' she said to him enthusiastically. 'So, can we look at mid-February for the release? Valentine's Day would be perfect for a romance novel,' she suggested, her gaze taking in both Abhimanyu and Peter. The latter merely shrugged and raised his eyebrows, letting her know that it was entirely her call.

Abhimanyu also smiled, nodding.

Maaya couldn't hold back her curiosity and asked, 'Tell me what it's about.'

'A love story,' Abhimanyu said with a straight face and then burst into a big laugh.

'Come on now!' Maaya playfully tapped the back of his hand, which was resting on the table.

Swallowing the bite of food in his mouth, Abhimanyu shared the plot of his story with his dinner companions.

'It's a love story between a young boy of nineteen and a woman almost twice his age,' he revealed with a flourish, and then stopped.

His chin rested on the back of his hand. His eyes looked right into Maaya's.

'Oh wow!' Maaya said. Her eyebrows rose, her eyes widened, and a smile appeared on her face, the curve of which grew bigger every nanosecond.

Instead of saying anything more, Abhimanyu only nodded gleefully, confirming that it indeed was going to be a very different love story – unlike anything he had ever written before. The plot was brand new and unique. He had succeeded in kindling Maaya's interest.

Suddenly, she was full of questions. *This is his strength. This is how he plays with the curiosity of a potential reader!*

'Where is it set?'

'Munnar, Kerala.'

'South India!' Maaya said excitedly.

'Yes. I realized that I hadn't written a story set in south India till date.'

'But why Munnar?' Peter asked.

'If I had picked Trivandrum, would you have asked me why Trivandrum?' Abhimanyu answered.

Peter turned his gaze towards Maaya and they both laughed.

'I still would,' Maaya said.

Abhimanyu reciprocated her smile and, turning to Peter, said, 'I visited Munnar on my last holiday. It was then that I decided that my next novel would be set there. It's breathtakingly beautiful.'

'It is,' Peter said, adding, 'I've been there.'

'Well, we can discuss Kerala's beauty some other time. Abhimanyu, tell us more about the woman in this book. What's she like?' Maaya asked eagerly.

Abhimanyu enjoyed the fact that Maaya was intrigued by his story. No doubt he had caught her fancy.

'Well, she is a homemaker.'

'Oh! She's married?' The smile momentarily left Maaya's face while her curiosity shot up.

'She is. In fact, she is a mother,' Abhimanyu said confidently.

Peter's eyes bulged at that. 'So the book is about an extramarital affair?' he asked.

Abhimanyu gave them a relaxed smile, musing privately about how eager people always were to judge others, even characters in a fictitious story. 'Well, not exactly. It's about one-sided love. The boy is in love with a married woman.'

That impressed Maaya even more. 'And what about the boy himself?'

'Oh! He is not married,' Abhimanyu said, well aware that the comment would make the other two laugh.

'I *know* he's not!' Maaya playfully slapped his hand again. 'But tell me, na, what is he like?'

This time Abhimanyu answered seriously. 'Well, he is in his first year of college.'

'So, does he live in her neighbourhood? I mean, how do they meet?' Maaya asked.

Abhimanyu smiled and looked away. Then, after a moment, he turned to face her again and said, 'You'll just have to wait to read it, Maaya.'

Maaya inhaled deeply and sat back in her chair. She knew that this was as much as she'd get from Abhimanyu for now. She picked up her drink and savoured it, along with the thought that the days before she got to read Abhimanyu's work were numbered.

Thirty kilometres away from all the celebration, gloom had found its home in Asmita's heart. It was as if luck had chosen to not be on her side. Every contact she had pinned her hopes on had either apologized for being unable to help her, or had plain shied away from even saying that, making weak excuses instead.

Fear had slowly begun to take over her audacity. Reality was beginning to dawn upon her and was making her revisit her decision to leave PaperInk.

Did I do the right thing? Can I take back the resignation? What will Maaya and Peter think of me then? What would Abhimanyu think? Is that asshole even aware of this? But then, what about my self-respect?

No! I won't swallow my pride. I won't fall in my own eyes. And if I bend now, they will make me bend forever.

Numerous thoughts like these wreaked havoc in her head and kept her anxious. Things were beginning to look troublesome, now that she was running out of options.

It was a bad time of the year to even look for a change anyway. Even though she was confident of her talent and skills, she had begun to mentally add up the money she had saved and invested, should there be a need for her to lead a jobless life for a while.

Meanwhile, she pulled up her old résumé on her laptop, updated it and uploaded it on the job portals she was aware of. She did that despite being well aware that they'd not really yield any results. Publishing was a niche industry, where people seldom applied for positions via portals. Hiring often happened through word of mouth within the industry network.

Her other concern was that unlike PaperInk, many of the well-known publishing houses in the country were based in Delhi/NCR. To relocate now would mean disturbing the peace in her life, leaving the cocoon of her family home and incurring newer costs, including the monthly rent.

She rubbed her stressed-out face and cursed the moment she had unethically and unknowingly snatched Abhimanyu's parking spot.

Why the hell did I do that?

How she wished she could undo it all!

Not leaving any stone unturned, Asmita also drafted a tweet. It took guts to let the world know that she was in trouble. But it was one other way of finding a job.

Editing & perfecting literary fiction is my passion.

I have been lucky to work on award-winning books by bestselling authors. I am looking for newer editing opportunities in Mumbai, including freelancing. If you have leads, please DM me. Or you can RT and help me spread the word.

The word was now formally out in the publishing circuit. Coupled with the one-on-one calls she'd made earlier in the day, this tweet now cemented Asmita's job search.

The editorial heads at the publishing houses that had once wanted her on board but were not currently recruiting, read her tweet dejectedly. *If only she could have come to them when they had needed her.*

The head of one of those publishing houses, though, still wanted to make an exception, the logic being that Asmita was desperate and they could get her on their terms.

However, that was not the path Asmita was destined to walk down. Something a lot more interesting was to unfold in the coming days, and it had to do with that very tweet.

It turned out that there was an opening in Rizwan's personal team. Yes, *that* Rizwan Siddiqui. The apple of Abhimanyu's eye. The reason Abhimanyu had abandoned his previous publishers.

Unlike Abhimanyu, Rizwan had an entire team of his own to help him with his books, social media and public engagements, outside of what the publishing house provided him with. Anirban Mukherjee, a seasoned PR person, headed it. He was the man behind Rizwan's robust brand-building. His primary strategy was to ensure that Bollywood celebrities tweeted about Rizwan's books. Of course, these were paid tweets that cost Rizwan a bomb, but were worth it in the end. Besides, Rizwan could afford it.

It was also Anirban who had found a freelance editor for Rizwan's works and newspaper columns. Recently, though, she had joined a print media house and had her plate full with new assignments. She no longer had the bandwidth to work for Rizwan.

Anirban had been looking to fill this position as soon as possible. So, when he came across Asmita's tweet, which had been retweeted by someone he followed, he immediately dropped her a direct message. Her reply came promptly, and soon, a meeting was scheduled for the next day at Rizwan's bungalow, which also had a separate office unit.

Meeting Asmita or deciding whether to recruit her hadn't been of any interest to Rizwan. He had Anirban to take care of such things. But when Anirban texted him about why Asmita was quitting PaperInk, he decided to attend the meeting too.

Asmita had not shied away from telling Anirban the truth during their chat. Instead, she was upfront about it. 'I don't wish to work for Abhimanyu. And if I stay at PaperInk, I will have to edit his book,' she had said.

To know that his competition was the reason behind someone's resignation at a publishing house was a thing of great interest for Rizwan. He had already been updated on Abhimanyu's move to PaperInk. The press release, which Maaya had put out on PaperInk's social media platforms, had caught his attention as well. However, to him, Asmita quitting PaperInk over Abhimanyu was the bigger news, and one he now wanted to use for his own benefit.

As soon as Rizwan walked into Anirban's office, he didn't waste a minute on small talk, or in greeting Asmita.

'Why don't you want to work on his novel?' he asked her.

Anirban immediately got up from his chair. Asmita lost track of what she had been telling Anirban and turned to look behind her.

She gazed at Rizwan. He was of average height and build and sported a thick, long beard, which was nicely shaped and well maintained. It was the most striking feature about him. The designer glasses, the shirt with the shiny cufflinks, the branded buckle of his belt, all broadcast his prosperity. Everything smelled of money and fame. However, his attitude was certainly a turn-off for Asmita.

What's wrong with all these popular authors? she thought.

Feeling intimidated by the directness of his question, Asmita too decided to get to the point with her answer. 'I don't like him.'

Asmita also stayed put in her chair while addressing Rizwan. This, when Anirban had gotten up from his chair to show his boss the respect he commanded.

A mysterious smile lit up Rizwan's face. He kept looking at Asmita, trying to read her face and admiring her guts. He then looked up at the ceiling and laughed. Asmita found the whole thing downright weird.

When he was done laughing, he asked. 'Have you read his work?'

Asmita shook her head silently and slightly defiantly.

'Any particular reason?'

'I am not much of a commercial fiction person ... at least not until now.'

'Rizwan writes commercial fiction,' Anirban jumped in, wondering if Asmita knew what kind of books his boss wrote.

'Yes, I know that,' she replied.

'So how will you work on my books, then, if you aren't "much of a commercial fiction person"?' Rizwan asked, leaning against the wall, a smirk on his face. His eyes were on Asmita, unblinking.

Asmita felt like she was under scrutiny. 'That's why I said not until now. Honestly, at the moment, I am in no position to be picky. I will have to take what comes my way.'

That indeed was true for her.

She chose to be honest. It couldn't hurt and anyway, Asmita had a feeling that this meeting wasn't going well, and she had little hope of getting this job. Hence, there was no point in trying too hard. As a matter of fact, she was eager to get out of this place as soon as possible. But just then, Rizwan said something which caught her attention.

'So, coming back to what you had said before – you don't like him. Why is that?'

Asmita took a moment to think about her reply.

'I wouldn't like to get into that. I thought this meeting was about my work. It was meant to be an interview for a job and not about why I dislike a certain author.'

Rizwan chuckled. He turned and looked at Anirban, who stood there silently, trying to figure out what was going on in Rizwan's mind. At the moment, he was letting Rizwan have his fun and lead the meeting. He would don his thinking hat after that.

'You are absolutely right, Ms Asmita. My bad,' Rizwan apologized.

Asmita kept quiet.

'So, have you already quit or are you on your notice period?'

'I am on my notice period.'

'Is there a possibility of you reconsidering this?'

'Reconsidering what?'

'This idea of quitting.'

'What do you mean? I don't see a reason why I should do that,' Asmita said, confused.

Rizwan looked at Anirban and asked him, 'Can you give us a moment?'

The latter nodded and immediately walked out of the room.

Asmita wondered what Rizwan was up to. She could already smell a rat.

Rizwan took the seat behind the desk that Anirban had vacated. He looked into her eyes confidently and, with a straight face, asked, 'What are you doing, Asmita?'

His words were simple but confusing.

'What do you mean?' she asked him.

'An author walks into the publishing house you work at, where you have shaped some of their finest works. And this new author becomes the reason you lose your career, the one you've spent so many years building?'

His words stung Asmita. Rizwan hadn't said anything that she didn't already know, but it stung to hear a third person confirm that she had been treated like a doormat. It made her blood boil and she felt like she'd been stripped of her self-esteem. But she couldn't admit as much to Rizwan.

'They didn't kick me out. It was my choice to leave them.'

That indeed was the absolute truth.

'A choice? Between picking two equally bad options? Why did it even come to this?'

Suddenly, Asmita was at loss for words.

Rizwan didn't wait any further to say what he had to next.

'How can any right-minded individual let some egoistic guy displace them for no fault of theirs? Why are you letting this happen to you, Asmita?'

Rizwan's words were sharp, invoking her pride and questioning her decision.

Asmita opened her mouth to say something but Rizwan interrupted her as he continued. This time, there was aggression in his voice.

'If I were you, I wouldn't let this happen to me. I wouldn't let someone else walk into my space and move me out. I wouldn't let my own folks leave me with no choice but to quit. I wouldn't let the world use me and throw me.'

Rizwan was terrific with his words and good at playing with minds. *He would make a good politician!*

Rizwan's words had an enlightening impact on Asmita. Instead of giving up and walking out, something which till then Asmita had felt was morally right, he was asking her why she didn't stay and fight.

'Why are you being so self-sacrificing? Why aren't you thinking about your own good instead?' he asked her.

Asmita wanted to do what he was suggesting but didn't know how to.

Rizwan went on. 'PaperInk ultimately got what they wanted. Peter and Maaya were willing to pay any price to get Abhimanyu on board. And that price was you.'

This time his words felt like they were stabbing her. His logical, probing questions pointed Asmita towards a new direction, one that she hadn't even thought of. He wanted her to hold her ground and defend her position and put her own good over theirs.

Rizwan was still not done. 'Be like Maaya. Be passionate about your passion and defend your ultimate goal by hook or by crook.'

He was inciting an urge to rebel, churning a slow revolution in her heart. With every new sentence, he called upon her conscience, her self-esteem and her confidence. He made her look bad in her own eyes for giving up on a career she loved for some guy.

'If you let a bunch of people shove you away today, how will you stop somebody else from doing this to you again? And if you would want to stop them tomorrow, why not stop them today itself?'

That was it. His last words made Asmita speak up, her own voice harder and more confident than before.

'And how do I do that?' she asked, looking into his eyes.

This was exactly what Rizwan had been waiting to hear from her. He let out a long sigh of contentment and took his sweet time before speaking again. He wanted the charged-up atmosphere to relax before he made his pitch to her.

'Care for a drink before we get to that?' he asked, his voice easy and casual now.

She was surprised by the sudden change and the invitation of a drink in the middle of what was meant to be an interview. Then she realized that this office was in Rizwan's luxurious bungalow. Besides, by then she had understood that this was a pretty unconventional interview anyway.

'No, thank you. It's too early in the day for that,' she said politely.

'Then a coffee maybe?' he asked.

'No, I am fine. Thank you.'

'Please. I insist.' He kept looking at her with expectant eyes.

Asmita wanted him to get going with what he had to say instead of wasting any more time over discussing coffee. So, for the heck of it, she agreed.

'Black, please,' she said.

Rizwan quickly made a call and ordered coffee for both of them.

After he'd hung up, he faced Asmita again and put forth an idea which was nothing like what she'd expected.

'I suggest you take your resignation back,' he said.

Asmita was silent, all ears as he continued.

'Work on Abhimanyu's book at PaperInk. But in reality, work for *me*.'

Her lips parted to protest. The worry on her face was clearly visible.

'And let me know what his book is about much before it goes to press,' he added before she could speak.

'No!' Asmita blurted out immediately.

Rizwan waited for her to go on.

'You want me to steal his work for you?' She didn't like saying that, but she said it anyway.

'Don't get me wrong. I am not suggesting plagiarism.'

'Then what?'

'Just a fair idea of his plot, the story and the characters. That's it. That's all,' he said.

In the world of publishing, a manuscript is always a closely guarded secret. Only a few people have access to it before it goes into print. Asmita knew what Rizwan was proposing and the reason behind it.

If he knew what Abhimanyu was writing, he could use the same plot and churn out a far superior story. That way, he could finally outdo the author he was always in competition with. And the masterstroke would be that he would release his work before Abhimanyu.

'I can't forward you anybody's work, Rizwan. I am sorry,' Asmita said firmly.

'You aren't going to forward me anything, Asmita. There would be no evidence of it,' Rizwan said, attempting to put her fears to rest, thinking that her refusal was because she was worried about being caught.

He added, 'I am good as long as we have meetings like today's, and you give me the gist of his chapters, as and when you work on them. I will be keen to hear the twists in his story. Narrate it to me verbally, that's it.'

That he wasn't asking for something that could be held against her was a relief to hear. Yet, getting caught wasn't Asmita's primary reason for refusing to do this. What bothered her was that the whole thing was *wrong*. And she didn't keep her thoughts to herself.

'Still, it is unethical and immoral.'

'Oh, so you mean what Abhimanyu and PaperInk are doing to you is ethical and moral?'

Asmita kept mum. She didn't have any words to refute that.

'Don't forget, they are your enemies. Don't forget that you didn't start this. This is only your reaction to their action. Give them a taste of their medicine. If they can mess up your life, you too can give it back to them.'

With those words, Rizwan had played with her mind again. He had seeded his idea and was now channelling her frustration.

'Right now, you are worried, just like Arjun was in the Mahabharata.' Asmita lifted her gaze from her lap to his face. Rizwan continued, 'He wasn't willing to fight back. But he eventually did. Krishna wanted him to fight to defend his stand, even if it meant killing the people he loved dearly.'

If you can't convince them, confuse them. Rizwan was incredibly good at provoking people, so much so that a strong-headed woman like Asmita had begun to feel the influence of his words. He had pulled the right levers and his argument was compelling. Or perhaps it was her adversity that helped Rizwan get the better of her.

'In a fight, you have to counter-attack. What should comfort you is the fact that you didn't initiate this fight. You didn't attack first. Somebody entered your house and attacked you. And you are busy wondering if it is right or wrong to counter-attack? You are wondering about *morality* here?'

Asmita got up from her seat. She nodded her head and said her final words, 'If I have to do this, I need to give it serious thought. I need some time.'

Rizwan's eyes glittered. He remained seated and nodded. 'You certainly do. I understand that.'

He could see in Asmita's eyes that she wasn't the same person he had seen when he first walked into Anirban's cabin. Something in her had changed. And he was the reason behind it.

'I will leave now,' she said.

Rizwan got up to see her out.

At the door, Anirban had just arrived along with a servant who was holding a tray with coffee cups. Asmita didn't feel the need to converse with him. Instead, she looked at Rizwan again.

'Maybe we can have a drink instead, when I meet you next time?' she asked.

Rizwan smiled and said, 'Can't wait to see you again.'

8

An SMS alert on Abhimanyu's phone caught his attention. In the world of chat apps, there are few occasions when someone bothers to check an SMS. Especially one that brings them joy when they do.

It was a confirmation from his bank. The big fat advance from PaperInk had finally been credited to his account. This marked a great start to his day. With a burst of renewed excitement, he decided to tackle his incomplete manuscript. However, before that there was a pending e-single, a short erotica, his first, which he had to finish for a digital publication. The story was to go live in two weeks.

It had been more than a month since Abhimanyu had written anything. He still didn't know how he was going to end his e-single. When he had begun writing it, he had wanted it to end on a happy note. But somewhere in the middle of the story, he wondered if, for once, he should try a sad ending. He was yet to make up his mind. Another possibility he was looking at was an open ending – leaving it to his readers.

What should I do?

Wrapped in his white bathrobe, he sat by the window of his flat on the twenty-seventh floor. The morning tea in his cup was already finished. He placed the empty cup on the table. Overlooking the balcony, the window framed the infiniteness of the Arabian Sea. The sea was at quite a distance from the building he lived in. But then that's what altitude does – it gives you an impression of being close to things that aren't so nearby.

Abhimanyu loved his home. He lived by himself and worked out of his flat. As he spent a good part of his day at home, sometimes all twenty-four hours, he had opted for a sea view studio apartment in a brand-new high-rise in a posh location in Mumbai. It was a clean, well-designed space, quite big for a single occupant, and the open-floor plan layout made it appear even bigger than it was. The flat had cost him a fortune, but it was worth it. It was modular and the interior was chic. And then, of course, it allowed him to gaze at the sea all day, till the darkness of night consumed it.

He had set up his workstation by the window. Ever since he had moved into this flat, he had begun to derive his creativity from the sea, which was why he preferred writing during the morning hours. He would often gaze at the endless waters as he thought about his story. The spectacle would relax his mind and inspire him. He would imagine artistic ideas sailing to him. This was enough return on the investment.

Abhimanyu opened his laptop and clicked on the last saved file of his e-single. Once the Word document opened, he scrolled all the way to the end. He checked the word count – 5,323 words, it read. He took a deep breath. His eyes scanned the last page he had written a couple of weeks back. He had to move the story forward and culminate it.

But how? he asked himself.

Abhimanyu then read the last page he had written in the voice of his character. He always did that in order to get back into the mood he had left the story in.

The part he was reading was a build-up to an intimate scene. He needed to immerse himself completely in the scene to write it further. He wanted to feel what he had been feeling the last time when he was writing it. He wanted to get his mojo back.

Abhimanyu let his imagination cruise across the sea in front of him. His mind was at work, trying to give birth to words. Words that would cast a spell on his readers. Words that would consume them. Words that would make them imagine themselves in that very scene.

He was a perfectionist. Much before he could expect his readers to fall in love with his words, he needed to fall in love with them himself. And, therefore, he made it a point every day to reread all that he had written the previous day. And in case he found himself thinking that his words didn't convey the feelings in the manner in which he wanted them to, he would delete them, sometimes thousands of them, without regret. Like that snail in the fable, Abhimanyu would often walk three steps forward and one backwards, at times two. This was why he always took so long to finish his books.

Now, as he looked out of his window upon the canvas
of the Arabian Sea, he was confident that he'd soon find
what he was looking for. However, that morning, it was
as if the words had chosen to play hide-and-seek with
him. His mind churned with the multiple ways in which
he could take the story forward, and that was precisely
what distracted him.

Options also bring with them the challenge of choice.
He struggled to zero down on that one line of thought
and decide the next course of his scene. He wanted it to
be a powerful one, something that would surprise his
readers, something that they would not want to get over
soon, something that would first tease them, then arouse
them and then leave them breathless.

He smiled while chasing the perfect set of words and
closed his eyes. His fingers moved lightly over the keys
on his laptop. His bare feet tapped the wooden floor
underneath. At one point, he leaned back in his chair
and stretched his legs. The loose knot of his bathrobe
unfastened and it flung open.

Possessed by thoughts of the intimacy which he had
to convey through his work, he looked down at himself.
His gaze travelled down the thin line of hair in the
middle of his chest. It moved down towards the cave of
his navel, surrounded by his rock-solid abs.

He took a good look at his athletic body and admired
it, something he always did when he looked at himself
in the mirror in his bathroom. He had worked hard on
it and resisted a lot of cravings to own this body that
he was in love with. His gaze travelled further down his

navel towards his black Brazilian-cut briefs. That was the only piece of clothing he was wearing under his undone bathrobe. His lean, muscular torso rose and fell with every breath. His thoughts strayed from the scene in the chapter to himself. His left hand, which till moments ago had been hovering over the keypad, descended upon his underwear.

Abhimanyu ran his fingers over himself. He was soft. His lips parted as his hand went down his trunks, to the middle area where it was slightly bulged. He adjusted his body against the back of the chair to find a comfortable position. He began to touch himself. At first, his hand moved slowly, then gradually picked up pace.

His eyes closed. After a few deep breaths, when he opened them again, the thin, frothy white lines of waves rising and falling in the sea in front of him flooded his vision. He wanted those untamed waves to break against his body and soak him.

Drenched with desire, he visualized the woman from the story he was writing lying near-naked on the seashore. He could see her – her body wet and covered in sand. He transported himself to the shore as well, lying next to the woman. They were on the edge of the sea, on the wet margin of sand where every few seconds the waves would come rushing and soak their bodies. She wore a white, transparent T-shirt, which clung to her body. Below that, she wore a black bikini bottom. In his imagination, it was sundown and there was nobody around. This was also the time in the scene he was writing.

They lay on their backs, their faces turned towards each other. Above them, the sky was preparing to welcome twilight. Her eyes looked deeply into his. She made the first move. Without uttering a word, she put her hand on his wet trunks. He gasped at her touch. In that moment, she owned him. He belonged to her. Her fingers felt him through his wet underwear and brought him to arousal. Her lustful eyes were glued to his. Her touch fuelled his manhood and it attained its full length.

Abhimanyu's eyes opened. He looked down and acknowledged how hard he was. He shut his eyes again and transported himself back to the shore. The woman slipped her fingers under the waistband of his wet underwear.

Aaaaaaah! He gasped and when his wild fingers brushed through his pubic hair, it was her hand that he imagined there. He wanted her fingers to feel him down there. Imagining her, he did to himself all that he wanted her to do to him.

He moaned and called out her name.

And then he moaned her name again, this time looking right into her eyes on the seashore. It felt surreal.

Inside his trunks, his fingers traced the stem of his aroused manhood. He held it in his palm and tightened his grip around it. It boosted his libido to admire its thickness.

In his thoughts, the woman rolled over him and sat on his chest facing him, her legs spread across his torso. She bent towards his head, taking a good look at his face. He stared back at her. His hand slipped inside her wet T-shirt. He held her right breast and lifted it. She was voluptuous. He let his hand discover the full shape of it. Her eyes shut in response.

His thumb and forefinger paid special attention to her nipples. They were already tightened and fully visible through her drenched T-shirt. All that while, she was busy stroking his throbbing manhood.

He lifted her breast again and this time let it fall. It collided against her other breast. They trembled like jellies, then came to rest. He couldn't resist any more and pulled the loose neck of her T-shirt down, letting her breasts bounce out over his face.

Right in that moment, Abhimanyu pulled down the waistband of his underwear. His big manhood unfurled. He was already wet and sticky. The pre-cum was on his fingers.

He couldn't take it any more. The tension that had built up now demanded a release. His breathing was heavy. His fist moved fast on the length of his penis while in his thoughts he stripped off the bikini bottom the woman was wearing.

The only piece of clothing she was left with was her wet white top. The loose neck was now tucked under the curves of her big breasts. To imagine her that way was deeply satisfying to him.

By then she had already pulled down his trunks till his thighs. She held his thick manhood in one hand and guided it to her vagina, aching for him. She let out a deep sigh when he entered her. It was just the two of them on the seashore, under the vast sky with the sea by their side. Nature had become their private bedroom.

She let out a deep moan as she let her lubricated body slip over his erection. She swallowed him in one go. A strong wave of salty seawater slapped against their bare bodies.

Abhimanyu's body trembled. His hips rose on the chair. His weight shifted from the base of his feet to his heels. His eyes remained closed, keeping him in the cocoon of the sensual experience on the seashore where she was furiously sliding up and down his erection, ruthlessly wanting him to cum for her.

He wanted her to slow down, but she showed him no mercy. She bit her lower lip while looking at him, as if she wanted to consume him. Her moans turned wilder. They were testimony to the heavenly pleasure she was deriving. She struggled to hold her ecstasy and dug her nails into his chest.

He couldn't take it any more. Back on his chair, his mouth opened and a moan escaped his throat. Hot semen rushed up the pulsating penis in his hand and exploded like a volcano upon his hard abs. When he was done, Abhimanyu fell back on his chair and gasped.

The next time he opened his eyes, the Arabian Sea looked calm. He got up and went to the bathroom to clean himself.

9

It had been two days since Rizwan had seeded the revenge theory in Asmita's mind. No matter how illegal and immoral the idea had sounded at first, towards the end of that meeting, she could see the satisfaction she'd get from it. She wanted to settle scores with the people at PaperInk, including its newly acquired author. She had walked out of Rizwan's office, breathing an air of revolt.

And yet there was something which continued to bother her. Her conscience! As more time passed since she had met Rizwan, her conscience began to tighten its grip on her thoughts.

Asmita sat in the office cafeteria with a cup of tea, looking out of the window and contemplating what she was going to tell Rizwan. She was beginning to have second thoughts about his offer. He had almost convinced her when they met, but now that she'd had time to think, the whole thing felt morally problematic.

The constant debate between right and wrong had taken away Asmita's peace of mind. Sitting there alone, she realized that this had to stop. Making up her mind suddenly, she decided that she wouldn't do it. She would call Rizwan and thank him for his offer, but politely refuse it. She immediately pulled out her cellphone to drop him a message but just then saw Maaya and Peter entering the cafeteria. They looked happy, laughing at something – perhaps an inside joke. The glow on their faces of acquiring a bestselling author felt like salt on the wounds on her heart. The regret of losing a good editor was nowhere to be seen. She put her phone back, deciding to delay her final decision on Rizwan's proposal.

Asmita was angry at herself for being unable to take a call. One moment, she wanted to say no and the very next, she wanted to accept. She found herself standing at the crossroads of morality and revenge, with no idea of which way she wanted to turn.

This sine curve of moving from one extreme to the other has to stop somewhere and soon, she told herself.

'Hi Asmita.'

Maaya's voice broke into her thoughts. Asmita had sunk so deep into them that she hadn't seen her boss coming up to her.

'Oh, hello,' she almost whispered.

Maaya took a seat on the other side of the table.

'Asmita, I am here to ask you if you had a chance to reconsider your decision?'

Little did Maaya know that Asmita had moved on to rethinking her decision about working with Rizwan.

There was no one else in the cafeteria. This opportunity had prompted Maaya to informally reach out to Asmita yet again.

Outside of the closed cabin glass doors, which suggested hierarchy and officiousness, a cafeteria provided them with an easier, more casual environment that could dilute the difference in their positions and let them have a conversation as two individuals.

Maaya's question made Asmita shift her eyes to the cup she was holding.

'You can take back your notice any day, Asmita. You know that, right?' she reminded the younger woman compassionately.

Asmita nodded politely, her gaze still fixed on the cup in her hands.

'Look at me. At least say something,' Maaya insisted.

Asmita said, 'I am concerned about my career. So yes, I have been thinking about all the options I have.'

'At times, in the heat of the moment, we end up taking decisions we regret for life. I don't want you to make that mistake. You know what I mean. Right?'

Asmita took a moment to acknowledge that. 'I do.'

'Good,' Maaya said, smiling and putting her hand on Asmita's, trying to comfort her. 'Should I reject your exit request today itself then?'

Asmita was taken aback by her directness. *How shamelessly insensitive are you, Maaya?*

She pulled her hand away.

'Would you like to reconsider your decision too?' Asmita responded, and this time, looking straight at her boss, she added, 'Perhaps that too was taken in the heat of the moment?'

Maaya stiffened.

'Had that been in my hands, Asmita, I would have done it. But it has to do with Abhimanyu. And you know that. It is a ridiculous demand from him ...'

'And you are supporting it,' Asmita cut her off, making her final point.

Maaya paused and then, looking unabashedly at Asmita's face, she nodded. 'Yes. Yes, I am supporting his ridiculous demand because I need him at PaperInk.'

Asmita gave a sarcastic smile in return and said nothing.

Maaya got up from the chair, but before she turned away, she looked at Asmita and said, 'I have to put PaperInk first. That doesn't mean I don't care about you. I do, which is why I want you to reconsider your decision. I can restructure your compensation and perks, if that's what would motivate you. This is an opportunity. Don't let your ego ruin it. Think about it.'

Maaya waited for Asmita to say something, but the latter didn't. She shook her head, and then, in clear words, let her colleague know that at any point in time, till the last day of her notice period, she could change her decision, should she feel like doing so. Then, after putting a hand on Asmita's shoulder, she gave her a single nod and walked away.

The reasons for Asmita to stay back at PaperInk had just doubled. After Rizwan, now Maaya had made the deal even sweeter. And yet, her conscience wanted her to ignore all of it, at least temporarily, if not permanently.

Later that evening, engaged in a phone call on her Bluetooth earphones, Maaya walked inside the washroom to wash her face and redo her make-up. It looked empty. She continued to speak while multitasking.

'Find a replacement for Asmita,' she said. On the other end of the call was someone from the consultancy in charge of hiring for PaperInk.

After listening to the reply from the other end, Maaya spoke again. 'I already asked her. But she is being too stubborn and an emotional fool as well.'

While listening to the consultant, she put on some lipstick and pressed her lips together. Then she said, 'No! I can't work this way. You know me. This is not a place for inflexible people. If you can't adjust, you will be shown the door. Good that she asked for it herself.'

As she heard the reply, she touched up her forehead.

'Yes! I know she is good. But I am sure there are even better people out there. Let's find them.'

She pulled out a comb and smoothened her hair with her hand as she brushed it.

'Oh, come on! Don't tell me it is difficult to acquire good talent. I just got Abhimanyu on board.'

There was a long pause. Maaya chuckled as she listened to the speaker on the other side.

'Great. Work on it then,' she said and disconnected the call.

She then sprayed some perfume on her neck and her wrists. She looked at herself in the mirror, rubbing her wrists against each other, completely unaware that a few metres away, the third toilet stall was actually occupied. In it was Asmita.

10

As if she already didn't have much on her plate, a new problem was waiting for Asmita at home. Her mother's health had deteriorated again.

Turned out that the doctor's initial opinion wasn't correct. Her mother complained once again of acute pain on the left side of her chest, and also in her left underarm. She was in bed, holding a hot-water bottle against herself, trying to relieve the pain.

Worried, Asmita sat next to her and placed her hand on her mother's forehead. She gently stroked it. Her mother complained that she wasn't being able to raise her left arm.

'It hurts,' she whispered and closed her eyes. Her only relief was that her daughter had finally come home.

Ever since her father's untimely death in a road accident, around the same time as Asmita's college graduation, the two women had looked after each other. Asmita had become the breadwinner of her family, while her mother continued to be a homemaker. The duo had done well for themselves, and their bond had become stronger than ever. As on previous occasions, the older woman knew that she would soon feel better now that her daughter had come home.

'Did you take your medicine, Ma?' Asmita asked, continuing to caress her mother's forehead.

Her mother nodded slowly, eyes still closed. Tucked inside a quilt, she remained calm, trying to bear her pain. Moments later, with great difficulty, she turned sideways. Asmita helped her. She then softly stroked her mother's back, trying to put her to sleep.

As Asmita watched her mother's body rise and fall with every breath, she realized that the fear for her mother had put her professional worries on the backburner.

She was lost in her thoughts till it finally occurred to her that she had not yet collected her mother's test reports from the hospital.

'Shit!'

The events on the professional front had kept her on her toes, giving her no time to drive down to the hospital, nor had she even remembered to do so. Besides, after their hospital visit, her mother had begun to recover, and therefore getting the test reports hadn't seemed urgent.

Asmita called up the hospital to ask about them now and realized that bad news had been waiting for her for the past three days. The lab assistant told her that he could send her the results on email. Asmita was relieved that she wouldn't have to leave her mother. She dictated her email ID to him.

Soon, her mother's angiography test results were in her inbox.

She realized that bad news had been waiting for her for the past three days. There was an above 90 per cent blockage in one of her coronary arteries and above 75 per cent in another. In the middle of all the medical jargon, these plain English words marked in bold font instilled a horror in her that she wasn't prepared for.

Asmita's heart was in her mouth. Her frenzied eyes scrolled up and down the PDF. She looked for more information online in order to get the complete picture. In the back of her mind, she kept praying that the lab had made a mistake; that what she was reading was incorrect; that something else, something mild, was behind her mother's deteriorating health.

The suggestive action part of the report mentioned a coronary artery bypass graft surgery. Asmita panicked and, in order to get rid of any misunderstanding, she called the hospital lab.

While the lab assistant was polite enough, he declined to explain the results to her. It was neither his job, nor was he equipped to handle such questions. 'Madam, you will have to consult the doctor tomorrow,' was all he kept saying to her.

The doctor had left for the day, and in the light of her mother's test report, *tomorrow* appeared to be far away. At once, Asmita thought of rushing to the emergency department in the hospital and getting a thorough understanding on her mother's report, but then she didn't want to leave her mother alone either.

What if she left her alone and …? Suddenly, Asmita's head was filled with too many unthinkable what-ifs.

She decided to call up Pooja, her physiotherapist friend, who also happened to be her schoolmate. Even though a physiotherapist would have no direct connection with an angiography report, her understanding of the report would be relatively better than her own. Besides, she couldn't think of anyone else to call up in this hour of crisis. She first forwarded her friend the PDF on her phone and then dialled her number.

Pooja, who had just finished her shift, asked her to give her some time to go through the report, and promised that she'd call back as soon as she was in her cab home.

And when she did, she confirmed Asmita's fears. 'Aunty is at great risk of heart attack, Asmita. I'm sorry.'

'We need to do a bypass surgery on her. There is no other way.'

It was the morning after Asmita had learnt of her mother's condition from the test reports. She was back in the hospital. And this time, she was in a heart surgeon's chambers.

The maid who came in the morning had stayed at home with her mother. Asmita had taken leave without telling anyone at the office. She didn't give a damn about it, especially not since she'd overheard Maaya in the washroom talking about replacing her.

The cardiac surgeon didn't mince words and Asmita had no doubts now that inside her calm-looking mother there sat a ticking time bomb.

She quailed before asking him the next question. The doctor was still going through the angiography report.

'Will she be fine?' she almost whispered. Her heart sank as soon as the words were out of her mouth. With bated breath, she desperately waited for his answer.

'Things look bad in this report,' the doctor said slowly, his eyes still on it.

The fear inside Asmita grew. Demons danced and wreaked havoc in her mind.

The doctor looked at her. 'It is challenging but curable. What makes this more complicated is her history of diabetes and high blood pressure. So, to answer your question – will she be fine? I can only tell you once we perform the surgery. Your current focus should be setting up that operation.'

'How soon?' Asmita's eyes were already wet by then. Yet, out of sheer strength of will, she held her tears back instead of letting them flow down her cheeks.

'As soon as possible,' the doctor said, handing the reports back to her. He could see that Asmita was on the verge of breaking down and finally said, 'Listen! There have been patients who were in worse condition than your mother. They are doing fine today.'

Finally, Asmita heard the words she had been desperate to hear. They instilled hope in her. And yet, the fact that she now knew that the doctor could tell she was on the verge of crying made it even harder for her to hold her tears back. Looking at the blurred face of the cardiac surgeon through her wet eyes, she nodded hard, trying to convince herself that things would be fine for her mother too.

The doctor scribbled something on his notepad and tearing off the page, handed it to Asmita. He had prescribed some new medicines and listed the tests that needed to be done before the surgery. Asmita went through them and then slipped the paper, along with the reports, in the manila envelope she was carrying.

She asked her final question. 'What would be the cost of this entire thing?'

'You can check the details with my assistant outside. Roughly, a few lakhs. Between six to seven.'

Suddenly, there was a new lump in the back of Asmita's throat and she struggled to swallow it.

11

'I have reconsidered my decision. I won't quit,' Asmita said, standing in front of Maaya the next day.

The moment Asmita had arrived in the office, she'd walked straight to Maaya's cabin. She hadn't even waited for Maaya to greet her before she said what she had to. Anger and misery had made her fearless.

Awaiting Maaya's response, she gripped the handles of her laptop bag, which hung from her shoulder.

Maaya was taken aback by the way in which Asmita had invaded her personal space, and the manner in which she announced her decision. It made her a bit uncomfortable. Besides, she found the sudden change of heart quite surprising. And yet, she chose not to react to the younger woman's temporary lack of manners, given that what she had just said was what Maaya had wanted too.

'Oh!' was Maaya's only initial response. She took a moment to absorb the news and then, taking off her glasses, she smiled at Asmita as she said, 'That is such wonderful news, Asmita.' She made a mental note to tell their consultant to stop scouting for new editorial talent.

Then she got up from her chair and walked up Asmita. In a gesture to acknowledge how happy she was, she put a hand on Asmita's shoulder and repeated herself. 'Truly! This is such wonderful news. Thank you.'

Not wanting to stay any longer in Maaya's chamber, Asmita turned to leave when her boss's voice came from behind her, reminding her of something.

'You know what this means, right?'

Asmita immediately stopped and turned around. 'You can send me Abhimanyu's manuscript, whenever it is ready,' she said.

Maaya breathed a sigh of relief. Everything was finally falling into place. She beamed at Asmita, who nodded and was about to pull open the glass door of the cabin when Maaya stopped her.

'As I'd promised, I will discuss restructuring your compensation and perks with Peter,' Maaya said, wanting to let her know that she intended to keep her word.

'Thank you, but that won't be necessary,' Asmita said.

Maaya was stunned to hear that. She kept looking at the woman before her, trying to read her eyes, when Asmita spoke again.

'Perhaps you can do so in the next appraisal cycle, based on my work.'

Maaya forced a smile on her lips as Asmita walked out of her cabin.

Back at her desk, Asmita let out a deep breath. She took a good look at her surroundings, the place she had planned to leave but couldn't any more. She shook her head, as if to rid herself of the past. She wasn't going to be the person she had been; for something vital within her had changed.

She pulled out her phone from her bag and typed a text. 'I have rejoined PaperInk.'

The message was sent to Rizwan.

Abhimanyu looked at his phone. It was a message from Maaya.

'Asmita has reconsidered her exit. She is ready to work on your book.'

A wicked smile bloomed on his face. He raised his eyes and stared out of the window at the horizon. A sense of victory filled his chest.

So, you finally went down on your knees in front of me.

Unable to hold it back, he let out a joyous 'YES!', celebrating his ability to crush Asmita's spirit. He was obsessed with her. He didn't realize how and when that had happened. Perhaps after she had put in her papers, because that act had been a big blow to his ego. But it was now restored. As much as he would have wanted to deny it, the fact was that ever since he had met Asmita, she had taken permanent residence in one corner of his mind. And now, to make her work for him was his victory.

Welcome back, Asmita Mullick.

He kept the phone back on his desk.

On the word document open before him, it was suddenly as if his words had been waiting for him to type them out. He couldn't wait to finish his manuscript and make Asmita read it. Eventually, that's what he had wanted in the first place – to make her go through his work by hook or by crook.

He clearly remembered what she had said weeks before, that she didn't like popular fiction. And now, after she was finally ready to edit his work, something strange happened to him. His pride, which had earlier demanded that Asmita read his work, now wanted her to like it as well. And he didn't want her to just *say* that she liked it, because she was going to be his editor. He wanted her to genuinely like it.

To make someone who hates you like your work is an insane kind of obsession. But that's exactly what was now playing in Abhimanyu's head. The chances of that happening were negligible; in fact, almost non-existent in this case. And yet, Abhimanyu was up for this challenge.

That she didn't consider his genre at par with the one she worked on had left a burning desire in his heart to prove her wrong. In his mind, he demanded from her the same respect, if not more, that she had for her literary fiction authors. If his work could change her mind and make her accept how wrong she had been to have that perception for so long about popular fiction, it would be an altogether different kind of triumph for him.

You haven't yet read a good enough commercial fiction book. Wait and watch, Asmita.

He had indeed begun to walk down the road of dangerous obsession. This mania fuelled him to finish his book much before he had planned to. It brought out the very best in him.

That day Abhimanyu wrote non-stop for hours. It was the same for the next few days. He didn't step out of his house, didn't go to the gym, didn't watch any web series or read any books. He ate, intermittently drank some wine, slept, bathed and wrote. After he finished the story, he went back to the very beginning. It was his final draft and yet he rewrote several chapters, thousands of words, in order to further improvise and take his manuscript to a level of far greater storytelling; something he had hardly thought existed. In six days, he was ready with the final manuscript of his next novel.

12

Four days after Asmita rescinded her resignation at PaperInk, she watched her mother being taken into the operation theatre. Over the last few days, her condition had deteriorated further and she was in terrible shape.

Worry ate at Asmita as she held onto the medical papers and took a seat in the small hall outside the operation theatre. The doctors had told her that it was going to take somewhere between four to six hours for the surgery to be finished.

Asmita hadn't eaten anything since that morning. Her mother had been admitted in the hospital the previous day, and since the last evening, had been put on a liquid diet. Even though the surgery was scheduled for 10 a.m. that day, it was already noon and things were just beginning.

One of the hospital staff advised Asmita to go to the cafeteria on the ground floor and eat something. Asmita nodded politely but remained in her seat. She didn't have the stomach to digest anything. Anxiety had already filled her belly. Negative thoughts crossed her mind every now and then. She recalled losing her father.

What if I lose Ma as well?

She shook her head, convincing herself that nothing of that sort would happen. Her mother would soon be fine. Asmita wasn't much of a religious person, but sitting alone in the cold hall of the hospital, she thought of God several times. Her silent prayers helped her distract herself from the negative thoughts. Occasionally, she took out her phone and tried to keep herself busy with a few submissions she was supposed to read. She failed to focus on them either. Her eyes moved from one line to another without absorbing a thing. She tried rereading what she had read moments back to understand what it meant. It was all in vain. Eventually, when she couldn't concentrate on work, she switched to Instagram.

She landed on Maaya's page. The last posted photo was of her with Peter and Abhimanyu. It was from the night they had signed the contract. The accompanying caption read, 'So excited to bring to you Abhimanyu Razdan's new novel. Stay tuned!'

Abhimanyu's handle was tagged in that post. Asmita tapped on it and, in no time, she was on his page.

She looked at the numerous photos of the man she abhorred. He looked breathtakingly handsome in all of them. Asmita's heart filled with not just hatred but jealousy as well.

She clicked a random photo and it expanded. There was an unending series of comments underneath. They were from his followers, almost all of them women.

She read a few. They were of all kinds – cheesy, heartfelt, flirty and a lot of them were without words, instead using a series of emojis, mostly hearts and kisses. She wondered if these women had any clue about the kind of person their favourite author was in real life.

Fall for the book, but not for its author. You have no idea who he really is.

Pitying his fan base, she closed that image and moved on to his next one.

Abhimanyu's latest pictures on his Instagram handle were from a portfolio shoot done at his home. In them, he was seen in the comfort of his ecosystem, creating stories. These were candid pictures in which he wasn't looking into the lens. The camera had captured him being himself, in his natural habitat. It offered Abhimanyu's readers an insight into his space and his mood while he penned down the stories they fell in love with.

She again scrolled through the comments section again. Her heart ached to read praise for the man she disliked so much.

Ever since their unfortunate parking lot run-in, this man had taken up permanent residence in her mind. And now, whatever the reason, for a while, Abhimanyu had successfully distracted her thoughts from her mother's ongoing operation. She realized this as soon as she closed his profile on her phone. With it, the uneasy sensation once again crawled up her spine as soon as her eyes looked at the door of the operation theatre in front of her.

Maaya's eyes twinkled when Abhimanyu's email arrived in her inbox. The subject line read 'First draft'. She couldn't hold herself back from clicking open the email. A smile spread on her lips as she double-clicked the attached Word document.

As soon as it opened, she began reading. Every subsequent step on her aspirational dream to publish an A-list author brought unparallelled excitement into her life. That she was one of the very few people to read Abhimanyu's first draft made her feel special.

Damn! This manuscript would have gone to some other publisher had it not been for me.

She wanted to cherish that moment, celebrate it. Maaya got up and got herself some coffee from the pantry. Then she pulled out the box of chocolate chip cookies from the cupboard underneath her desk. Once she sat back in her chair, she was ready to read what Abhimanyu had cooked up.

In the company of his words, the coffee and cookies tasted even more delicious. In the opening paragraphs, he introduced her to the town of Munnar. She could clearly visualize it through his words. At once, she was virtually transported to that hilly town of Kerala.

As she read on, she felt like she lived in one of the houses he was describing. And, from the terrace of this house she lived in, she could see the vast tea estates all around. It felt amazing to travel through Abhimanyu's words. That opening scene assured Maaya that the price they'd paid to get Abhimanyu on board was worth it. *You are magical, Abhimanyu!*

He had written the story in first person, from the young boy's perspective. Maaya roamed the hilly tracks of Munnar through this boy's eyes. He was nineteen. He had dreams, just like many boys his age. He had his own set of challenges, like others in his peer group.

He was single; he'd never had a girlfriend. He wanted one but didn't have the courage to look into the eyes of a girl and hold a conversation with her. He often found himself in one-sided love affairs.

One reason he never acted upon his desires was due to his upbringing. The boy belonged to a low-income family. In his mind, romance was for the rich – boys who could afford to take their girlfriends out on dates and dinners, buy them gifts and flowers. He could not even treat himself to good food in a restaurant, forget taking someone else on a date.

In the next chapter, Abhimanyu had described him as a decent boy, one who seemed to be focused on his studies and stayed away from anti-social elements and acts. What Maaya liked the most about this boy was his shy and earnest nature. Women, no matter how much he yearned for their company, intimidated him. Most of the time, he would keep to himself.

Maaya loved the character sketch of this boy. She couldn't believe it was fiction. It appeared to be a true story. She felt sure that such a boy lived somewhere in the hills of Munnar. Now that the boy had been introduced to her, she couldn't wait for Abhimanyu to bring in the middle-aged woman he had talked about, the female protagonist. One of the reasons Maaya waited for her so eagerly was to see if she could relate with her; if she could step into the shoes of this woman, a person her age, and get to know what this boy felt for her. She already liked this boy so much. And now she wanted to see how this affair between him and the woman would start. Getting to know their initial chemistry thrilled her.

By the time the first two chapters had come to an end, Maaya had finished her coffee. Her plate was left with only cookie crumbs. She was thoroughly enjoying the story and wanted to move on to the third chapter, but the calendar alert on her mobile told her that it was time for the weekly editorial meeting.

13

After letting Maaya know that she wasn't quitting PaperInk, Asmita had applied for a week's leave. It had been granted to her immediately.

Fortunately for her, her mother's surgery went well. Immediately after her operation, she was taken to the ICU and kept there for two days. Once her vitals had stabilized, she was shifted to a semi-private room. The moment she was in a condition to talk properly, the first thing she wanted to know was how much money had been spent on her.

Asmita told her that she was yet to find out and pay the bills. The truth was that, as per the hospital policy, she had had to deposit Rs 5 lakh before her mother was admitted. Her mother also reminded her to thoroughly check the bills, for she feared that the hospital would try and increase the amount by charging them for tests and medicines she hadn't even been prescribed.

Asmita smiled and put a hand on her mother's forehead to calm her down. She was relieved that her mother was now out of danger. Her health was the only thing she cared about.

That week, Asmita had stayed at the hospital throughout. Every day, she'd go back home to take a shower and change her clothes, and then return as soon as she could to be with her mother. Understanding her situation, the maid in her house had agreed to time her arrival as per Asmita's need. Not only that, she had also helped Asmita by cooking her meals accordingly.

Five days after her surgery, Asmita's mother regained enough strength to sit up on her bed and have some solid food. Instead of using the bedpan, she insisted upon getting up and walking to the bathroom with the help of a nurse. As soon as that happened, she started asking for an early discharge. She asked this of every doctor who visited her to check on her progress. And when she didn't hear from them, she complained to the nurse that the hospital was trying to make money. Asmita and the nurses exchanged smiles whenever this came up. To Asmita, her mother beginning to protest against staying at the hospital was a sign that she was getting better, both physically and emotionally.

Her mother hated the taste of the hospital food. She abhorred the air in her room, which smelled of medicines. She hated that all she could see were the white curtains circling her bed, the overhead IV fluid bottles that hung from a stand, the medicines and the food tray by her side. She was bored of staring at the TV for hours on end.

On the sixth day, when Asmita's mother confronted the head of the cardiac department and alleged that he was unnecessarily trying to make more money by keeping her in the hospital, the doctor smiled and asked her, 'Would you prefer going back tomorrow or tonight?'

Asmita was delighted to hear those words. Her mother was surprised. Then she thought for a while and asked, 'Why not today afternoon?' It was 10 a.m. by the clock.

The doctor burst into laughter. Asmita went around the bed and gave her mother a hug.

By the time evening fell, mother and daughter had left the hospital together and a harrowing week had come to an end.

Once home, Asmita assumed complete responsibility for her mother's health and well-being, doing everything for the older woman herself. She would give her sponge baths and dress the area around her stiches. She administered her medicines, monitored her blood pressure and fed her fruits and non-oily food.

On the ninth day, she went back to work. She had hired an attendant to look after her mother in her absence.

'Hey, how's your mother now?' Shalini, the commercial fiction editor, asked Asmita.

'She is doing better now. I have left her with an attendant for today. I am a bit worried, though. It's the first time I've been away from her for this long since the operation.'

'I hope she gets well soon.' That was Maaya, who had walked up to Asmita's desk to check on her mother's health. She put a hand on Asmita's shoulder as she spoke.

'Thank you,' Asmita said.

Maaya smiled and, after a brief pause, asked, 'Ready to work?'

Asmita looked down, shutting her eyes and nodding.

'Great, then! Abhimanyu's manuscript has arrived. Can I send it to you today?'

Asmita was surprised to find out that Abhimanyu had already finished his first draft. *Had he already finished it before signing the contract with PaperInk?* she wondered.

Holding Maaya's gaze, she nodded again. 'Yes, please,' she said confidently.

'Wonderful! I will email it to you right away. You will love it,' she said and walked away.

'I hate you for this.'

That was Shalini. She drew Asmita's attention back the second their boss had left their worktable.

Asmita turned and looked at the other woman in confusion. 'Sorry?'

Shalini smiled and made her point. 'For working on Abhimanyu's novel.' She raised her eyebrows twice, as if pulling Asmita's leg.

'And the irony is that I didn't want to work on it,' Asmita responded, rolling her eyes.

'I heard that.'

'So don't be jealous of me. If anything, sympathize with me.'

Shalini smiled and turned her eyes back to her laptop.

The forwarded email carrying Abhimanyu's manuscript arrived in Asmita's inbox in the next few minutes. She tried not to be sensitive about it and deal with it just like she would have with any other manuscript.

Asmita scrolled down Maaya's email to read Abhimanyu's original email inline.

At first, it felt strangely uncomfortable to see his email in her mailbox. In many ways, it announced to her that he'd finally intruded upon her space. That she *must* click on the attachment in his email was proof of his victory over her.

Realizing that she was beginning to give in to negativity, she reminded herself of the fact that things were finally looking better. Her mother was on her way to recovery. That was what mattered the most to Asmita. The rest was secondary. She pushed herself to move on and double-clicked the file. With that began her journey into Abhimanyu's professional life. Or, at least, that's what she thought.

She had never done before what she was doing now – reading a manuscript while holding a very strong dislike for its author. She had only read the first five paragraphs when she felt that the beginning could have been a lot better than what it was. She had expected a lot more from an author whose work sold in such crazy numbers. *You haven't impressed me, Mr Bestselling Author.*

Even his beautifully crafted sentences fell short of impressing her. In her subconscious mind, she thought – *It has to be your personality and not your art that charms women. Huh!*

Against the backdrop of her bias against him, Asmita finished reading the first two chapters. She took a short break and got up for some coffee.

Shalini noticed her and excitedly asked, 'So?'

Asmita responded with one word: 'Trash.'

Shalini's eyes widened in utter disbelief.

'You want to read it yourself?' Asmita offered.

Shalini badly wanted to, but hesitated. Taking up Asmita's offer seemed inappropriate to her. It would mean judging Asmita's judgement. But then, she couldn't resist either. After all, it was Abhimanyu Razdan's novel's first draft. She quickly nodded her head. Her huge smile and twinkling eyes revealed her excitement.

This very excitement pissed off Asmita. With a push of her hand, she swirled the back of her chair.

'Okay, just give me whatever you have read so far. I will delete the document after reading it,' Shalini said.

This very excitement pissed off Asmita. With a push of her hand, she swirled the back of her chair. 'Cool! I'll send it to you once I'm back with my coffee,' Asmita said.

While she punched the buttons on the coffee machine, Asmita talked to herself. *What's so great about him? What exactly do people like about him? Or his work?*

Now that she had gotten a taste of his writing, she had even begun to judge his readers and everyone who was smitten by him, including her colleague Shalini.

Is this what India loves reading? Is this what makes a bestseller?

The questions still on her mind, she walked back to her desk with her mug full of coffee. She forwarded Shalini the two chapters she had read. 'There you go,' she said, looking at her colleague.

Shalini rubbed her hands in excitement, thanked Asmita and immediately turned to her laptop. Clearly, she couldn't wait to go through the chapters. Gazing at her, Asmita smirked, observing her excitement.

God! What has this man done to women?

Shalini's eyes were glued to the screen. Asmita shook her head, smiling, and turned to her own laptop. She opened Chapter Three. But before she could begin reading it, something occurred to her and she looked back at Shalini.

'Do you find him good-looking?' she asked her colleague.

Shalini looked up from the screen. 'Who? Abhimanyu?'

'Mm-hmm.' Asmita nodded.

The big smile on Shalini's face gave Asmita her answer. She wished she could stop Shalini from answering it in words now. But Shalini didn't know that.

'Obviously! He is so hot. Don't you think?' her eyes widened as she said.

Asmita stuck out her pursed lower lip and shrugged.

'What does that mean?' Shalini confronted.

'Umm ... I mean he is kindaaa okaaayish ... you know ...' she dragged her answer and then quickly added, 'I mean ... not bad.'

'Really?' Shalini said and then added. 'You are an outlier, then. You know that, right?' she added.

Asmita smiled. Before Shalini got back to reading Abhimanyu's work, she said one final thing.

'And what makes him sexier is his mysterious mind, his thoughts, his words. Wait for him to make his characters fall in love. You will see,' she said and then her attention was once again on the words in front of her.

For once, Asmita didn't mind the innocence with which her neighbour praised the author whose work she was to edit. Perhaps she was bored and tired of loathing him, or maybe she wanted to be able to edit his work without hating his guts. Besides, sustaining anything with the same aggression beyond a point is difficult, even when it's hate. *If I have to get the job done anyway, why not do it without letting my blood boil?* she thought while looking at Shalini.

Asmita turned to carry on with Chapter Three. She sipped her coffee and relaxed in her chair.

There was something different about this chapter. Unlike the previous two, this one sparked an interest in her. Abhimanyu had introduced a middle-aged, south Indian woman in this one. She was a homemaker and a mother of two kids, a girl and a boy, aged seven and five.

It was somewhere towards the end of the very first page of this chapter that Asmita found herself unknowingly drifting with Abhimanyu's words. There was a scene in which the young narrator of the book sees the middle-aged woman for the first time. Somehow, that scene began to consume Asmita.

All that the boy did was simply look at this woman. And that was it. But there was something magical about the way Abhimanyu had written the scene.

The boy sees her for the first time at a bus stop. She stands under a shed, talking to someone on her phone. It's late afternoon. There is nobody around them. Underneath the messy hair, his eyes are stuck on that woman, mesmerized by her beauty. Even though she is on a call, she notices him notice her. And, for the first time in his life, he doesn't take his eyes off a woman.

Abhimanyu had described that moment marvellously.

Not that he didn't try to steal a glance at her and then look the other way. He did, but found that he couldn't look away. And now he is stuck on her. He is hypnotized. As if the connection between his mind and his body has been cut off and he can't do anything about it. The only sense that's working for him is his sight.

Then, slowly, it all makes a step-by-step comeback. He feels an undercurrent in his skin, a tingling in his fingertips, but it's too early for him to be able to relax his fingers. Meanwhile, the woman has chosen to look the other way.

Unable to help himself, he admires the grace with which she carries on with her call. He is aware that perhaps he is making her feel awkward, but he just can't help it. He is sorry about making her feel uncomfortable. He wants to tell her that this is not him; that something has happened to him. His lips part, but not a single word comes out of his throat. There is a lump in the back of his throat, which he wants to swallow, but he isn't able to do that either.

The next second, his brain restores his hearing, as if he has just come up to the surface after diving into a body of water. He can now hear her voice. She is talking to someone close to her in Malayalam. It is his mother tongue as well. She is soft-spoken and her words make her seem like a caring person. There is so much love in what she is saying and the way she is saying it. He yearns for her to talk to him like that. He is drawn to her.

Awestruck, his eyes take in her fine white silk saree, which has a golden border to it. The sight of her naked, slim and soft midriff consumes him. Then suddenly, something makes him look down at himself, at his untucked shirt over his wrinkled pants. He is ashamed to present himself this way to this beautiful stranger.

The string of white and orange jasmine flowers that she is wearing in her hair has become slightly askew. How he wishes to fix that while she keeps talking on the phone. He wants to take care of her.

He has been attracted to beauty a number of times, but never before has he wanted to take care of it, to protect it.

Silently, he observes her other free hand, how it moves in the air as she talks. He smiles, looking at the random invisible figures she is unknowingly drawing in the air. He notices every minute detail of her posture, even how she shifts her weight from one leg to other. He is in love with that as well. Occasionally, when she tucks her strands of hair behind her ear, he wishes that he could do that for her. He needs to be close to her. He wants to smell her hair.

There is something very different about this woman. He doesn't understand why he is so fascinated by her. That she isn't a girl his age doesn't matter to him. Instead, he senses a far superior level of warmth in her arms because of her very age; in the fullness of her body, which perhaps would have nourished and raised human beings. The contentment that a woman like her can provide him is unmatched to that of girls his age from his college.

By the time he comes back to his senses, a tender feeling for her has engulfed him. Deep within him, something raw has been exposed and it demands attention. It can't be left unattended now.

All that Abhimanyu had described in that chapter was just one thing – the boy's gaze. But the rawness of that gaze kindled something intense inside Asmita. The way Abhimanyu had described the scene kindled her fantasies.

For her, the sight of a young boy beholding an adult woman like that was innocent as well as intense. She wanted to read on and find out what happened next, but a call from home interrupted her plan. It was the attendant back home, and she needed to know where her mother's medical reports were.

It is evening. Most of the people at work have left for home. Asmita has stayed back in office. She is wearing a saree. A white saree with a golden border. It is way past her usual time to leave the office. But she's stayed back to finish reading Abhimanyu's manuscript. Moments ago, she scrolled all the way down to the last sentence and read it.

She knows it is already late. Outside her office, she can see night taking over twilight. The chairs around her are abandoned. She hears faint conversation at a distance. It comes from the far end of the office, where the sales team sits. Someone there has turned on the music on his laptop.

It is unusual for her to stay back in office in order to finish her work. However, she is rejoicing in the delay. It isn't like she's chasing a deadline. Nobody has asked her to finish reading the manuscript early. It was her call. Or to put it in the right way, she simply hasn't been able to resist finishing it. It is unputdownable.

She hates herself for being consumed by the words of a man she abhors. It feels like a guilty pleasure to step inside his creative mind and explore it. It feels like a sin, an act of adultery, to enjoy so much what she has wanted to hate. There is a strange sense of regret within her, and also an insane level of excitement. She wants to read the whole thing all over again. That's what his words have done to her.

It gives her a sense of thrill; the excitement of breaking rules, the very rules she had unconsciously made for herself. She stretches her legs and sinks into her chair.

Even after she's finished reading the manuscript, she isn't in a hurry to go back home. She is in some sort of a trance; one that she doesn't want to come out of. Looking up at the ceiling through the lights strung on the jute ropes, she is still with the characters in Abhimanyu's world. They dance on the cemented ceiling, perch on the cast-iron panels that run across its length. She stays there for a while, watching them.

When she is finally ready to leave, she gets up from her chair. She turns back and her eyes meet Abhimanyu's. She is shocked to see him in her office, especially at this time of the day. The truth is that ever since she has read past Chapter Three of his manuscript, she has wanted to see him … badly. And now he is here. Right in front of her eyes.

Abhimanyu stands at a distance, looking at her. For some reason, he is wearing the same attire he wore the day the two of them had met for the first time.

His sharp eyes tell her that … he knows; he knows what she is going through in the aftermath of reading his work. He can see it clearly on her face. He knows that somewhere deep inside her heart, his words have touched her. And now he is here to measure the damage he has done to her.

Neither of them says a word. The faint music from the far end of the office continues to play in the background. Abhimanyu's intense gaze penetrates her, as if he's trying to read her mind, as if he is reverifying whether or not his words have kindled her desires. Has he left her happy, high and craving for more from him, of him? Did she burn in the ecstasy of his narration when he brought the two characters so close and pulled them asunder? Was there something left incomplete in the chapters, which she now desperately wants to complete as he stands in front of her? Did she imagine him gazing at her in that white saree, the way the boy in his novel stared at the woman?

She desires him so much. He can see her losing control of her body. Her legs shake. She is unable to stand. This is what Abhimanyu's proximity is doing to her.

He sees it all and steps forward. Still looking into her eyes, he puts his hand on the nape of her neck. Asmita can't believe what is happening. Her lips part and the next moment Abhimanyu takes her lower lip in his mouth. She can't take it any more.

She orgasms in her sleep. Her thighs, that were rubbing against each other, come to a sudden stop.

She wakes up.

14.

Through her sources, Maaya had prudently checked the calendar of upcoming big releases in the popular fiction category across publishing houses in India. It appeared to her that PaperInk could rake in the moolah if they brought out Abhimanyu's book within the next two and a half months. She immediately called Abhimanyu to discuss this with him.

'*Two and a half months?*' Abhimanyu reacted with shock.

'Yes! Five months from now the market will be flooded with numerous popular fiction titles. Across genres,' she said.

'So what?' Abhimanyu asked.

'If we bring out your novel as soon as possible, you will lead the bestselling charts for a longer duration.'

'Maaya, are you doubting my ability to lead it otherwise?'

'If I did, I wouldn't have fought my battle at PaperInk to get you on board, Abhimanyu.'

Abhimanyu kept mum.

Maaya pressed on. 'But I do know retailers and distributors.'

'What about them?' he asked.

'When it is only you out there, our sales team can push them to open their wallets for your work. When there are others along with you, their spends will get divided.'

'Hmm,' he acknowledged and his mind began to churn.

Meanwhile, Maaya continued, 'I don't doubt your ability at all, but you know how the industry and some authors go to the extent of manipulating sales figures to remain on the bestselling charts. It isn't a secret any more.'

'I do,' Abhimanyu confirmed, recalling Rizwan for a moment.

'This is the first time PaperInk will do such a huge print run. We have to renegotiate things with our distributors. It benefits us to release the book as soon as possible. And I am saying this because the first draft of your manuscript is ready. Asmita is already working on it.'

The mention of Asmita made him forget the point he had been going to make.

'Okay,' he said instead, and then quickly added, 'but then we will have to speed things up.'

'Absolutely. I will ask Asmita to brief the cover-design team while she gets on with the edits alongside. She would have read it by now, I believe.'

'Wait,' Abhimanyu stopped her and said, 'I would like to be a part of this cover briefing meeting.'

Abhimanyu was a control freak. When it came to his books, he wanted to drive everything and monitor everything. Unlike many authors, he never felt that his job finished only at writing. He would participate in every step of the process till the book hit the market, and even beyond to sustain its sales. Maaya liked this about him, but at the same time she was also wary of handing over every decision to him. She had seen the other extreme of this spectrum as well – authors hijacking the entire process and ruining it all. However, keeping in mind the crazy numbers Abhimanyu's works had sold in the past, she liked the idea of his presence.

'Should I schedule a telephonic meeting for tomorrow then?' Maaya asked.

'Ah, no. Schedule a meeting at your office. I will come. In fact, as time is of the essence, let us loop in marketing and sales as well to close things?'

Whenever the stakes were high, Abhimanyu preferred a face-to-face meeting. He wanted to read the expressions on the faces of the stakeholders and understand their body language. He wanted to verify if they were getting it right and if they meant what they were saying. A meeting at PaperInk would also give him an opportunity to get to know the mind of the person he was most interested in – his editor. Now that she had his manuscript and had most likely finished reading it.

'Makes sense! See you then,' Maaya said and disconnected the call.

The next morning, Abhimanyu walked into the office of PaperInk. Maaya had already sent the meeting invite to the team. Asmita was also included, but she had somehow missed the invite in her inbox. When the meeting alert popped up, she was in the cafeteria.

'You coming?' Nakul asked.

'Where?' Asmita asked back.

She looked pretty in her blue printed kurti and white leggings. Her short hair looked sexy and defined her diamond-shaped face even more. The white-strapped watch on her right hand, which held the coffee mug, completed her chic look. Her face had a glow. There was something different about her that day, something sweeter and more attractive.

Nakul smirked and said, 'The meeting. We are discussing Abhimanyu's book cover. Right?'

'Is there a meeting?' Asmita asked, surprised.

'Yeah. And you are in it,' Nakul said. 'I just saw Abhimanyu walking in,' he added.

'Wait, *what*? He is here?' Her jaw dropped open.

'Mm-hmm,' the designer said, nodding. 'Hurry up,' he said and left.

Asmita ran to her desk. There was a calendar invite waiting for her. She quickly clicked on it and opened the email. Maaya had mentioned discussion pointers in it – book jacket, editing deadlines, marketing and sales discussion.

'Shit! How did I miss this one?' she cried, checking the time on her laptop's screen. The next second she closed it, pulled out its power cord and rushed straight to the Romance Room.

She recalled telling Maaya the day before that she had finished reading the manuscript. But then that had been a very brief chat on text messages. She was yet to give her boss detailed feedback on the book and then begin editing it.

On her way to the meeting room, she found herself experiencing a strange kind of conflict within herself. After all, she was going to see the person whose words she had fallen in love with and whose personality she hated. She had no clue how to deal with this bizarre situation and face the man who had turned her world upside down, in more ways than one.

As soon as she saw him through the glass façade of the meeting room, a sudden chill shot up her body. Abhimanyu looked dapper in his light-blue blazer and off-white khaki pants. His long, curly hair shone in the sunlight, invading the room through the big window.

She pulled open the glass door and walked in.

People in the room were already busy, either setting up their laptops or opening their notebooks. Maaya was chatting with Abhimanyu, who sat next to her.

'Hi!' Asmita said politely to no one in particular. Her eyes met Abhimanyu's for only a microsecond and then shifted away. Her heart was beating loudly and she felt off-kilter.

With his designer glasses and that three-day-old stubble, Abhimanyu looked smoking hot. Asmita couldn't deny that he was handsome.

Abhimanyu acknowledged her arrival in the room with a small nod, without breaking his conversation with Maaya. He did this purposely, making it a point of ignoring Asmita in front of the people he had greeted cordially just a few moments ago.

This first spectacle of the cold war between the author and his editor went unnoticed by the others. The only empty chair in the room was bang opposite Abhimanyu. Overcoming her discomfort, Asmita pulled it out and settled on it.

Maaya began the discussion, opening with praise for Abhimanyu.

'I have finished reading the manuscript,' she said, looking at him and, closing her eyes in a theatrical display of pleasure, she finished, 'I can't tell you how amazing it is!'

When she opened her eyes, she saw Abhimanyu smile. 'It really is,' she repeated.

'Thank you, Maaya,' he acknowledged.

She went on to update everyone else in the room. 'We are going to release this book in the next two and half months.' She dropped the bomb on the table.

Everyone looked shell-shocked. Abhimanyu noticed the little drama unfold, all the while consciously ignoring the person who sat right across from him.

The very first resistance came from the production team.

'That's impossible,' Rajeev Subramanian, the production head, spoke up.

'Impossible?' Maaya asked, her eyes widening.

'Almost impossible,' he amended.

Maaya waited for him to go on.

'I don't see how our printers will agree to such short notice,' he said.

'But we have done this in the past. You know the drill, Rajeev.'

'Those were rare occasions, Maaya.'

'Well then, this is going to be the rarest of the rare,' Maaya said firmly.

Abhimanyu liked this treatment.

'Yes, and that's exactly the problem,' Rajeev said.

'What do you mean?'

'On those rare occasions, our highest print run was fifty thousand copies. This time it is two lakhs. You see the problem?'

Rajeev's words filled Abhimanyu's chest with immense pride. By putting down a print run four times higher than their biggest books so far, PaperInk was really going all out for him.

Asmita noticed Abhimanyu cautiously concealing his pleasure. She didn't miss the twinkle in his eyes, which were glittering with satisfaction.

Maaya pondered for a while and then said, 'Rajeev, can we please check once with the printers first? I would like things to be made crystal clear, instead of just acting on preconceived notions. I don't doubt that they are based on our past experiences. But I am open to taking exceptional calls, should I need to, to make this happen. We can pull out our current orders to them to make space for this one.'

Rajeev nodded. 'Sure! I will check our current orders with them in the pipeline. However, we are only 5 per cent of their business. Other publishers place bigger orders with them. So that's another caveat.'

Maaya hated to see her team telling her the challenges instead of offering solutions. This was the one drawback of inviting an author to these meetings. Everything came out in the open. However, Abhimanyu liked the fact that he was getting insights into their constraints. A print run this big, in such a short span, was indeed a tough ask. He knew that he was staring at a challenge, but a sweet one nonetheless.

At the same time, Abhimanyu strongly believed in the fact that it wasn't the publishing house that would make or break him, but his writing, which he had full confidence in.

'Whatever it is, Rajeev. Talk to them after this meeting and let me know,' Maaya said firmly, effectively ending the production part of the discussion.

'All right, let's talk about the cover now!' she announced and turned towards the author. 'Abhimanyu! Do you have any ideas in mind?'

'I do,' he started, and the room fell silent. Everyone waited for him to tell them how he visualized the cover of his upcoming book.

Abhimanyu smiled. 'Honestly, guys, there are actually too many ideas in my head, and I haven't been able to zero down on any single one. Right now, I'm really keen to know what you think.'

'Hmm ...' Maaya said.

Abhimanyu jutted his chin towards Asmita and said, 'I would love to know what the *editor* thinks of it ...'

Asmita looked at him, noticing his dismissive way of singling her out without even directly speaking to her.

Abhimanyu continued, '... now that she has finished reading the story.'

Asmita could see the devil in his twinkling eyes. 'Sure,' she said and looking straight at him, began.

'There is this scene in the story where this young boy plucks a purple jasmine flower from a stranger's garden. Unlike white and orange ones, the purple jasmine is rare. He does this because, the previous day, the middle-aged woman he calls aunty and is also in love with had expressed her desire to adorn her hair with a jasmine flower of that colour.'

Asmita's eyes moved around, taking in everyone at the table. That was the best way for her to avoid constant eye contact with Abhimanyu.

She continued. 'While he is plucking the flower, the dog in the house barks at him and starts chasing him. The boy jumps the fence and eventually falls on the ground. He has bruises on his elbows and knees, and yet the flower in his hand stays safe. All its petals are intact.'

Abhimanyu noticed the spark in Asmita's eyes as she narrated the scene he had written. It felt different, a good different, to hear his words in her voice. And the manner in which she was narrating the story felt even more important – almost spiritually so.

Leaning forward and resting his head in his hands, he listened to her with immense interest. The words she spoke were drenched with feelings, as if she had truly empathized with his characters. There was a great sense of affection in how she portrayed them, especially the boy.

Asmita continued further. 'Moment later, he enters this woman's house. Her husband is out of town on work and her kids are in school. He looks around for her but can't find her. He calls out for her, but there is no response. He is suddenly worried about her. The entire house is open. He searches for her from one room to another. Then finally, he enters the kitchen, located in the extreme end of the house. That's where he finds her. He sees that she is busy cooking, her earphones plugged into her ears. She is listening to music. He exhales a sigh of relief.'

An innocent smile lit up Asmita's face. Abhimanyu noticed it. And the second Asmita noticed him noticing her, she looked away.

For a moment, she lost track of what she had wanted to say next, but then recovered and got back on track.

'She is wearing a nightie and is humming along with the music. Without making any noise, the boy keeps staring at her from behind, watching her in this candid mood as she goes about her chores. There are bruises and blood spots on his arms and legs. His clothes are stained with dirt, and yet there is joy on his face. The joy of bringing a stolen flower for the woman he loves!'

Listening to his story being narrated with so much conviction and emotion was a different high for Abhimanyu. Asmita remembered the finer details and almost made that scene come alive in that meeting room for everyone. Abhimanyu's eyes were glued to her. She had his undivided attention. And unknowingly, with every word that she spoke, she was stroking his ego.

Well aware of his scrutiny, Asmita carried on making her point.

'This is a very powerful scene. It portrays love in its most raw and innocent form. I think we should make this visual the cover of our novel.'

That '*our*' felt like music to Abhimanyu's ears. He didn't say anything and, ignoring everybody else, continued to gaze at Asmita.

This time, looking at Nakul, Asmita added, 'We shoot this boy from behind, covered in the glory of dirt and bruises and maybe with a thin streak of blood on his elbow. We show this purple jasmine securely held in his hand. His bruises are his badge of honour and this flower his reward—'

'Incorrect!' Abhimanyu intervened at once, a hint of a smile on his lips. Looking right into Asmita's eyes, he slowly said, 'His reward is the happiness of that woman, which he will get when she turns around and sees him.' The smile on his lips widened, as if seeking Asmita's acknowledgement.

Asmita took a second or two to absorb what he said. He was right. She half-smiled back at him and thoughtfully nodded her head.

Maaya gleefully watched her editor and her author finally restoring their much-needed bonhomie. She breathed a sigh of relief.

Everyone went quiet for a while. Heads turned and looked at Abhimanyu. When he realized he had to say something, the delight on his face vanished and he said two words. 'It's good.' And that was it.

His eyes were glued to the table. He still appeared lost in thought.

Asmita couldn't understand what to make out of his '*It's good*' comment. *Is that some sort of a sarcastic remark I didn't get or did he really mean it?* She didn't know how to react to it. And yet she forced a smile on her face, which vanished as suddenly as it appeared.

'I don't think ...' Abhimanyu spoke again. His eyes were still lowered to the table. '... that there can be a better cover idea than this,' he finished and looked up at Maaya.

Thrill and joy ran through Asmita. The man whose words she had fallen for just confirmed in everyone's presence that there couldn't be a better cover than the one she had visualized for his novel.

'You like it?' Maaya double-checked.

'I *love* it,' he said, finally looking at Asmita, who was beaming.

'Should we add some romantic elements to this middle-class kitchen scene? You know, to make it clearer that it's a love story between this boy and this middle-aged woman?' Maaya added her two cents.

Asmita immediately felt that this was needless but didn't know if she could say that. To her rescue came Abhimanyu, who immediately interjected, 'Let it be just the way she's briefed it. I think those bruises and that flower are enough. Any romantic addition to it would actually be subtracting something from it.'

Once again, Abhimanyu wooed Asmita with his choice of words as he spoke up in her support.

Maaya took solace in the fact that it only made things easier for her. Authors seldom agreed to the first cover brief, and bestselling ones almost never. They always wanted more options to cherry-pick from.

'Great! We are done with the book jacket concept discussion then,' Maaya announced, throwing her hands in the air, cheering the completion of a difficult task so effortlessly.

'Now, do you have a title in mind?' she asked Abhimanyu.

'No,' he lied.

He had thought of one, but now fancied something else. 'I believe she will do justice to it,' he said, shifting his gaze back to Asmita. People in the room, who till a few days ago had heard of how Asmita had put in her papers because of Abhimanyu, were now sure that those had only been rumours. Everything appeared more than cordial between the two.

Maaya turned to Asmita. However, the latter wasn't prepared for this one.

'Ah ... I haven't thought about it,' she said and then looking back at Abhimanyu, added, 'but I certainly will now.'

'Eagerly waiting,' he responded.

'And where are we on the edits, Asmita?' Maaya asked.

'I am yet to start. I didn't know we were going to have this tight a deadline.'

Abhimanyu itched to ask for her views on his work and yet chose not to. He would keep that for a later one-on-one conversation, he decided.

'I know. We figured this out only yesterday,' Maaya said, and then added, 'How soon can you get started on this?'

'I have two books in the pipeline.'

'Can we pull up this one? I will push the deadlines of the other two accordingly,' Maaya asked.

Asmita agreed and said that she'd need about three weeks to finish the edits of the book, which was around ninety thousand words long.

Abhimanyu looked at the calendar on his phone and calculated the time he would have in his hands to go through Asmita's edits. As per his initial plan, he was going to override all her edits with that of his personal editor, whom he trusted more than anyone. However, in the light of Asmita's recent cover brief, he now wanted to wait and see what Asmita sent him.

Working backwards from the release date, Abhimanyu found himself with a tight window of only two weeks. He made a mental note to call his editor as soon as he stepped out of the office. *I will ask him to edit the manuscript alongside Asmita. Keep it ready, just in case.*

'Seems like we are done for the day,' Maaya announced. On that note, she dialled the cafeteria's number. She hadn't forgotten to order food from Abhimanyu's favourite bakery again. When it arrived, along with piping hot coffee, people grabbed their plates and Asmita, finding everyone's attention on the food, excused herself and left.

Around fifteen minutes later, when everyone was ready to leave the room, Abhimanyu bid them goodbye and then quickly asked Maaya the directions to Asmita's desk. He said that he needed to discuss a few things with her before she began editing. Maaya was willing to escort him, but Abhimanyu insisted on finding his way himself.

Outside the Romance Room, he looked for Asmita. Employees at PaperInk looked back at him in awe. In return, he smiled and moved on, fully aware of what it meant for him to walk around in a publishing house that had been so eager to get him on board.

He found Asmita. She was working at her desk with her back to him.

'Hey,' he said.

Both Asmita and her neighbour, Shalini, turned around to look at him.

'Oh, hi,' Asmita said hesitantly. She immediately got up from her chair.

Shalini waited for Abhimanyu to notice her and as soon as that happened, she greeted him with more words than Asmita had anticipated.

'Oh my God! It is such a pleasure to meet you. I have read your books and I just *love* them,' she said, extending her hand.

Any other time, Abhimanyu would bask in the glory of her admiration, but that day he was distracted. He shook hands with her but didn't bother to even ask her name.

Asmita wondered if he knew that Shalini was the editor who would have worked on his book had he not made his odd request. She kept that thought to herself and let Shalini cherish the joy of shaking hands with the author she was gaga about.

Abhimanyu gave Shalini one final smile and then turned to address Asmita.

'Can we talk?' he said.

Asmita looked around and then nodded. 'Sure,' she said, while not sounding sure at all.

'Should we sit in the cafeteria, then?' he proposed.

'Oh yes, the cafeteria would be fine,' Asmita said, relieved.

She didn't want a one-on-one discussion with him within the earshot of her colleagues.

Abhimanyu waited for her to step out into the aisle.

The two walked side by side. Abhimanyu was saying something to her, but Asmita's eyes and mind were busy scanning the office floor, watching her colleagues noticing her walk with him.

The cafeteria was empty. They found a corner table and sat across from each other.

Abhimanyu initiated the conversation.

'Listen ... I ... ' He paused as soon as he began, and then added, 'I liked the way you described that scene.'

'I didn't describe it. You described it. I only narrated it,' Asmita said.

Just a week ago, even in her wildest dreams, she wouldn't have imagined having such a warm conversation with Abhimanyu.

He smiled, looked down at the table and then back at her.

'You are right. I meant that I liked the conviction with which you narrated it,' and even before she could have somehow countered that one, he added, 'I mean the way you visualized it as the cover ... It's ... it's amazing.'

Across that table, Asmita's eyes kept playing hide-and-seek with Abhimanyu's. Revealing a small smile, she nodded and said softly, 'Thank you.'

'So, you have finished reading the entire story.'

'I have, yes.'

'And?' he prompted.

In her heart, Asmita fell a small thrill at being asked for her opinion by someone who otherwise was so full of himself.

'It's nice,' she said. And that was it. She didn't add anything else.

Abhimanyu hadn't seen that coming. *Have I misread her body language?*

He didn't know how to react to that 'nice'. After the conversation in the Romance Room, this was very different from what he'd expected. And those two words fell short of bringing him the joy he was there for. In fact, if anything, they felt bitter.

It would have been better if instead, she had said she didn't like it; just like she had said the other day that popular fiction wasn't her cup of tea. In that case, he would have attributed it to her lack of interest. A negative and critical review would have been more fulfilling than a positive one, which firmly put the book in an average box labelled 'nice'. Criticism, coming from a fan of literary fiction who didn't have an appetite for the beauty of simple language would have been a badge of honour. However, with that 'It's nice', she didn't leave him room for that. Abhimanyu somehow swallowed those two words and looked at her.

Asmita knew well enough that her words had hurt his ego, which was why she had said them in the first place. The truth was very different from what she had revealed. But how could she give this man his due, considering everything he had put her through? She enjoyed playing with his ego and making a dent in it. This! After she had unknowingly inflated it moments back in the meeting room.

Abhimanyu was at a loss for words. Asmita knew that for once, she had caught the bull by the horns. *I will hold him there for a little longer before setting him free.*

The king of romance sat right in front of her, consuming that tiny morsel of appreciation grudgingly. His discomfort was visible on his face. Asmita derived pleasure from it. In fact, she was glad that he had walked down to her desk and invited this upon himself. *You had come for a pep talk. But His Majesty will have to wait.*

'I see. So ...' he paused and then said, 'were there parts in the manuscript that were not so nice for you as well?'

Asmita kept looking at him. *I know what you are trying to do.*

He was playing it smart. If she revealed to him what she hadn't liked, she would also have to tell him what she'd found more than nice. And Asmita was determined not to make him feel good about anything, not after she'd already given him that by narrating the kitchen scene.

She spent a few seconds trying to recall specifics from the book.

'Hmmm ... I don't think so. All of it was equally nice,' she finally said with a smile, her eyes dancing.

Equally nice! That rubbed more salt on the open wound.

'I see…' Abhimanyu's knuckles tapped the table as he spoke and his face looked grim. *Do I look gullible? Because I am not.* 'I see…' he said.

Asmita noticed that but pretended that she didn't. She waited for him to speak, in case he had anything else to say. She was enjoying teasing him.

'But that's my opinion. As its creator, what do you think of it?' She turned the question around.

Abhimanyu looked at her with his dark eyes. *Are you messing with me because I am being nice to you?*

'I always believe there is scope for improvement,' he said, playing it modest.

'Hmm …' Asmita slowly nodded. *Come on, cut the drama and come to point.* She then quickly asked, 'Aren't all creative people self-critical of their works?'

'Can't speak for everyone.' He chuckled, and she couldn't help smiling back.

'Creativity is subjective. Besides, there is no end to improving. Even the best of the best works can be improved further. Don't you think?' he asked.

'No doubt about it. However, the point is whether or not there is any need to do so. One has to draw a line somewhere and move on to creating newer things. No?'

Abhimanyu nodded in agreement. The two kept talking for a while. Asmita was enjoying their conversation, but Abhimanyu was still dealing with the discomfort of not hearing what he had sought her out for. Given the signs he'd noticed in the meeting room, he had mellowed down in front of her and shown her a nicer version of himself. Now he hated himself for that. He had locked himself in his flat and put himself through a marathon of rewrites, had worked on his book over and over again, improving it as much as he could, just to change her preconceived notions about popular fiction. And now he saw that he had failed. *She had denied James Bond the right to feel like James Bond.*

It was a lot to take in, though he tried to put on a brave face. There was silence on the table. He had had the distinct displeasure of conversing with her. Abhimanyu had nothing more to say and he decided to leave, but not before reminding Asmita of the parking episode.

'Listen,' he said. 'I think we can forget how we met the other day at the parking lot and make a fresh start.'

He wasn't very sure why he said that. *Perhaps this will let you say nicer things about my work, just in case you are not telling the full truth.*

His words touched her heart, or perhaps it was the way he said them. Asmita hadn't anticipated this gesture and it was refreshing.

She felt a sudden and strange impulse within her that made her want to pull his stubbly cheeks and tell him that she was sorry for behaving like an idiot that day. *What the hell, Asmita!* she scolded, instantly checking herself for even thinking that way, lest the thought continued.

'I am sorry too. And indeed, we should make a fresh start,' she said instead, smiling to soften her words.

'I am glad,' Abhimanyu said, extending his hand towards her.

She took it in hers and shook it warmly.

That day, on his way back home, Abhimanyu carried a bittersweet feeling in his heart; more bitter than sweet. He wondered why he had behaved the way he had in front of Asmita. And even though she hadn't made him feel like a hero, there was something in their conversation that he had liked. He couldn't figure out exactly what it was.

Perhaps it just had to do with how she had envisioned the cover of his novel. He had genuinely loved that; he wasn't going to lie to himself. And the manner in which she had recited that scene from her perspective made it clear that she felt close to his characters, that she felt for them. Yet, when asked directly for her opinion, she had summed up his work in just two words – 'It's nice.' That continued to bother the hell out of him. He couldn't connect the dots. *What am I missing? There has to be more to this than 'nice'.*

Later that evening, long after he had reached home, a message arrived on his phone. It was from Asmita. She had taken his number from Maaya.

It read:

'I lied. It isn't nice. It is beyond brilliant. Your new book.'

15

Abhimanyu gently bit his lower lip as he stared at the message. It brewed a whirlpool of joy in him. The twinkle in his eyes and the grin on his face revealed his feelings.

He shook his head in ecstatic disbelief.

You were playing me all this while.

Reading what he had desperately wanted to hear earlier demanded an instant acknowledgement. But he held himself back. An immediate response would make it look like this message was a big deal for him – which it was. And being Abhimanyu Razdan meant he needed to deal with such admiration pragmatically; no matter how desperate he had been for it till just moments ago.

He decided to take his sweet time to respond to Asmita's message. After all, she too had taken hers to tell him this. *It's only fair that I return the favour.*

At first, he was annoyed with himself about opening a chat request from an unknown contact on his phone. Those ticks had turned blue and she would know that he had seen her message so quickly. *Grrrrr!!!*

Then he realized that perhaps it would be more fun ignoring it for a while if she knew he'd seen the message.

Miles away from him, in her office, Asmita knew exactly what was going on in Abhimanyu's mind. She shook her head, smiling as she saw his status change to offline without his typing a reply. *Such a kid you are!*

Asmita kept her phone down and got busy with the first chapter she was going to edit. She couldn't wait to reread the words that had kindled something exceptional in her.

Thoughts of Abhimanyu kept playing hide-and-seek in her mind as she went through his work for the second time. The image of him extending his hand as he asked them to move past the ugly chapter of how they'd met frequently brought a smile on her face.

She read the preface of his book in his voice. She read the introduction to the town of Munnar in his voice. After a while, she talked to herself in her head in his voice.

Soon, it became both sweet and annoying for her, and Asmita tried her best to keep Abhimanyu's voice and his words separate. She'd consciously keep it out and then find herself promptly drifting into doing the exact opposite. Every damn time!

What the hell? She was angry with herself.

At last, she took a break from editing, and went through her unread emails and responded to a few of them. Finally, when she returned to the edits, she was sure that she'd be able to keep Abhimanyu's voice at bay, but just then he finally responded to her message.

She smirked and picked up her phone.

'A woman is never more truthful than when she acknowledges herself a liar,' the message read.

She giggled at the words. And because she too was a well-read woman, she immediately responded, 'Isn't that exactly what Mark Twain said?'

'Not *exactly*! He had said it for men. ☺'

'Ah! I see! In that case, this is completely different from what he said. ☺'

'Totally!' he shot back.

'I envy your guts,' she typed.

'And my writing?'

On his phone's screen, Abhimanyu saw Asmita typing. After a while, she stopped. Then she began typing again, only to delete it. He waited in anticipation. His cunning mind told him to not remain online for this long, but his heart had other plans.

Finally, her text arrived.

It was a row of heart emojis.

Almost involuntarily, Abhimanyu spun in his writing chair, and after covering the 360-degree landscape of the three walls and the Arabian Sea visible from his window, his eyes returned to his phone screen.

'Glad to know,' he replied.

When Asmita didn't write back, he messaged her again.

'What was your favourite part?'

'All of them ☺,' she wrote back.

Abhimanyu chuckled as he read the words. He was about to reply but then he saw her typing and waited.

'Honestly, I loved the way the boy loved the woman. That innocent love of adolescence ... it is so refreshing to read about. We don't see this kind of love today, beyond the world of books.'

Once again, Abhimanyu refrained from replying because Asmita was typing. Now that the dam was broken, it seemed like she had a lot to say, and he didn't want to interrupt her.

'The way he is obsessed with her ... I wish adults experienced that kind of intense love. Also, this woman, even though initially she doesn't have any such feelings for him, in the second half, there is a part of her which wants to reciprocate and shower all her love upon him. That transition of hers from his guardian angel to his lover is exciting in a new, different kind of way. It breaks my heart that in the end the boy has to leave town, and that he doesn't even get to kiss the love of his life. That all he gets to cherish forever is that one long hug that he demands from her in the end. And she obliges. It's a heartbreakingly beautiful love story. When I finished reading it, I felt sorry for him. I wanted to hug him tight as he cried his heart out.'

This text from her was the drug Abhimanyu had been craving. *How well she's captured the essence of my story!*

This time Abhimanyu couldn't hold himself back and landed up sending a kiss emoji, tailing which was a text – 'You made my day.'

Of course, it was subject to interpretation, but he believed that Asmita would take it in the spirit of the moment; as a warm acknowledgment of her admiration of him. But as soon as he hit send, he wasn't so sure and regretted it immediately.

So fickle is the heart! It wants things and then the mind overpowers it. He thought about quickly deleting it, but by then it was already too late.

Asmita felt a thrill when she saw that emoji on her screen. She was an intelligent and mature woman and knew how to read between the lines and understand context, instead of over-interpreting things. She took that kiss emoji in the same spirit with which she had sent him the heart emojis; the feelings were not personal, but about work and his book. *And anyway, maybe he uses this emoji very frequently*. She didn't know.

Even though Abhimanyu didn't want their chat to end, he realized that it was probably wise to cut short the conversation and not overdo things. 'Looking forward to your edits,' he typed.

'Very soon,' came the reply.

That evening, before leaving office, Asmita looked up Abhimanyu's other books online. She talked to Shalini, who was an expert on both Abhimanyu and his work, and asked her which was her favourite novel by him.

At first, Shalini said that she loved them all but then contradicting herself, she told her that his most recent, one was his best so far. Asmita decided to pick it up from a bookstore on her way back home. She didn't want to order it online and then have to wait for it to arrive.

That night, she went to bed around 10 p.m., but slept at 4.30 a.m. in the morning, after finishing Abhimanyu's most recent release.

16

Asmita brushed her teeth, looking at herself in the mirror. She felt hungover, the effect of Abhimanyu's words still clouding her mind.

His novel had done something to her – something significant and irreversible.

She couldn't help thinking about Abhimanyu and being consumed by the world of his fascinating words. This was the second time he had done this to her with his work. The more she resisted him, the more he persisted. *What have you done to me?*

The man had conquered her mind. No one had affected her so deeply with just their words – simple, honest words. She had lost control over herself and when she looked into the mirror, she came face-to-face with the stark reality – she had fallen in love with Abhimanyu. And, with that troubling truth, all hell broke loose within her.

In that book, the story wasn't the innocent one-sided love of a young adult boy for a mature woman. It was the love between a woman and a man, both Asmita's age. Intense and passionate!

The thought that she was working with the author who had created those fabulous moments made her feel special. Shalini had been so right about him and his work, she realized. She could now see what she had been denying herself all this while. Scenes from the chapters she'd read the night before flashed through her mind. Scenes in which she had, while reading, replaced the protagonists with Abhimanyu and herself.

One of those scenes had been set near a washbasin, and now Asmita was standing at her own washbasin, the very same one that she had pictured as Abhimanyu's words had unfolded before her.

That's what reading his novel had done to her. She had overlapped her own world over the story Abhimanyu had created. Asmita had imagined that scene taking place in her own washroom, where she now stood wearing a black spaghetti top and pink panties.

Her eyes scanned her body in the mirror and stopped at her midriff, visible between the waistband of her underwear and the hem of her top. That's where Abhimanyu had made the male protagonist in his story kiss the girl, before bending down and taking the waistband of her panties between his teeth. He had ended that scene in the very next sentence, writing, 'And through the oasis between her legs, he reached her mind.' *Gosh!*

How much she had enjoyed reading that one line, and how much she hated that he had ended the scene with it.

She wanted more. No, she *needed* more. She would have begged him for it, had he been in front of her. *Why did you leave the rest to my imagination?*

The feelings he had left her with made her restless. In the absence of his words she had been denied closure, and she had desperately wanted it. She desperately wanted it *now*. Something within her still pulsated in anticipation of it.

Standing by the washbasin, she touched herself exactly where Abhimanyu had described the kiss – two inches below her navel. Her mouth opened slightly as her fingers crept down and she looked at herself in the mirror, her gaze following her fingers.

Just then, her mother called out for her.

Against her wishes, her imagination escaped the clasp of Abhimanyu's intense world of romance and went straight to her mother. She quickly wore her shorts and stepped out of the washroom.

Asmita was on her way to her office. As the car stopped at the red light, she had this strange urge to revisit the chat she had had with Abhimanyu the previous evening. She immediately pulled out her phone and went straight to it; to the kiss emoji he had sent her. She smiled when she saw it. The pad of her thumb moved over that emoji, caressing it.

Only when the vehicles behind her honked and summoned her attention did she realize that the lights had already turned green. She nodded apologetically in her rear-view mirror and pressed the accelerator. As soon as she picked up speed, her lips gradually stretched into a wide smile. She laughed at her stupid self.

What the hell!

Asmita couldn't stop blushing. She wasn't this person; the person she was now becoming.

After she reached office and before she resumed her editing, she had this sudden urge to text Abhimanyu. She wanted to talk to him, but then decided to fight the urge and put her phone away.

Moments later, she was debating with herself, asking why she couldn't do what she wanted to. Finally, giving in, she picked up the phone, but wondered what to write to him.

At first she thought she would write something about the manuscript she was editing, but on second thoughts, she thought of telling him about the novel she had finished reading the previous night.

'Hey, I happened to read your last novel,' she wrote and pressed send.

Asmita had to wait to read his reply. Abhimanyu, who had just finished his workout in the gym, was packing his bag to leave when her text arrived on his phone. He smirked as he read it.

'And?' he sent.

'I don't have words to describe it,' she typed, smiling to herself.

If only she could tell him how she had felt standing alone in her washroom, visualizing the scene from the book!

'That bad?'

She smiled wider and sent three laughing emojis first, following up with, 'Unfortunately, that *good*.'

'Thank God!' he wrote back and then quickly added, 'But why unfortunately?'

'Because it wasn't edited by me.'

Abhimanyu took a deep, satisfied breath before he replied to her. Clearly, he was achieving what he had wanted – to change her thoughts about popular fiction.

'In that case, I wish you had at least a few words to describe it. Isn't it unusual for a literary fiction editor to run out of words?'

'Can you take my "no words to describe it" as the best few words I can find?'

He chuckled. *You are smart, Asmita.*

'Last time, the first feedback I received from you on my work was a lie,' he playfully taunted her.

'And I don't repeat my strategy.'

'Why so?'

'Because that will make me so predictable.'

'I see.' *You love playing with words, don't you?*

'So, be assured this feedback isn't a lie,' she answered.

'I'll be heartbroken if it was.'

How she loved reading that message.

'Thanks for the warning. ☺' she typed back.

'But why did you do that the last time? Tell a lie first and then the truth?'

'Hmm … A yes is so much better if it starts with a no. No?'

The man of words was very impressed to see her way with words. Smiling, he wrote back, 'And whose quote is this?'

'Oh, hello! This is my original.'

He loved the way she addressed him. That informality made him feel closer to her. 'You should write a book,' he told her.

'Someday!'

'What kind of book will it be?'

'Like your last one.'

'You liked it so much?'

'I meant it when I said I have no words. Stop trying tricks to make me say more.'

'Okay, I won't. But at least tell me what it was that you enjoyed the most about it?' He always had this need to know where exactly, on which page, he had touched the heart of his reader, be it anyone.

'The intense, mad romance. That's what I enjoyed the most.' As soon as she hit send, Asmita couldn't believe that, carried away in the flow of their chat, she had actually written those words. A part of her felt shy, but the other part felt relieved about letting it out.

'I see! What about the guy in the novel? Did you like him?'

'I fell in love with him.' *I fell in love with you.*

She let out a deep breath as soon as she sent that.

Abhimanyu felt ecstatic as he read her reply. He wrote back, 'And the girl?'

'I imagined her as me. I had stepped into her shoes while reading.'

'That explains why you fell in love with that guy.'

'Hmm ...' *You! It was YOU, idiot!*

Till just a few days back, how desperately he had wanted to make her read his work and like it, and here he was today. Not only had she confessed to admiring his work, but also to experiencing it by living the life of the female protagonist; by falling in love with another character in it.

Nothing raised his self-esteem like the warmth of that acknowledgement.

'I'm so happy to know that, Asmita.'

In her head, she read her name in his voice. It felt good.

'I hope that now, it will be you who takes my latest work to that level.'

'I will give it my best,' she wrote, and then added, 'But I do have a complaint with your last work.'

'Which is?'

She wrote something, but then deleted it. Then she typed instead, 'Let's meet and discuss it?'

Abhimanyu liked that invitation. He was game.

Asmita sat on her chair finishing her day's work. It was quite late. Abhimanyu was initially supposed to arrive around 5 p.m., but got delayed due to traffic. Asmita felt guilty for making him come to the office during peak hours. She had suggested that they postpone their meeting, but he insisted on seeing her that very day.

One reason was that they were running short of time and the publication deadline for his new work was drawing closer. He was already impressed by her idea for the cover. Maybe she had more valuable feedback on his work. And if there was something important about his writing that she wanted to discuss with him, he wanted to know it sooner rather than later. And, well, he wanted to meet her because he wanted to meet her.

By 6.30 p.m., the office was already almost entirely empty. The sales team, which would otherwise leave later, had a party to go to and had already left. The glamorous office looked abandoned, with only Asmita in it. Outside, a lone security guard stood at the main entrance as the darkness increased with every passing minute.

Abhimanyu called Asmita and said that he would take another half an hour to reach. He was remorseful about making her wait for him. Indeed, she was getting late for home, but the yearning to meet Abhimanyu made her put up with the delay.

In anticipation of his arrival, she kept looking at the time on her laptop. As it neared the estimated time, she began to feel butterflies in her stomach. They fluttered strongly the second she received a text from him.

'In the elevator, coming up,' it read.

Asmita stood up and thought about replying to him, but her fingers seemed to freeze. A chill crawled up her hand. She struggled a bit and then gave up when she saw Abhimanyu walk towards her.

Oh my God. He is here.

He looked cool in his round-neck T-shirt with a pair of denims and sneakers. This was perhaps the first time she was seeing him without a jacket. It made him look younger, more casual. His curly hair shone from a distance, slicked back in place with gel. It was unusual for someone to look this fresh at this time of the day. But then she'd spent a whole day at work and he was coming straight from his home.

Abhimanyu waved at Asmita as he walked in and looked around at the empty office, surprised.

Asmita felt a thrill of guilty pleasure as she watched him walk up to her. His coming to meet her like this, when there was nobody around, was somehow almost wickedly fulfilling. It wasn't as if she'd timed things that way, but circumstances had conspired to make it so. She was thankful for this blessing in disguise. The fact that in that moment he looked so handsome served to amplify the feeling of guilty pleasure.

'I am so sorry for this delay,' he said, shaking his head. There was real guilt in his voice. He put out his hand to shake hers.

'It's okay,' Asmita said softly as their hands met.

His hand was warm. It soothed Asmita's cold fingers and her heart secretly did a somersault, warming up too.

The V-neck of her designer kurti, which flaunted her sharp collarbones, grabbed his attention temporarily. Afraid that she'd notice him staring, he immediately looked around.

'People have left,' Asmita said, guessing what he was thinking.

'Yes, I figured. I think you are getting very late and you should ...'

She spoke over him with ease and confidence.

'Abhimanyu!'

He paused. For some reason, hearing her say his name felt immensely satisfying.

Asmita smiled and for a split second, closed her eyes, before opening them to look at him. 'It's okay. I am fine. Don't worry,' she said with conviction.

Something in the manner in which she said those words told Abhimanyu that she didn't regret waiting; that she had wanted to wait for him. That she had wanted to meet him as much as he had wanted to meet her, no matter how late. Happily surrendering to this knowledge, he threw his hands up.

'Okay!' He grinned at her.

'Should we sit in the conference room?' she asked as she picked up her laptop.

Abhimanyu looked at the array of vacant chairs across the length of her long desk. He asked, 'Is there a problem with right here?'

His eyes scanned her desk. With photos, awards, a tea mug, coasters, cute toys, tiny plants and numerous stacks of books, her bit of the table was stamped firmly with her identity. Noticing this, Abhimanyu felt like sitting there rather than in a boring conference room.

'Uh ... okay. No problem at all,' she said, looking around.

'Sure?' he double-checked.

'Yes, sure.' She pulled up a chair for him.

'So! Tell me,' he said, making himself comfortable.

Asmita felt at loss for words. She didn't think he would come to the point so directly and so soon. She had just leveraged the idea of discussing his work as a way to meet him. In reality, she had wanted this to be a general conversation. She hadn't prepared anything beforehand and only had some vague ideas of what she could say to him. She scrambled for ways in which she could begin the conversation.

'You had a complaint about my work, didn't you?' Abhimanyu reminded her of her last message to him that morning.

'Oh yeah.' She chuckled, slightly nervous.

'So, go ahead. Tell me.'

'You … brew a perfect romance,' she began, her eyes thoughtful. He noticed how big they were, how deep.

His lips curved into a smile and his own eyes twinkled.

'Your protagonists are so strong that people fall in love with them. Your readers are bound to be shattered when your characters are left in pain. The chemistry between your protagonists is intensely emotional, something that is rare these days. You take your readers to the summit of love before you put your protagonists together in each other's arms …' Her eyes once again met with his as she spoke. There was utter silence around them. Abhimanyu felt transfixed by her eyes.

She continued, '… but then you drop your readers from that cliff just when you have to describe the lovemaking scene.'

Abhimanyu's eyes widened. He took a couple of seconds to take in what she'd just said. He recovered but was still not sure if that's what she had meant. Smiling and biting his lower lip in a mild embarrassment and yet thoroughly enjoying the moment, he responded.

'Okay ... I am not very sure ... but I think ... I am ... I think I get what you are trying to say ...' he said slowly and cautiously.

Asmita smiled mischievously. 'I am not *trying* to say anything. I am saying it.' She too was enjoying this conversation now. Her initial worry had been replaced with a secret thrill at talking to him this frankly. 'Why do you shy away from describing the intimate scenes till the end?'

Abhimanyu stiffened. Shots had been fired at him at point blank range!

The simplicity with which Asmita raised that bold question was admirable.

Quickly recovering from the shock, Abhimanyu shook his head to clear it. *So you have called me to your office to complain about the lack of lovemaking scenes in my book!*

He attempted to frame a response but failed. Instead, he asked her a question.

'Would you like to read them till the very end?'

That was a dumb one, he thought as soon as he asked that. *Why else would she ask for them?*

'Of course,' Asmita said, pursing her lips and crossing her arms.

Like a fool, Abhimanyu nodded his head wordlessly. What a joy it was for Asmita to pin him down with her words.

'I see,' he said finally. And then, as if defending himself, he added, 'I never felt the need to write them.'

'So, is that the case with all your books?'

He nodded, smiling slightly. She found herself thinking once again about how cute he looked and, to distract herself from that thought, she decided to move away from the banter and have a serious conversation.

'But you do realize that you make your reader crave for more and then leave her disappointed ...' He noticed how she had chosen a female reader in her example. '... by denying her what she wants?' she completed.

He knew without doubt that this female reader was Asmita herself. It thrilled him to listen to her thoughts, to look into her eyes when she was confessing what she craved for.

It was a sensitive conversation. He was pleased that they had their privacy to freely talk about it.

'I see ... but ... isn't it worth it to only fan the flames of the burning desire instead of dousing it?'

'What you call dousing, others may call fulfilling. And what's the point in setting it aflame if you aren't going to fulfil it?'

'But she, my reader, can fulfil it in her head. No? I mean, I don't stop her from imagining what comes next,' he countered.

'You do stop her by not writing it. You do stop her by not feeding her your words, which she craves for in that very moment.'

'Don't you appreciate the fact that I provide her with an entire canvas and let her fill it with the colours that she wants, with her imagination? Isn't that fascinating?'

In the dead silence in the office, the exchange of those soft, thoughtful words with intermittent smiles was intoxicating for both of them. Neither noticed that their voices had dropped by several notches, that they'd drawn their chairs closer together and that their knees were almost touching.

'I think the fascination lies in stepping into the shoes of the protagonist and getting to experience things you have described, and not in imagining what happens next.' Asmita leaned forward as she made her point and her whole body went on high alert as she realized that she could now smell his musky cologne.

Abhimanyu relished this proximity. Inches from her, he could sense the electricity in the air between them. He hadn't seen this side of Asmita before. He hadn't expected to see it either. But now that he was, he admired her ability to speak so freely and with such confidence. For a while it put him on the back foot.

He opened his mouth to speak, but then stopped. He momentarily closed his eyes and chuckled. It was as if he was giving up on defending himself.

'You want me to write the finer details of these scenes?'

Nobody had ever asked this from him and certainly not with this conviction. For him, there was also an intense sense of fulfilment in discovering that Asmita was so demanding. In that moment, he couldn't deny that she had an irresistible effect on him. All he wanted was to go on listening to her.

'It is up to you. I strongly believe one can write about lovemaking without making it gross. To write out a whole scene instead of ending it with a single sentence – "And then they made love",' she ended on a playfully furious note, making a face as she spoke.

Abhimanyu laughed, listening to her fake anger. Meanwhile, Asmita spoke again.

'You see, for me the pleasure is in imagining what you tell me to,' she said, unmindful of the fact that she had now openly referred to the reader as herself. It was all too direct now.

Abhimanyu was attentive enough to notice this. His sharp gaze pierced her eyes as if wanting to look beyond them into her mind, her soul.

And, as if she had read his thoughts at the very instant, she said, 'As your reader, my pleasure lies in exploring your mind and getting to know how you imagine the protagonists in your head. After all, they are your characters.'

It impressed Abhimanyu, how she put her thoughts across so lucidly. He thought of something and then, in a self-critical mode, asked, 'I fear I might ruin it for you, Asmita.'

'What if you don't?' she immediately countered. That silenced him.

She went on, 'And why do you doubt yourself? You are a master storyteller.'

How he loved that last sentence!

'That doesn't mean I am good at everything. Not at writing sensual scenes.'

'And how do you know that?'

He smirked. 'Do you want me to try and do it in this new manuscript?'

'Well, there's no scope for that, considering the kind of story it is,' Asmita said. 'They don't even kiss.'

'Exactly,' he agreed.

'Maybe for your next one, whenever you write it.' Secretly, Asmita wished that he could go back in time and write such a scene in the earlier novel.

As if Abhimanyu had read her thoughts, he asked, 'So, which part of my novel that you read yesterday did you feel needed an elaborate sensual scene?'

Asmita's heart raced. In an attempt to not reveal her feelings, she stole her gaze from his on the pretext of taking out his novel from her handbag. She turned around and pulled out the book. Abhimanyu was pleased to see that she was carrying it in her purse.

'Here.' She opened one of the many folded pages.

That she had marked pages of his novel was a delight for him. *You really have loved it a lot, haven't you?*

There were sentences that she had highlighted with a fluorescent marker. His eyes quickly scanned the page. This copy of his work was now personalized, marked by her. It was an altogether different feeling to realize that something which in a way belonged to him now also belonged to her. It was an intimate affair. She had embedded a part of her being, her taste, in his work.

For Asmita, to show all of this to him was to make herself vulnerable in front of him, but then she desired exactly that – to be vulnerable, to let him know how his words had affected her.

Abhimanyu drew even closer and looked at the book lying open on the desk. He enjoyed how closely they sat next to each other while she flipped a page. The armrests of their chairs rubbed against each other but there was enough distance between their elbows. Abhimanyu was cautious and made sure he didn't accidentally touch her arm.

She passed him the book and put her finger on the paragraph where the boy and the girl were in the girl's kitchen. The boy had come to her house and was making tea for the two of them.

'Here.' Asmita pointed at a line. She said, 'In the patriarchal world we live in, you describe the boy making tea for the girl. That too, at her place, while she sits on the slab swinging her legs, watching him bustle around the kitchen. You know how astonishingly romantic you make it appear in my head?'

Abhimanyu smiled gingerly, his teeth biting his lower lip and his gaze shifting from his novel to her eyes. When their eyes met each other, Asmita felt an adrenaline rush. She immediately shifted her gaze back to the paragraph she was referring to.

'So then why do you only make them cuddle and end the scene with just a kiss? I long for the details. What follows that kiss ...' she said. Her voice was soft and expressive. It was a different kind of thrill for her to share what she desired, to make herself powerful and vulnerable at the same point.

She continued, 'Borrow the steam erupting from the boiling tea and make the romance steamy. Make way for passionate love while the tea boils. Just like the tea, set their hearts on fire. Let them burn in those flames of desire. Describe that intense kiss in tender detail and then take it forward.'

The manner and her choice of words stunned Abhimanyu. He couldn't focus on the page any more. His lips parted and his breath quickened. The next second, he fearlessly looked at Asmita's face as she looked down at the book, turning the pages again. It was as if this time she had set his heart on fire with her words.

Abhimanyu gathered the courage and let his elbow slide over to her armrest. Their elbows touched. Asmita felt him but didn't pull back her arm. She continued to speak but her words failed to register in his mind. All he could feel was her touch, burning him.

Ignoring what she was saying, he challenged her. 'I would need a reference for the kind of kiss you want me to describe.'

The unmissable frankness in his words immediately shut her up. She slowly turned towards him, interpreting what he had just said. He let out deep breaths. His intense eyes were fixed on her, as if he was trying to read her mind.

There was no way she was going to be able to resist that intense gaze of the man whose work had moved her so much. She was still under his spell, an even more powerful one than before. Asmita turned the book upside down.

Almost as if she couldn't help herself, yielding to her strong urge, she stretched her neck and went straight for his lips. One of her hands held the back of his head and pulled him towards her.

Abhimanyu surrendered at once and let her carry him away. She invaded him like a tornado and trapped him in her whirlpool. To see her take the lead was a different kind of high for him. Asmita's strong longing to have him was evident in the manner in which she held him. One of her hands was on his cheek and the other ran wildly through his curly hair, pulling it so that she could kiss him more deeply. And she did. She kissed him as if she would die if she didn't. She needed him to survive.

Indulging in that deep, long kiss, Abhimanyu ran out of breath. He tilted his head to breathe, but Asmita's sturdy hands held him back. Her other hand grabbed and pulled locks of his curly hair above the nape of his neck. The pain was sweet and as he opened his mouth to take a breath, Asmita's lips were still on his, sucking his lower lip. He thoroughly savoured this level of demanding dominance from her. He held on to the edge of the desk, keeping himself steady.

The next time he tried to bring his lips together, Asmita's tongue separated them. She invaded his mouth. She was possessed. Time had stopped ticking for her. Nothing else mattered in that moment. His warm breath had further left her intoxicated. Oozing with desire, she explored the cave of his mouth.

She was ruthless. He was kind. His one hand crept upon her upper back to support her while she savoured the kiss. He liked how her skin felt on his stretched palm. He had this sudden craving to slip his hand inside her kurti and feel the skin of her back. Just then, his chair rolled back a bit. Abhimanyu immediately gripped the floor with his feet. He spread his legs and this time he pulled her to him, positioning her chair between his legs.

His hand finally slid down inside her kurti, while his other hand let go of the desk and caught the back of her neck. Asmita savoured being desired by him. He reciprocated the energy with which she had kissed him. Holding her tightly in his grip, he went deep into her mouth. He felt Asmita's palms caressing both sides of his neck. He could feel her fingers slipping inside his T-shirt. *God! This feels awesome.*

When Asmita was left breathless, she slowed down and gradually pulled away. Abhimanyu let her catch her breath. They looked at each other. She was gasping. The gloss on her now-swollen lips was gone; all that was left was his mark. Her intense eyes looked into his.

When she was finally in a position to speak, she spoke. 'You got your reference to the kind of kiss I want you to describe?' she asked in between breaths.

The sheer audacity with which she said those words was the most sensual thing about her; more than what she had done moments back. It attracted Abhimanyu so much that he wanted to pin her down and make mad love to her. He licked the taste of her mouth on his lips and swallowed it without taking his eyes off her. The two kept staring at each other for a while, letting the fire slow down.

'What are you?' he asked. Those words weren't meant for her but for himself. She was a mystery he was trying to solve.

'Instead, ask me what I want to be,' she said.

His eyes still fixed on her, he asked, 'What do you want to be?'

Without taking her eyes off him, she answered, 'Your muse!'

Abhimanyu was trying to read her thoughts when she pulled away and sat up straight. She pursed her lips and, for the first time since their bodies had separated, she looked away from him.

Asmita spotted the copy of his novel placed upside down. She picked it up and slowly ran her fingers over the paragraph she had been pointing at. In her head she was touching his intangible mind, his thoughts, through his words. It was a delight for Abhimanyu to watch her lean fingers sweep over his written words. It was an intimate spectacle. In his head, he was imagining her hand slipping inside his T-shirt and her fingers running down his chest. He could sense her sharp nails brushing through the tiny hair on his chest. *Have you already become my muse?*

Asmita shut down his imagination when she closed that novel.

The next time she looked at him, quietness had sailed into her eyes. She felt relaxed. The hormones, which had been dancing wild inside her, had subsided. For a second, she found it difficult to look into his eyes, but then she overcame it.

She opened her mouth to say something, then shut it. 'What?' Abhimanyu asked.

Words came out of her mouth softly. She was slow but confident. Her head shook left and right when she said, 'I don't regret what I did, unless you think I ...'

'Shhhhhhh ...' Abhimanyu put his finger on her lips. She looked up at him. He smiled.

She didn't smile back but acknowledged him with a tiny nod.

'I am sorry, I had called you to discuss things about your current manuscript as well, but ...' she paused.

'But?' asked Abhimanyu.

'... but I don't think I will be able to focus on it any more today,' she confessed.

Abhimanyu chuckled, more so to make her feel comfortable. 'I understand. We can do this later. Don't worry.'

As he said that, they heard quick footsteps approaching them. Behind Abhimanyu's shoulder, Asmita noticed the security guard coming towards them. She had completely forgotten his presence. *Thank God he didn't show up earlier!*

Quickly distancing herself from Abhimanyu, she rearranged her hair and restored her posture. With a touch of her forefinger, she brought the dormant screen of her laptop back to life. She had to show the guard that they had been working.

'Madam, how long you plan to stay?' he asked, looking at both of them.

Asmita looked at Abhimanyu and asked, 'I guess we are almost done?'

His eyes moved between the guard and Asmita.

'Oh yes! We are.'

Asmita looked back at the security guard and told him that they would leave in five minutes.

He nodded and walked back to the gate.

Asmita looked at Abhimanyu. He smiled. She smiled in return. They had a little secret of their own. They realized this. He had a thousand things to talk to her about in the aftermath of what had transpired between them, and so did she.

'We can talk about everything later,' she suggested, reading his mind.

Abhimanyu smiled and let out a deep breath. A part of him loved how, without him saying anything, she seemed to know what he wanted to say.

'It's going to be a long conversation,' he said.

'It will be.'

Asmita packed her bag. Ten minutes later, the two stood in the same parking lot where they had met about two months back. A lot had changed since then, so much so that it felt like they had taken a U-turn right there.

It was dark. Asmita was about to step inside her car when Abhimanyu pulled her by her arm. He gave her a hug.

17

The night was bound to bring them together on a phone chat. The evening had been leading to it. There was no way they could have let the night pass without reaching out to each other.

It was past 11 p.m. and Asmita was in bed. She'd turned out the lights in her room and it was bathed in moonlight. Every time she closed her eyes, she remembered reaching for Abhimanyu; remembered how his lips had felt on hers. She could picture his face clearly – how it had looked in that moment. And she remembered how she'd felt, as if she was floating into an unknown universe. That feeling returned as she remembered every second of their moment together with agonizing clarity. All that remained now was for her to actually feel the taste of his mouth.

That evening, she'd brought back visions of him. They had first entered her head as soon as she was out of the office and behind the wheel, driving back home. And now, in the cosy comfort of her bed, where she lay in her flimsy nightclothes, it was exciting to revisit what had happened in the office. This Asmita did, again and again, in the greatest possible detail. She could still smell his cologne on her breath and feel his curly hair between her fingers.

The thrill kept sleep at bay. She hadn't had an experience like this before with anyone. In fact it had been a long time since she had kissed a man. Her last relationship had ended three years ago and since then, she hadn't felt the urge to date. Well ... not until she had read Abhimanyu's work.

Interestingly, it wasn't Abhimanyu himself but his words that had made the difference. Not in her wildest dreams would she have fallen for a man whom she had hated from the very day they met. But here it was – the strangest of events unfolding before her. *Life is full of surprises.*

For Abhimanyu, kisses weren't a distant memory. He had done it all, numerous times. He had dated enough women and had had quite a few one-night stands as well. However, what separated this occasion from the rest was the person and the manner in which she had approached him. Nobody had ever dominated him the way she had. Nobody had ever not waited for his approval, but Asmita did. She had claimed him. Right in her very office.

What also stood out for him was that unlike the other women he'd been with, Asmita hadn't been a diehard fan of his from the beginning. As a matter of fact, she hadn't even recognized him. For this reason, she became the sole woman he'd wanted to woo with his work. And now he had outdone himself, for his words had propelled her to a different level altogether. There couldn't be any bigger victory for a man who had always wanted to be admired. Asmita had unintentionally excited him the way nobody else ever did.

Later that night, while he was at a party that he wasn't enjoying much, Abhimanyu's thoughts kept returning to her. He pulled out his phone and dropped her a message. It was 11.45 p.m.

'Awake?'

In her dark room, Asmita once again remembered their kiss as she read Abhimanyu's message.

How she loved seeing his name on the phone screen!

'Very much,' she immediately wrote back.

Abhimanyu was delighted to read that. He walked away from the loud music. On his way out of the club, he typed, 'Call?'

By the time he was outside, Asmita had responded. 'How about a chat?'

He pondered on that for a moment and then wrote back, 'Long chat? Short chat?'

'Why put a time limit on it?' she responded.

'Perfect. Give me twenty minutes,' he wrote, getting into his car.

The next time he sent her a text, he was home.

Abhimanyu poured himself some wine and sat on his bed, leaning back on the headboard. He unbuttoned his shirt and unhooked his trousers for comfort.

'I have been thinking about you all evening,' he typed.

He didn't have to wait much to hear back from her. Asmita had been waiting for his text with bated breath.

'That feeling is mutual,' she replied.

A few seconds passed. Then he wrote, 'After we kissed, why did you mention the no-regrets thing?'

'You didn't let me complete.'

'I didn't want us to digress and ruin the moment.'

'I understand, but let me say it now.'

'If you insist …'

'I didn't regret doing what I did, but I did think later that I should have sought your consent.'

'Ah! I now see where you are coming from.' Abhimanyu smiled as he typed.

'Hmmm.'

'It's generous of you to say that, but the fact that I let you do what you wanted to do *and* that I participated equally in it should let you know that you had my consent. And now you have this in writing, so you can produce it in the court of law if I put a sexual harassment allegation on you.☺'

Asmita giggled and turned in her bed.

'Oh boy! I didn't see that coming,' she replied.

'Did I scare you?'

'Not exactly, because now you have also given me the evidence to defend myself, if I need to.☺'

'There will never be a need to do that, Asmita.'

As usual, she enjoyed reading her name in his texts.

'The other thing I was wondering was,' she wrote and pressed send without completing the thought.

'?'

'... if you are in a relationship. It would be inappropriate of me to do what I did if you are.'

'Would you not have wanted to kiss me then?' he asked, enjoying putting her on the spot.

'I would have. Perhaps even more so, because not being allowed to do what you want to makes you want it even more.'

Abhimanyu chuckled as he read her words. He removed his shirt and, after gulping down the last of his wine, stretched his legs on the bed. He then slipped out of his pants and, stretching his hand to the side of his bed, switched off the lights and pulled a bedsheet over himself.

Meanwhile, Asmita had sent more texts. 'But wanting is one thing and going through with it is another. And I wouldn't have, had I known you have a girlfriend.'

'What would it be like? To hold on to your desires and not act upon them?' he asked.

'Suffocating.'

Reading that one word made him want to hold Asmita's face in his hands and kiss her deeply, leaving her breathless like she had him. He wanted to suffocate her with pleasure. It was as if not doing so would make *him* suffocate. He wondered how it would be to hold her in his arms in that moment, in his bed.

When Asmita didn't see a message from him, she sent another.

'What happened?'

'Nothing,' he responded.

'What are you thinking?'

'Can I be honest?'

'Is there a reason you shouldn't be?'

This was another thing about this woman, something he cherished so much – she had a way with words, just like he did. The two vibrated at the same frequency.

That she spoke her mind so effortlessly was what affected him the most. It had impressed him even when, months back, she had technically insulted his craft in comparison with literary fiction. Of course, she had been wrong then, but she had had the courage to speak her mind to an author her publishing house was trying so hard to acquire. She was a strong woman and she had left a deep impression on him, influencing him and making him crave her good opinion. And now, *she* had fallen for *him*.

'I am thinking about how I would have kissed you if you were next to me right now, in my bed.'

With those words, Abhimanyu eagerly awaited Asmita's response, but he didn't get one for a while. 'Don't worry, I am not in any sort of committed relationship, in case you are still concerned about that,' he typed.

The next second, he saw Asmita typing.

'How would you do it? The kiss,' she wrote.

He took a deep breath and typed back. 'I'd roll over you. Slide my hand under the nape of your neck. And take your lips in mine.'

She sighed as she read that. Her left hand crept up to touch the back of her head, while she typed with her right. *What are you doing to me?*

'Hold me tight,' she texted.

'I am doing that. Feel the weight of my body on yours, crushing you.'

The shift in his choice of words – *would do* to *doing* – made her crave him even more. The change in the tense made the moment even more intimate. She treasured how he made a distant dream unfold before her like reality. She dug her nails into her own skin, pretending that they were Abhimanyu's fingers. Her naked thighs rubbed against each other. In that moment, she knew she wouldn't be able to stop at just a kiss this time.

She wasn't this person. She hadn't even known that this person existed within her. She felt possessed by Abhimanyu, as if some kind of resilient energy made her desire him so much that she didn't want to keep a check on herself. To drift away with this powerful attraction was a kind of satisfaction and joy that she couldn't even try to resist. She sailed along with him to wherever he took her.

'I dig my face in your neck,' he wrote.

Her fingers inched towards the side of her neck.

'I feel your stubble caressing my soft skin,' she replied. 'Is it very rough?'

'I like rough.' Her nails scratched her soft skin as she sent the text.

'I kiss your skin where my stubble had rubbed against you.'

'Ahhhhh,' she moaned out loud and wrote, 'And then?'

'I take your soft skin between my lips and suck it, healing it and taking away the burning sensation.'

'No,' she wrote back.

Abhimanyu waited for her to add more. And she did.

'Suck it hard, Abhimanyu. Leave your mark on me.'

That lit a fire in his body. He was so warmed up that he pulled the thin cover off him. He was already hard. His bulged briefs restricted any free movement of his manhood, which demanded more space now. He wanted to set himself free.

'I am going to mark your skin with my lips, sucking it so hard that you moan.'

'Mmmmm … do that. Please!'

She desired to burn; she was like a moth to the candle that was Abhimanyu. The intensity with which she wanted to make love to him was overwhelming for Abhimanyu too. All that he wanted in that moment was to satisfy her fully.

'What are you wearing?'

'A spaghetti top…'

'And?'

Abhimanyu watched her status change from 'typing' to 'online' and then back to 'typing'. She took some time and finally wrote back:

'My panties.'

'I want you to pull them down.' He was direct.

So was she. 'No. Do it yourself.'

'God, Asmita!' he wrote and then began typing again. She waited for him.

'Open your legs and make space for me.'

She craved for more foreplay and didn't want to climax so soon. She thought he was going too fast, but the next moment she found out that she had misread him.

'I want you to imagine my face between your thighs.'

Oh Abhimanyu! She moaned aloud as she read that. At once, she could picture him like that and it made her dive into a sea of deeper pleasure. She could foresee what was coming – a tsunami of satisfaction.

'Feel my teeth,' he wrote.

'Where exactly?' she asked.

'At first digging in the flesh of your inner thighs.'

'Ahhhh! And then?'

'Then pulling the thin waistband of your panties.'

Her other hand sneaked down her neck and over her cleavage, skipping her breasts, which begged for her sensual touch. She lowered her hand between her legs. Her fingers crawled over her underwear, to the place where the fabric was already damp.

'I can smell you,' Abhimanyu typed.

The rawness of his words made her even more excited. Asmita couldn't hold herself back any more. She slipped her hand inside her panties. There was no returning for her now.

'God, it feels so damn good,' she wrote, biting her lips.

'I will give you better than good.' Abhimanyu was obsessed with the thoughts of fully satisfying her.

He wrote on. 'I pull those panties down, with my mouth, till your knees.'

Her body trembled with joy. Just like he said, she pulled her underwear down till her knees and went back to touching herself.

'You bend your knees, with the base of your feet flat on the bed and see my head in between the triangle of your legs and your stretched panties.'

He had a wild imagination and Asmita cherished playing by it. She bent her knees like he had said. Her hand didn't leave her sweet spot for even a second. Her fingers were wet in her secretion.

'I take the folds of your wet lips in mine,' he wrote.

A loud moan escaped her open mouth as soon as she read that. She needed him in that moment, in her bed. She clenched her teeth. Her middle finger made circles on her sweet spot. She was in the agony of pleasure.

'Feel my strong hands holding your thighs firmly, while my tongue runs up and down your lips.'

'Aaaaaaaaaah Abhimanyu!' is all she could type back.

'I pull the juicy wet folds of your soft skin in my mouth. I taste you, Asmita.'

She was trembling fiercely as a strong thrill of pleasure built up within her. It was difficult for her to hold her legs in the same posture Abhimanyu had put down for her. Her stretched underwear was taking the weight of her legs. She wanted to take off her panties completely, let her knees drop on the bed and spread her legs apart. But the epitome of her pleasure was to be controlled by his words. In that moment, he was her master. She wanted it that way.

In his bed, Abhimanyu had taken off his briefs. He held himself tightly. He couldn't wait any more.

'Pushing your lips apart, my tongue presses against your clit.'

She pictured him reaching between her legs and touching her oasis. She rubbed her supersensitive spot. Her eyes closed a few times between typing and reading. She was losing all her energy. He was so wild with his imagination, he was going to give her an orgasm with only his words over a chat.

She could almost feel his stubble rub against her wet skin.

'I can't hold it any more,' she begged.

'Come for me, Asmita. Come for me.'

With those words, he brought forth an earthquake in her. She glided two of her fingers inside and vigorously helped herself. The pad of her thumb rubbed her clit. Her hips rose off the bed as her fingers moved faster and outrageously mined deep pleasure from the cave of her body. She imagined him doing everything he had said to her.

In his bed, Abhimanyu's mouth opened and let out a deep sigh of satisfaction. His body quaked as he climaxed.

In her bed, Asmita screamed his name as if he was there in her room, riding her. She erupted in pleasure. Her hips finally dropped back on the bed. Between deep, long breaths, her legs stretched to find comfort. The immense tension had finally been released from her body.

The screen light on their phones had momentarily gone off. They were gasping for breath. It was going to take some time for them to recover and text each other again.

Asmita basked in the aftermath of the climax, thinking about what it would be like to feel Abhimanyu's stubble between her legs for real.

His words kept her wet for the most part of the night. Sleep conquered the remaining.

18

smita had begun editing Abhimanyu's manuscript. For her it was not just editing the work of an author, or even a bestselling author, for that matter. She was now editing the work of someone she had been intimate with. It was a different experience altogether. Of course, it was her responsibility to do a good job on every book, but with this particular manuscript, she no longer felt like it was only Abhimanyu's work. She felt like she was part of it, that it was *their* work, in a whole new sense.

She wanted this book to stand out from all the others he had written till date. She wanted him to stand out.

The question of ethics, of whether it was right for her, as an editor, to kiss her author and make love to him over midnight chats didn't bother her. Till date she had never mixed work with pleasure, but now that it was happening, she was enjoying every bit of it. Every time morality stared at her, she looked at her bosses at PaperInk and recalled what they had done to her. She was better off, she deduced. The irony was that she had fallen in love with the person her bosses had wanted her to care about so much. And now she was doing exactly that, at a whole new level.

Life *is* stranger than fiction, after all. How else was it possible for an editor who had abhorred an author so much to fall in love with him because of his work? *It's a great plot*, she thought. *Maybe, someday, this too could become a book – an editor's affair with her author.* She smiled to herself, shook her head and returned to her edits.

Asmita channelled all her enthusiasm into shaping Abhimanyu's work. She saw herself as accountable for the success of this new book. She wanted to become the woman behind this man's success. That was her sole goal. This time she wanted to impress the man who had captivated her with his words. She wanted to bring him more of what he cherished the most – fame.

Abhimanyu was busy working out in the gym. With every repetition, he rejoiced in the intimacy he had shared with Asmita the night before. His life had suddenly become as mysterious as the love in his novels. An affair had come at him from the corner he had least expected. PaperInk had only been meant to influence his professional life, not personal.

Every time he got up, lifting 100 kg of weights on his shoulders, he pictured Asmita craving him as she read his words. It boosted his self-confidence. On his way back home, he dropped her a text.

Asmita read his message as soon as it arrived but didn't respond. As he took the elevator up to his flat, Abhimanyu thought that by the time he would step out of it, he would have his reply, but that didn't happen.

He couldn't wait any longer and dialled her number. To his surprise, she disconnected the call. *Must be in a meeting.*

He was wrong, for he soon received a text back from her.

'Editing your work. And you are a serious distraction,' it read.

'Don't take chances then. We will talk once you're all done,' he mischievously wrote back.

'I'll be done in a week. Can you wait for that long?' she participated in the banter.

Indeed, he *was* a serious distraction.

He began to type, but on second thoughts, deleted it. In a sheer display of self-control and giving preference to his work, he wrote back, 'I can. Even for a month. How about you?'

Asmita's lips parted as she read that. *Are you throwing a challenge at me?* She took her time to think and then responded.

'I can. If you promise me that when the editing is over, you will meet me like you met me over our chat last night. I want to feel your stubble in between my legs.'

He treasured her boldness. Smiling, he typed back, 'I will. And this time, for real.'

'See you on the other side of the edits, then. You are already distracting me.'

'Good luck.' And that was it.

Maaya was not in office that entire week. Yet, she continued to track the progress of Abhimanyu's book's edits. Asmita would send her a daily update on email, which Maaya made sure she read.

Neither Abhimanyu nor Asmita got in touch with each other for the next twenty-four hours. Day one was very difficult for Asmita. She wondered what it was like for Abhimanyu.

The next day was tough but relatively easier, and she could again abstain from talking to Abhimanyu. She did not even clear her doubts about the manuscript with him, something which she would usually discuss directly with the authors. For the time being, she marked her comments on the manuscript and parked them so that she could show them to Abhimanyu after the editing was over.

Perhaps she should have avoided the playful ego battle she was in with him. After avoiding each other for two straight days, on the third day, she realized that she had needlessly taken it upon herself to make Abhimanyu believe that she could live without him with no trouble. She could have struck a balance, working during the day and chatting with him at nights. It could have been wonderful. *What a waste!*

In his absence of the author, Asmita was left only in the company of his words. She looked for him in them. She revered them. She took them with her to bed, worked on them and, the next morning, woke up with them. She was obsessed with the idea of continuously nurturing them and making them better. It was as if it wasn't only Abhimanyu's book, but her baby too. She collected all the longing she had in her heart for him and blended them with his words. She poured all her yearning into her edits, deleting the sentences that were redundant, refining the language, improving the sentence structure and fixing the grammar wherever needed. At several places, she added words of her own to the manuscript.

She hoped Abhimanyu would like them when he read them.

Another task on her plate was to supervise the cover work on the book. Based on her inputs during the last meeting, Nakul had already done a photoshoot. In fact, he had also prepared three different cover design options.

She straightaway rejected one of them and was confused about the other two. She liked both of them equally and even after looking at them again and again, couldn't make up her mind about which one was better.

Asmita took colour printouts of both the designs and placed them on her desk. They were going to be there for a few days. Seeing them frequently in front of her eyes would help her make up her mind, she thought. A part of her excited brain desperately wanted to reach out to Abhimanyu and show him the images that would possibly become the wrapping for his story, but she was bound by her own words to not call him.

Hard as it was, she held herself back. At the same time, she asked the design team not to forward the cover options to either Abhimanyu or Maaya. She wanted to be the first person to introduce Abhimanyu to them, and she very well knew that Maaya wouldn't wait for a single second to forward them to Abhimanyu and ask his opinion. Thankfully, her absence in the office had let Asmita place the cover options so openly on her workstation.

On the other side of the city, it was becoming difficult for Abhimanyu to hold himself back from reaching out to Asmita. Had it not been for his big ego, he would have texted her on the second day itself. He missed her. Terribly!

Like a tsunami, Asmita had wreaked havoc in his life with that kiss in the office. She had further drowned him later that night over the intimate chat. And now she had abandoned him on the shore and retracted. He craved for her to take him with her, to not leave him alone like this. After he had gotten to know what she felt about him and what she wanted from him, all he wanted was to see her in person.

How tortured and restless he was, spending his days without being able to reach out to her. But then, he was also a man who couldn't swallow his pride and contact her first. He eagerly waited for the seven days to end. Secretly, he wished that Asmita would finish her edits much before that. He dropped subtle hints for her on his Instagram posts, which he wrote every day, believing that she would read them and understand them. He wrote them only for her. The last one read:

Here I am, writing these words for you
Remembering the words I had left with you
Get done with them as soon as possible,
for I am waiting to hear a word from you.

That week changed so much for him. This time, it was he who burned for her touch.

19

By the end of the fifth day, Asmita had finished editing the entire manuscript. It had been a fascinating marathon run. Her heart raced when she began editing the last chapter. On the other side of the finish line she could see Abhimanyu with his arms open, waiting for her. He was the sole reason that she finished editing the 70,000-odd words in record time. She was dying to talk to him.

As she excitedly pressed the enter button one last time, she let out a long, satisfied sigh. She was in bed. It was 1.30 a.m. And it was all done.

Her enthusiasm about finishing work on Abhimanyu's book was mixed with the thrill of winning the challenge. She had successfully avoided talking to him all this while. Moreover, the fact that Abhimanyu too had kept his part of the bargain made the whole thing competitively interesting. A man who could restrain himself like that was her sweet poison. She couldn't wait till the morning to tell him that the edits were done. On second thoughts, she decided that she couldn't wait till the morning. *Let's see if you are awake, Abhimanyu.*

She opened the WhatsApp chat window. The date above their last shared texts was a reminder of their will power. She was finally going to end the abstinence.

'It's done,' she wrote and bit her lip, waiting for the ticks to turn blue.

A full one minute later, her phone's screen darkened. She unlocked it again and there was no change in the read status. *Oh no, have you slept?*

She kept her phone away and switched off the bedside lamp. She tried to sleep but couldn't. Her anxiousness to receive a reply kept sleep at bay. She tossed and turned in bed, wondering if she should give him a call instead.

On impulse, she picked up the phone and dialled his number. The next second, she disconnected it. *Should I or shouldn't I?*

Instead, she went to his Instagram handle. Asmita wasn't much of a social media person. In the past five days she had barely logged in, for she was immersed in Abhimanyu's manuscript. Also because she wanted to avoid him completely. However, now that she was on his handle, she read his recent posts. She could make out that they were written specifically for her.

'*The only solace I take is that my words are with you, while you and I have decided not to exchange words,*' read the latest one. It was posted only a few hours back.

Oh God!

Out of curiosity, she checked all his latest quotes and slowly, her face broke into a big smile.

'I imagine you playing with my words,
rearranging them as per your wish,
deleting a few, adding some new.
Be done with it soon, for I want to come back to
you.'

And just the way she had demanded from him, after their kiss in the office, she had become his muse. For someone who had fallen in love with this man's words, to discover herself in them was a divine and overwhelming feeling.

When she was done reading all his recent quotes, she checked his Instagram stories. In them, she found him running in shorts and a gunjee on a beach. It didn't look like a beach in Mumbai.

'Goa looks beautiful,' the next story read.

What the hell! You are in Goa? So, you are chilling,
Mr Author!

After browsing through all his stories, Asmita was intrigued and returned to his posts to read the comments from his followers. There were hundreds of them under every post. As always, the most used emoji was the red heart. Many of his followers had also left questions for him, asking him about the girl for whom he was writing the posts for.

Asmita cherished reading those questions. They warmed her heart. Interestingly, these were the very girls she had judged when she'd first looked at his page outside the operation theatre where her mother was undergoing a surgery. However, everything had changed since then. She finally went to sleep with a smile on her lips.

Around five in the morning, when she was in deep sleep, a message from Abhimanyu arrived on her phone.

'Awake?' it read.

Abhimanyu waited for a response. When he didn't get any, he dialled her number. There was no way he was going to wait for the Sun to rise. He had to speak to her right then.

Asmita picked up his call, still half sleep. Hearing his voice felt like a dream.

'Hey,' she said drowsily.

'Hiiiiiiiii,' Abhimanyu sang into his phone. His voice lacked any hint of sleepiness.

'Where are you?' she asked, turning in bed.

'God! That voice of yours,' he groaned.

'What about it?'

'It's hoarse.'

'Bad hoarse?'

'Nice hoarse.'

'So, you like it?'

'I love it. It's sexy.'

'Then you should wake me up in the middle of the night more often, so that ...'

'Shhhhh ...'

'What?'

'Don't speak too much. We will lose this raspy voice of yours.'

She adored that he'd said *we* instead of *you*. *You continue to take my heart away with your words, Mr Author!*

In her still-dark room, Asmita smiled and said, 'Okay. How do I ... talk then? How do ...'

He found it cute, how innocently and readily she agreed with him and was now wondering about things. All that he wanted in that moment was to take her in his arms and love her.

'Damn! Words that have stopped short on your lips, wish I could taste them on mine,' he said.

'Just the words?'

'To start with.'

'Are you always this romantic?'

'Is that a bad thing?'

'I didn't say that.'

'You didn't say it's a good thing either.'

'Mr Writer, stop playing with words with your editor.'

'Not playing. I am flirting with my editor.'

She giggled and shifted the phone to her other ear.

'Have we not passed that stage? The flirting one?'

'We never got to that stage, actually.'

'Haha ... you mean I didn't let it come to that stage,' she retorted.

'Technically, that's true.'

'So, would you have enjoyed it? Flirting with me? Before reaching this stage of intimacy between us?' Asmita asked.

'Umm ... I believe that I would have enjoyed it very much.'

'That brings me to my next question,' she said.

'Which is?' he asked.

'Why would you have wanted to flirt with me? There is no dearth of women who adore you and desire you, who send you hearts on your Instagram posts.'

'Shhh! You're talking too much again! I don't want to lose that voice.'

'Answer me,' she pressed.

'So, someone has been going through my Instagram posts.'

There was a brief pause again.

She couldn't wait longer and said, 'Answer me, na.'

'Honestly? No.'

'What no?'

'I had not thought of flirting with you.'

That woke her up properly. She didn't say anything back.

'I mean, I had not desired you ... this way ... till I got to see this side of you.'

'Which side of mine?'

'This bold you, who could call me to her office and kiss me at her desk.'

'So, is it all about that kiss?'

'Noooooooo!'

'Then?'

There was silence again.

'I am listening ...' Asmita whispered, reminding him to speak.

Abhimanyu replied in a soft voice, 'It is about your being an alpha female. About you living on your terms. Honestly, I had envied your guts when you chose to quit PaperInk instead of working on my book.'

The mood of the conversation had now changed from playful to slightly intense.

Asmita absorbed his words and the complete honesty in them.

He went on. 'Perhaps, deep down, I was obsessed with proving you wrong. With making you like my work.'

She smiled, listening to that.

'And I guess somewhere down the line, when you did love my work, this obsession, mixed with the pull of your bold nature, turned into a strong attraction. I mean the audacity with which you kissed me without thinking twice, it had a serious impact on me ... made me desire you so much. Newton said it. Every action has an equal and opposite reaction.'

She chuckled.

He continued. 'Nobody had ever done that to me. How could I *not* fall for you?'

Hearing his reasons made Asmita feel good about herself. It also made her want to confess some stuff of her own to him.

'I am sorry for having such preconceived notions about your work. Clearly, I was wrong, and I am sorry about it.'

Abhimanyu smiled, and Asmita could sense that he wasn't taking her seriously.

'No, I am! Seriously! Your words are so powerful. They are so simple and yet *so* impactful.'

'Shhhhhhh! Don't ruin it.'

'I will. And you will hear me out.'

He smirked and let this bold woman have her say.

'I am not a woman who would kiss a man just like that. I mean, I didn't know this about myself till the time I did this to you. I don't think I can do this to any other man I have ever met in my life before. Honestly, I hated you. And you know it. Actually, hate is a small word. I loathed you, to the extent that I preferred quitting my job than working for you. But then your words changed everything for me. Completely! To the extent that I fell for you. I don't know how to explain this, but this crazy thing has happened. I am possessed by your words, Abhimanyu.'

With his phone stuck to his ear and his heart somersaulting in delight, Abhimanyu continued listening to her.

'While I missed you terribly in these five days, I had the solace of being in the company of your words. I saw what you had posted yesterday on Instagram.' She paused, trying to collect her thoughts and let him know exactly how she felt about his words. And when she was ready again, she said, 'You know, I lived with your words! I wish there was a way I could make love to them. I don't know how you choose them, or how they appear in your mind, but they get me every time. I am not sure how I can make you understand this. Am I even making any sense to you right now?'

There was pin-drop silence at his end. And then he spoke.

'A lot.'

The way he summed it all up in only two words and went quiet again made Asmita want him even more.

'What happened?' he asked.

'Nothing,' she spoke into her phone and then kissed it. 'Muaaaah!'

He smiled and then asked, 'So, where is the edited draft?'

It took a while for Asmita to remember that she had forgotten to send it to him.

'Oh no! Sorry, I forgot!'

'Oh! Is it? Okay, so now I get it,' he said sarcastically.

'What?'

'You lost the challenge.'

'You mean to say that I am talking to you without finishing the edits?'

'That's what it looks like. Given that I don't have the proof that you finished it.'

'That you don't have the proof isn't proof that I have not finished my work.'

'Lady! I only speak on the basis of fact.' He chuckled.

'Says the author of *fiction*.' She laughed too.

'Call me whatever.'

'All right, Mr Writer, I will send it to you right away, while you are on this call.'

'Relaaaaax! I am kidding. Do it when you wake up.'

'I don't think I'll get any more sleep.'

'And I am yet to go to sleep.'

That reminded her of what she'd wanted to ask him.

'Oh hey! What are you doing in Goa?'

'So, is someone really spying on me?'

'Spying? Well then, Instagram should rename the followers' tab to spies' tab. No?'

'No, but on that note, I am going to bite your cheek.'

She giggled and said, 'And then are we going to have a cushion fight?'

'If you have those Hollywood movie cushions.'

'Why so specific?'

'The Indian ones are hard.'

She burst out laughing.

He added, 'And what's the fun if the stuffing in them doesn't fly around in the air?'

'So true! But tell me, na, what made you go to Goa?'

'You won't believe me.'

'Try me.'

'Okay. So! I went because I had to take my mind off you. I have a friend who runs a café here. I came to meet him …'

All that he said after that went unheard. She was swept away with his opening line. The way he put it so candidly touched her heart.

'I want to kiss you, Abhimanyu,' she said, cutting him off in the middle. 'Right now. A deep kiss! I want to hold your face in my palms and suck your entire breath away with that kiss.'

'What's stopping you?' he asked, his voice hoarse with desire.

'The distance,' she said, and added, 'Come back to me, na.'

That morning, neither of them got any sleep. They kept talking till the sun came up.

20

Abhimanyu was to go back to Mumbai two days later. When he had planned the Goa trip, he hadn't known that Asmita would finish the edits sooner than he had anticipated.

He wanted to run back to her as soon as he heard that she was through with her edits, but Vikram, his chef friend in Goa who had recently opened his own café, stopped him. He said that Abhimanyu couldn't do this to him.

'You can't just plan things and then leave midway. All for a girl. I've taken two nights off just so that we can party together!' he complained.

'She isn't *just* another girl. And it's not about her.'

'Then?'

'Dude! I am running short on time. The book needs to go to press ASAP.'

'Asshole! Don't give me that shit. You were anyway going to get your edits two days later. The book would have gone to press in time then also, na?'

Abhimanyu laughed, giving it away that Vikram's logic was foolproof.

Pointing his knife in one direction, Vikram said, 'That's the sea and here is the sand. Put your ass in this recliner under the giant umbrella and work as much as you want to for the rest of the day. But for the next two nights, you are here and we party. My other friends are arriving today evening. Got it?'

Abhimanyu couldn't come up with a better excuse, so he stayed back for the weekend.

Asmita had already emailed him the edited manuscript. He spent the next two days going through it. When he was through, he was sure about one thing – for the first time since his career began, he wasn't going to his personal editor.

Asmita's treatment of his work had surprised him. At one place, she had struck out an entire paragraph and replaced it with one simple line. And damn! It read a lot better than before. There was an element of art with which she had brought brevity to the whole thing. He loved it. When he read her lines, he was sure that those were going to be the lines the readers would stop and reread, for they were such beautiful statements. They were so well crafted that he wondered whether he'd have to give the credit to Asmita, should people fall in love with those sentences.

While accepting and rejecting changes made by her, Abhimanyu constantly kept asking himself if he was being unnecessarily biased towards Asmita. But in his mind, he knew that he wasn't. He wouldn't let his relationship with her affect his work in any manner. For him, his book took precedence over anything in this world, even himself.

In the end, there were only certain things he rejected. He had accepted most of the changes made by Asmita. This wasn't his initial plan the day he had first asked Maaya to pick Asmita as his editor.

If she had been mistaken about his work, then he too had been wrong about hers. *You are brilliant!*

Abhimanyu noticed how she had further intensified the chemistry between the boy and the woman in his story. And yet, she had retained the element of innocence, something which was so close to his heart, in that love story. The character graphs of his protagonists were more defined now than before. Indeed, Asmita had added a lot of value to his book. There were sections where Abhimanyu had his *aww* moments while going through her words. He was so happy with them that he took pictures of those edits and sent them to her on WhatsApp. Under them, he wrote what he loved the most about those parts. Asmita relished the instant gratification she received from Abhimanyu on chat. She felt satisfied, knowing that all the hard work she had put into the book had been worth it.

Late Monday afternoon, Abhimanyu arrived back in Mumbai. The only thing on his mind was the need to see Asmita. He couldn't wait any longer. As soon as he got back, he texted her.

'I need to see you.'

'The feeling is mutual,' came the response.

'I am glad it is.'

'Where do we meet?' Asmita asked.

'Dinner?'

'Sure. But where?'

'I am making pasta at home, tonight,' Abhimanyu said.

Asmita bit her lip at the infinite possibilities of what could happen over dinner, given where he was inviting her to.

Dragging herself back to the present, she asked, 'So, you cook too?'

'And quite well!' he responded.

A man she had fallen for was inviting her over to his place for dinner, which he was going to cook himself. The thought itself was an incredible one. At once, she imagined him in the kitchen, doing the chores, flitting around in front of the gas as she sat on the edge of the kitchen slab and spoke to him, touching him lightly as he passed her. The scene from his previous novel, where the boy made tea for the girl, came alive in front of her eyes.

Is there any end to your charm, Abhimanyu?

There was no way she was going to miss the chance of seeing him in action in the kitchen, and also experiencing what might come later. A smile bloomed on her lips as she texted him. 'I will judge that once I taste it. Eight p.m.?'

'Can you make it seven?'

'Okay. Text me the address.'

21

A little after seven in the evening, Asmita stood alone in the elevator of a high-rise residential complex, holding a bottle of red wine in one hand. She wore a fitted knee-length light-grey pencil skirt. It had a double-layered waistband and a concealed zip at the back. On top, she wore a black, full-sleeved figure-hugging turtleneck top that flaunted her small, perfectly shaped breasts and lean torso. In the office, she had worn a jacket over it, but now that she was here for Abhimanyu, there was no need to hide it any more.

As the lift raced up, her heart sank under the weight of anxious excitement. After the eventful happenings of the past few days, from the kiss in the office to the days of abstaining from even talking to each other, finally getting to see her man was sheer bliss.

She kept checking herself in the mirror that formed one wall of the elevator. Her hair was tied in a bun at the back of her head. She thought about letting it loose, but then resisted the impulse. The second the elevator came to a stop and the doors opened, she let out a deep breath and walked out. Abhimanyu's flat was right in front of her. She rang the bell. She could hear music drifting out from the other side of the door. Her heart was beating loud and fast. She wanted to suppress the sound, lest she give away her condition to Abhimanyu in the very first glance.

Asmita heard the doorknob turn. *Oh my God!* she murmured to herself and the next second, she found him before her, in the flesh, finally. *Abhimanyu!*

He stood there in a black printed vest and blue denims, holding a flat wooden spatula in his hand.

The fact that he had not made an effort to dress up was strangely appealing to her. She had always seen him in formals, often with an additional layer of a jacket or a blazer. And here he was in his designer vest, which showcased his muscular physique. The realization that he didn't feel the need to treat her formally was a happy one. He wasn't treating her like he would others. There was a strange intimacy about that move, like he already felt closer to her than anyone else.

Asmita understood it as a gesture on his part, like he was welcoming her into his world, fully and completely. He wanted to be himself in front of her.

'Look who is here!' he sang with his signature charming smile.

The next second, he checked her out, his gaze sweeping over her. The look on his face revealed how stunned he was. He breathed in sharply and then said, his voice husky, 'You ... look ... *gorgeous.*' Something about the way he spoke made her feel like his reaction had taken him by surprise too, as if the words had come out of his mouth even before he could consciously think about them.

He meant every word. That look on his face revealed how stunned he was. He had never seen Asmita in this stunning avatar. He hadn't even known that she could transform herself like this, that she could look like a ramp model, her body lean, her face shining. Asmita had sharp features, but she had seldom leveraged them to her advantage or put much effort into looking her best. She mostly wore decent but simple and loosely fitting clothes to work – Indian attire more often than not. To Abhimanyu it felt like today, someone had flipped on a switch within her and she was glowing. She smiled at him.

'Thank you,' she said, leaning against the doorway.

Abhimanyu leaned further to give her a warm hug before standing back to let her inside.

Asmita's eyes scanned the beautiful space Abhimanyu called his home.

'Wow!' she said as her eyes moved from side to side, taking everything in and exclaiming over the expansive and beautifully done space.

It was all pearly white – the sofas, the recliner, the cabinets and even the cupboards in his open kitchen. To break the monotony of the white, there were plants in different sizes placed here and there.

'Oh my god! This is fabulous, Abhimanyu!'

Abhimanyu smiled and said, 'I am glad you like it.'

The soft, warm light of the modular chandelier suited the evening mood, and the strains of jazz music, playing in the background, made the place even cosier.

On her right was the open kitchen. It was a substantial space for a studio apartment. In front of the kitchen slab fitted with a four-burner stove was a gorgeous rectangular kitchen island meant for chopping vegetables and serving a buffet. And, because this Italian marble finished island was in the centre of the kitchen space, there was enough room to walk around it. Asmita instantly fell in love with this part of the flat.

'Is there anything here that is not perfect?' she asked, walking around the kitchen.

Abhimanyu chuckled.

'Here! This is for you,' she said, placing the wine bottle on the island.

'Thank you so much,' he said, walking up to her.

She enjoyed how effortlessly he came close to her and stood by her side. She secretly checked out his chiselled collarbones, broad shoulders and muscular biceps.

'I had put some white wine in the fridge,' he said. 'Works for you?'

'Sure,' she replied with a smile.

'Great!' Abhimanyu went to get wine glasses from the bar at the other side of the drawing room. Meanwhile, Asmita noticed a bunch of spaghetti sticks in a serving bowl. Next to it, in a smaller bowl, was red sauce. She discovered some tomato peels in a plate next to the washbasin. Looking at it, she smiled and exclaimed, 'You made this sauce from scratch? Like right *now*?'

Abhimanyu nodded and said a soft yes as he walked up behind her.

Smiling, she turned around to look at him.

'You thought I will use some readymade sauce?' he asked, placing the glasses on the countertop and pulling out the chilled wine from the fridge. He then grabbed some nachos and pita bread along with hummus from one of the cupboards.

Abhimanyu poured the drinks and they cheered, their glasses clinking musically. He suggested that she sit on the sofa in the living area, but Asmita insisted on staying put in the kitchen. There was something alluring about seeing him cook and she didn't want to miss that. She wanted to be there by his side as he moved around the kitchen, chopping and stirring and garnishing.

They both held their glasses in their hands as they talked. Asmita rested her body against one edge of the island while Abhimanyu stood right across from her, also leaning against the kitchen slab.

He loved having her in his space, at his home. It was his oasis, and there was something intimate about being able to share it with the woman who had captivated him so. Asmita, in her turn, cherished his proximity and the opportunity to see his life and personal space so closely. In the back of her mind, images of their first kiss flashed in her head. She observed his lips touching the edge of the glass as he drank from it. To hide her thoughts, she averted her eyes and looked down into the glass, anticipating the events of the evening which had just begun seemed filled with promise.

However, for the moment, the two kept their chat casual, discussing only light, unimportant things. In the aftermath of their intensely intimate moments, in person and on chat till a week ago, this was a bit anticlimactic and not really the way that either of them had expected the evening to go. In fact, given that they had abstained from reaching out to each other for a good chunk of the week gone by, both of them had expected a fiery, passionate reunion. They were supposed to have their arms wrapped around each other in an embrace that made them weak in the knees.

Abhimanyu was holding back because he thought it would be unfair of him to not let her adjust to his space first. Asmita, on her part, wanted him to take the first step this time. And so, the initial inhibition that had come into play, and which the two had to overcome, lingered, making the mood almost formal. They had to break this ice, and the idea excited them, making the evening even more interesting. After all, there was no denying where the evening would go, but the fun lay in finding out how they'd get there.

'So ... finished Draft 2?' she asked.

Abhimanyu closed his eyes and, with a smile, nodded wordlessly.

'That's great!' Asmita said with a twinkle in her eyes.

'Yes. But hey, tonight we don't talk about work,' he said.

She liked that suggestion, especially since it meant that he was taking the lead and moving the conversation to a more personal place.

'Then what do you suggest we talk about?' she asked happily.

'About us. Let's get to know each other better?'

Looking into his eyes, she said, 'That's a great idea.'

Strange as it was, their relationship had had a catastrophic start and then taken an intense U-turn. They had been intimate but were yet to get to know each other in person, outside of their professions.

Standing in that kitchen and sipping wine, they asked each other questions and slipped into their respective pasts. They passed through the magic of their childhood, the thrill of their adolescent years and how they had arrived where they were now.

They talked about the places they had lived in, the people they had dated; Abhimanyu had plenty of those, Asmita only one. They laughed over the huge gap in the number. As time passed by and the bottle of wine was emptied, questions weren't needed any more. In a happy, relaxed frame of mind, they began sharing things on their own, without being prompted. The conversation had gone on autopilot mode. The background music too was doing an incredible job of adding to the ambience.

Forty-five minutes later, Abhimanyu recalled that he had to cook the meal as well. Engrossed in the conversation, he'd also lost track of time. Besides, the light snacks they'd been having had helped them keep hunger at bay for a while.

'Let me help,' Asmita insisted.

'There is nothing much to be done here,' Abhimanyu said, putting the water to boil.

The sight of a handsome man preparing a meal for her was seductive; more so when she felt so happy already. She noticed every fine detail – how elegantly he held the spaghetti sticks, how he let them sink in the water when it had come to a boil, how he moved while grabbing things from here and there. While Abhimanyu kept talking, she was losing her focus on his words. Perhaps for the first time, her emphasis was on the man and not his words. Intoxicated by his aura and the chivalrous manner in which he was conducting himself, she couldn't wait any longer.

Abhimanyu walked past her to fetch some herbs from the closet behind her. The way she looked at him gave her thoughts away. Asmita had let herself become vulnerable, and she was aware of it. Her eyes were big and black, and they were focused on him, unblinking. The second he noticed her unwavering gaze, his eyes widened. She didn't flinch and continued to stare at him, almost challengingly, unabashed. She didn't even need the wine to exhibit her desire so boldly, but it had certainly had a role to play. Her lips parted. She let out a deep sigh and placed the glass of wine on the edge of the countertop. It was an invitation he could not ignore.

Silently, he pushed the drawer back without a word and, without taking his eyes off her, switched off the gas burner. The pasta could wait. He had to address something a lot more important in that moment.

'Asmita.' Just one word, in a soft voice. That's all that was needed.

He stepped closer, took her in his arms and went straight for her lips. The ferocity with which he kissed her made her surrender herself to him. She closed her eyes and felt his touch, inhaled the musk fragrance emanating from the skin of his neck. She loved how he gripped her so tight, every inch of their bodies cushioned against each other. He pushed her against the kitchen island. His lips frenetically sucked hers, dissolving them both in throes of pleasure. At once the passion had turned fierce, raw, as if they had waited way too long.

Their tongues took turns to invade each other's mouth and wrestle, trying to dominate the other. It was a game they played breathlessly, staying in the other person's mouth for as long as they could. When there was a dire need to breathe, they called truce.

Their eyes opened and they looked at each other. Their chests rose and fell. Their hearts pumped like they'd both run a marathon. The sound of their deep breaths overpowered the music in the background. All this while, not for a single second had they looked at anything else but each other.

They weren't done kissing yet. Their hunger for each other ran deep within them. Their lips met once again. Abhimanyu's hand ran down Asmita's neck, onto her shoulders and further down over her breasts. She thrilled at how he was exploring her. He felt her soft flesh from over her top. She pushed herself against his palms, making him feel her better. He grabbed and squeezed one breast and she let out a sweet cry. Her lips parted and she pulled back. Left on their own, Abhimanyu's lips glided down her chin and onto her neck. He kissed her there. Swimming in an ocean of pleasure, Asmita looked up at the ceiling, making space for his head in the cave of her neck.

He was rough. She wanted him to be rough. He pulled the neck of her top down and sucked the soft skin of her neck, marking it with his teeth. Asmita felt herself go wild with pleasure. She wanted to be marked. She wanted to carry those bruises of his love on her skin back home with her. They were going to be her souvenirs. He then moved to the other side of her neck and his rough stubble brushed against her soft skin and burned it. Like an animal, he was all over her, fulfilling his hunger and hers.

His free hand crawled down over her top. He pulled its edge out of her pencil skirt. Without giving her any time to react, he slipped his hand under it. Brushing past the skin around her navel, his hand went higher. He clutched her breast over her bra and squeezed it. Asmita trembled on feeling the uninhibited touch of his hand on her body. She wanted it so much. At first, he struggled to slip his hand beneath the wired cup of her bra, but then he pushed it out of his way and grabbed her breast. Only then did he find momentary peace. Asmita groaned with pleasure when she felt his wild fingers inside her bra.

He took her tender breast in his hand and felt her hard nipple. His thumb circled around it. He teased her and left her hungrier for him. Her loud breaths told him how much she wanted him to continue.

'Don't stop,' she reiterated.

The intensity grew within her. It was getting difficult for her to stand on her feet any longer. She was gradually slipping into an uncomfortable posture, hurting her back.

Abhimanyu noticed her discomfort and immediately pulled away from the island top. His hands now moved over her hips. In his strong arms he lifted her and placed her on the countertop of his kitchen.

Sweltering in her desire, Asmita loved how he took care of her. She wanted to offer herself completely to him. She wanted to be his.

He then held the hem of her top in both his hands and pulled it up. Seeing it coming, Asmita readily straightened her arms above her head. She wanted this more than him – to be undressed by him, to be seen by him.

She was wearing a navy-blue bra underneath. Abhimanyu took a good look at her near-naked body. He loved the sight of the pits around her collarbones, giving a sharp definition to her lean structure. They held immense appeal.

He ran his tongue around her collarbone. His wet touch burned her. She closed her eyes, savouring it. He traced his tongue down her cleavage. At the same time he tried to unhook her bra and when he failed to do so, he felt her hands trespass his. Abhimanyu let her help him help her. In a second she unhooked it and let him take it from there.

Nibbling at her cleavage, he took off her bra and placed it on the countertop. He then moved back a little to take a good look at her.

Her breasts were small and perfectly shaped. He loved the crescent moons over her ribs. He didn't want to leave any inch of them. Her nipples were pink, rosy and swollen. He couldn't wait any longer. He looked at her and his gaze burned her. Her face was flushed with desire. The deep ache in her hardened nipples needed to be satiated. Her brazen eyes conveyed all this and more to him.

Abhimanyu latched onto her breasts. He took her soft flesh in his mouth and squeezed the other, leading to an intense shiver of arousal. She moaned for him.

He took turns at her breasts, not letting either one be deprived of his mouth for too long. At times, unmindfully, he dug his teeth into them. On one occasion, when he clenched her nipple and pulled at it, a gasp escaped Asmita's throat. She shut her eyes, turned her face towards the ceiling and let him have her his way.

As her legs spread wider, her pencil skirt rode up her legs, exposing her thighs. She could feel herself getting more and more wet. This man was doing things to her that were beyond her imagination. She felt lucky to have found him.

Asmita ran her hands through the curly locks of his hair and then on his cheeks, while he was busy nibbling at her. Her hands further descended to his shoulders. She pulled him up by the straps of his vest. When he got up, she pulled it off. Her eyes scanned his athletic body, the undercut of his chest and the abs popping out and sinking in with every breath he took. She explored his rock-solid chest and nipples with her fingers.

She ran her hands over his back and pulled him closer. She wanted intimacy between their naked upper halves. She wanted her soft breasts to thrust against his hard chest; their nipples to rub against each other. She wrapped him in her arms. Her sharp nails dug into his back and carved tiny crescent moons. She began kissing his chest and followed the thin line of hair at its centre.

The platform she sat upon restricted any further movement. She landed on the floor and switched places with him. Abhimanyu now stood, taking the support of the countertop, while Asmita went straight down to unbutton his denims. She opened his zipper and saw his protruded underwear. She craved for him. Standing above her, Abhimanyu watched her grab the waistband of his briefs. She looked up at him. A wickedly delightful smile appeared on her lips. The next second, she stripped him.

His erection throbbed the second the briefs slipped down. Soon, it stood in all its glory for her. From up close, Asmita observed his manhood closely. She grasped it in her fist and felt him all over. Then she again looked up at him. There was no shame or shyness in her eyes. And, with her gaze still locked on him, she took him in her mouth.

Abhimanyu lost his mind. He could only watch her for a few seconds before his eyes shut and he transcended into a different world.

Asmita slid her lips across his length, from tip to root. She made him discover the deep interiors of her mouth – the depth his tongue could have never explored. She swallowed him. She tasted him. He was soaked in her saliva and pulsating in her mouth. She began to brew an orgasm in him. Each passing second, he struggled to hold himself. When he couldn't take it any further, he held her head and signalled her to hold on. Asmita let him pull out.

She rose up. Abhimanyu grabbed her. Her skin had turned hotter than before. He turned her around, pushed her against the countertop and took her spot. His hand travelled to her lower back where he found the zipper of her skirt. He didn't waste any time in pulling it down. Asmita's skirt slipped off and fell on the floor, leaving her in her lacy navy-blue bikini briefs.

Abhimanyu lifted her by her waist and placed her on the countertop. He spread her legs out. One hand ran down her left inner thigh. Asmita sighed heavily, looking into his eyes. His fingers moving on her fleshy thigh was deeply satisfying. When his hand finally reached for her underwear, her sigh was loud and sensual.

He could feel her wetness when he clasped her underwear in his hand and rubbed it against her skin. That carnal act made Asmita even more excited.

'God! You are so wet,' he murmured.

Asmita swallowed the lump in the back of her throat. She attempted to speak but her vigorous breathing suppressed her faint voice. She only nodded while looking at him through half-closed eyes. Abhimanyu held the back of her neck. It was hot. There was sweat on her forehead.

'You're feeling hot?'

She put her hands on the countertop to find support and hesitantly nodded. She did not want to deviate his attention.

Abhimanyu wanted to help her out. He intended to go find the AC remote, but Asmita immediately held him back, not letting him go. On second thoughts, he stretched out his arm, opened the fridge fetched out a few ice cubes.

Looking at her, Abhimanyu slowly ran them down her cheek, onto her neck and then her breasts. He worshiped every inch of her body. She was his Goddess.

'Aaaaaah!' A furious wild moan escaped her mouth.

'What are you doing to me, Abhimanyu?' she murmured, closing her eyes.

The edges of the ice cubes chilled her soft breasts. He ran them in circles around her nipples. She couldn't wait any longer. Asmita held his hand and guided it downwards.

The ice cubes in his fist had already melted. With his other hand, Abhimanyu opened the fridge again, pulled out both the ice trays and scattered the ice cubes all over the countertop. He picked up a few cubes and slipped his hand inside her panties, pressing them against her vagina.

Asmita had not seen that coming. He did it at lightning speed. He didn't circle those cubes against her skin this time. Instead, he held them against the length of her wet lips, letting a freezing wave run through her.

It was an electric sensation, as if a mild current had passed through the bottom of her spine. It was sweet and unbearable at the same time. She howled but didn't protest. Her body demanded that he pull his hand out. Her mind overpowered that urge for its pleasure. He was insanely wild and she was madly in love with him. Everything he did turned her on. The spectacle of this naked man, playing with her this way, was intensely arousing.

With the heat of her body, the cubes began to melt. Abhimanyu rubbed them over the folds of her lips. He wanted to crush all the ice and slip it inside her.

'What are you doing to me?' she murmured again, sounding as if she was high.

'Corrupting you.'

As the ice between his fingers and her skin melted, it took his numb fingers a few seconds to realize he was touching her. He found her clit and began circling it with his thumb. Right in that moment, Abhimanyu churned a whirlpool within her. The sexual tension building up in her was intense. It begged for a release.

'Get inside me. Now! Please! *Please*!' she urged him.

Standing between her spread legs, Abhimanyu took off the last piece of clothing on her. Asmita gripped his erect manhood in her hands and aimed it towards her. His crown nudged through the soft folds of her skin and invaded her. She helplessly moaned for him. Wet and lubricated, she consumed him to the fullest without any struggle. He brushed past her pleasure nerves that transported waves of ecstasy to her brain.

His pelvis began to move in rhythm.

The man whom she had fallen in irresistible love with was finally making love to her. Not on chat but for real! He stoked pleasure in her. She cried in sweet agony.

When Abhimanyu picked up pace, Asmita struggled to support herself. She spread her arms behind on the countertop, trying to balance her torso. The ice cubes had melted on the countertop. Every time Abhimanyu pounded himself into her, her butt slipped further behind on the wet surface. She raised her legs in the air and circled them around him. She clung to him and moved with him. It still didn't help her. She was slipping behind, taking him along with her.

Holding her waist, Abhimanyu slipped her far behind on the island, making enough space for himself. He then mounted the surface. The two had turned the kitchen into a bedroom. She laid down on her back on the kitchen island, while he positioned himself up over her. Beneath Asmita were a dozen scattered ice cubes, intensifying her sweet agony. She quivered under his body weight and moaned louder than before, faster than before, in tandem with every stroke.

'I love you, Abhimanyu.'

'I love you too, baby.'

'Come inside me!' she screamed, tightening the grip of her legs around his butt. He could sense her force.

With panting breaths, he reached deeper inside her.

'I am coming, Asmita,' he said and repeated it loudly, 'I AM COMING!'

She acknowledged it with wild moans. 'Aaaaaaaahhhh … Abhimanyu…' The walls of his kitchen echoed her loud moans.

An orgasm rushed through his pulsating manhood and erupted inside her. A tremor rippled through his body and he collapsed over her. Asmita too climaxed in that moment, finding a deeply satisfying relief to her tension. They both lay on the cold, wet countertop for a while, trying to catch their breaths. She continued to hold him in the lock of her legs, while her arms circled around his back.

A while later, they cleaned themselves up. Asmita had been the first one to jump off the countertop. Abhimanyu watched her as she walked away from him, stark naked.

Moments later, she shouted from inside the washroom. 'Can you please get me my clothes?'

Abhimanyu looked around for them. 'Why don't you come out and get them yourself?' he said mischievously.

'Abhimanyu, please!' a coy Asmita replied.

He smiled and picked up all her belongings. He found it cute, how she had transitioned from being horny, till moments ago, to shy now. He tried to push open the washroom door, but it was latched from inside. A second later it opened and he saw her hand slip out. The smile on his face widened into a grin and he handed over her clothes before Asmita quickly shut the door.

Sweet! He walked to the bedroom and got himself a towel. Wrapping it around himself, he waited for Asmita to step out.

Later that evening, Asmita sat on the kitchen slab, listening to Abhimanyu tell stories. They were back at it – telling stories. These were not narratives of his novels, but reminiscences from his childhood. He enjoyed telling them to her, and she was hooked. The two drank up the leftover wine, while he finished cooking the spaghetti for them. All that while, Asmita's curious eyes kept looking at Abhimanyu and trying to imagine the little boy he would have once been.

At one point, he shared an embarrassing event from his school life. He told her how, during PT class, while exercising, his pants had fallen in front of everyone. He had become a laughingstock for the other kids. Asmita laughed , picturing the incident. She couldn't stop herself from reaching over and pulling his cheeks.

Later, Abhimanyu told her about his first heartbreak. It wasn't a break-up, for he had not even expressed his feelings to the girl from his school whom he had a serious crush on. For two years, he'd secretly loved her and by the time he gathered enough courage to tell her, she had left the school and the city. He was fourteen and she was his senior.

'I cried for her for many days,' he said with a smile now, while serving the spaghetti.

'Awww!' Asmita said, genuinely feeling for him. With her eyes focused on him, she said, 'Come here.'

He walked towards her. She gave him a peck on his cheek and hugged him. Abhimanyu loved how she treated him.

Thirty seconds later, she whispered in his ear, 'I am starving now.'

They giggled. Asmita jumped off the kitchen slab and picked up the plates. The two walked towards the dining table adjacent to his workstation. There was a window in front of both tables. Asmita gazed at the neighbouring lit-up skyscrapers and then at the infinite darkness beyond. It took her a few seconds to understand what it was. Her eyes widened.

'Hey! Is that the sea?'

He rolled some spaghetti into his fork and held it closer to her lips. It was unexpected. Asmita cherished that he was feeding her the first bite.

'It is,' Abhimanyu answered.

Her eyes widened.

She chewed fast. 'Oh my God!' she screamed when she could. 'I didn't realize it when on the way here but …' she paused, her eyes wide.

'Is it good?' he asked, holding back his smile.

'But … YOU LIVE IN A SEA-FACING FLAT?!' she said, completely ignoring his question.

'And what about the spaghetti?' he said, ignoring her question.

She immediately stopped chewing and gave a few big nods to let him know it was delicious.

The two kept talking over dinner and bonded with each other like never before.

When it was time for Asmita to leave, Abhimanyu held her hand. He was going to see her off till her parked car, but stopped just before they stepped out of the flat.

'Don't go. Spend the night with me,' he said. He meant it. She could see it in his eyes.

Asmita herself didn't want to leave that place. After the evening they had had, it was already very difficult for her to walk away from him. She looked at the sprawling bed at the other corner of the studio. How she wanted to sleep holding him in her arms and in the morning, wake up to the sight of the Arabian Sea and make tea in the very kitchen where they had made love!

'My mom! She would be waiting for me,' she said, making a face.

Abhimanyu understood and didn't push her, though a sad look dawned upon his face. Asmita noticed that and looking at his gloomy face, she smiled mysteriously.

'What?' Abhimanyu sought.

'I am not going to leave you on that note,' she said, her smile widening.

'Then?'

'I want to show you something and I hope it will cheer you up.'

He was intrigued. Asmita unlocked her phone and went to her email. Abhimanyu eagerly waited.

'Here,' she said, turning her phone towards him.

It was the cover of his upcoming book, the one she had finally zeroed upon.

Abhimanyu's eyes widened. Asmita watched the smile grow on his face. He took the phone from her and looked closely at the cover. The kitchen scene from his manuscript had come alive. It was raw and innocently romantic, just the way he had wanted it. He read the title once.

'*The Boy in the Neighbourhood*. You have finally chosen the title for my novel!'

And then he read it out again, a little louder.

'*The Boy in the Neighbourhood*.'

He bit his smiling lower lip and held it like that while gazing at the cover. His eyes were sparkling. Asmita's heart flipped on seeing that. *He likes it!*

Abhimanyu finally took his eyes off the mobile screen and looked at her.

She raised her eyebrows, seeking his confirmation.

'This ...' he paused and said, 'is heart-warming.'

'Did you like the title I picked?'

'I looooove it.' He cupped her cheeks in his palms and kissed her for giving him that joy.

22

The manuscript had finally found its identity – the title by which it would be known in the coming days. Maaya was also back in office and had approved the title and the cover jacket. Her only concern was whether Abhimanyu would like it. How could she have known what was going on between her editor and her author?

Time being of the essence, Maaya couldn't have afforded her author disagreeing on the cover. And if there were any objections by him, it would only mean spending more time either in persuading him or, worse, redesigning the whole thing. She gave Abhimanyu a call the minute the cover arrived in her inbox, just like Asmita had anticipated.

On the phone, Abhimanyu did a good job of making her believe that he was seeing the cover jacket for the first time. Asmita had prepared him well for this. He read out the title a few times, making her believe that he was absorbing its vibe. In the end, after taking some time, he said, 'I love them both. Let's go ahead.'

Maaya felt a tinge of pride at having been able to offer him something so splendid that he didn't need to ask for any changes. It was a cakewalk she hadn't anticipated.

The sales team too was happy with the cover jacket. They felt it was impressive and the book would fly off the shelves.

The production team had an update from the printer, though. The printing press was in no position to take such a huge printing order for Abhimanyu's new book.

Peter and Asmita looked at Maaya, worried

The production team apprised everyone that even if PaperInk postponed all their current orders, amounting to a total of 75,000 copies across titles, to make way for Abhimanyu's book, the printer would still not be able to deliver the kind of quantity they wanted.

'Folks, can we not go to a different printer?' Maaya suggested.

'We can, but printing such numbers in such a short time will be difficult for anyone. Besides, there is no guarantee of quality and we may not get the kind of discounts we get at our regular printer. The payment terms will have to be negotiated from scratch. And that kind of a risk for this book isn't advisable.'

For some reason, Maaya felt that the production team hadn't done enough on their part. She never liked 'no' for an answer, always preferring people taking charge and delivering results.

'Did you ask them to make this an exceptional case? We are willing to pay for the entire print run in advance. How about that?'

Peter turned towards her. He feared she was going to set the wrong precedent with that one.

'No, Maaya. Please understand, we are hardly five percent of their business. They wouldn't disrupt the other big publishers' work for us.'

Maaya hated it when anyone referred to other publishers as *big* publishers; more so when it was her own team. It always made her feel as if she hadn't done enough to make PaperInk 'big'. She would have commented on that reference right then and there in the meeting room, in front of everyone, if she had had a solution to their current problem. It bothered her to not be able to find one.

'Can I suggest something here?' Asmita pitched in.

'Go ahead,' Peter said.

'Instead of postponing the print runs of the entire 75,000 copies across titles, can we look at doing that for 50,000 copies?'

'How does that solve our problem?' Maaya asked.

'Let's not totally stop production of other titles. Our other authors would not like it if, at any point in time, their work goes out of stock. At the same time, instead of printing 2,00,000 copies of *The Boy in the Neighbourhood*, let's print 50,000 in one go and take it to the market. I suggest we work on a zero-warehouse stock model and place every single copy straight on the bookshelves.'

'What about the rest?' Peter questioned.

Looking at Asmita and acknowledging her line of thought, Rajeev Subramanian spoke up. 'I would buy her suggestion, Peter. We still won't be able to get the remaining 1,50,000 copies in the month after that, though. I can only push and get another 50,000 copies.'

'So that means our order of 2,00,000 copies would take four months to be out?' Maaya summed up for everyone.

'I will try for three instead of four,' Rajeev said.

'What is our major con then? If we move ahead in this direction?' Peter asked.

'We sell low to distributors, we earn low,' the sales head stated.

The whole rush to release such large numbers of the book in such a short span finally began to bother Peter. It appeared to be a bad idea to him. 'Maaya, can we not delay the book and bring it out when we have enough bandwidth?'

For Maaya, this was not a possibility. They had moved way too far to come back. They were in the last week of September. In two months, the literature festivals' season was going to kickstart. As per her initial plan, she wanted every leading literature festival in the country to host a book launch for Abhimanyu. It would mark PaperInk's arrival in the list of premium publishers. And Maaya was not going to waste that opportunity. She knew very well that Abhimanyu went to all these festivals almost every year, but only as a speaker. Never before had he brought out a new novel at this time. She would milk the opportunity, even if it meant going to the market with 50,000 copies.

She had already talked to the directors of several leading literature festivals in the country. As per her recce till then, there was no other popular author whose book was to be launched in the upcoming season. It was a delightful discovery for her; it might not happen again next year. She was obsessed with the idea of doing something different, something big with Abhimanyu, other than his usual multicity book launches at bookstores. A bookstore launch would bring him a hundred or two hundred readers, but a literature festival would have a footfall of thousands. She didn't want to lose the opportunity to create a buzz. So she remained adamant.

'Changing the date now will disrupt what we've already put in motion, Peter.'

Peter knew her attitude well. He wasn't going to challenge it. If Maaya had decided on doing something, she would do it anyway. It was best for him to invest his energies in making that happen instead of objecting to it.

That's when the sales head began talking again. 'Asmita's idea of a sequential print run is, in fact, a good one. If the book is a runaway bestseller, which we all want it to become, it will make the retailers and distributors value it a lot more. A scarce product with a huge demand! In that case, we can reduce our discounts to them.'

With that, the idea of postponing the publication date of Abhimanyu's novel was put aside. More pros and cons of bringing it out at the scheduled time were discussed.

Amid all the choices available, Asmita's idea found everyone's agreement.

The team at PaperInk was excited and anxious. They had constraints but they had found a way to adjust to them by optimizing their resources. It was a difficult choice, and only time would tell if it was the right one.

The team dispersed and Asmita walked out of the meeting room, excited. She couldn't wait for the day when the initial readers of *The Boy in the Neighbourhood* would post their reviews.

23

'So, what do you think?' Asmita asked, giggling.

The two were in a Mumbai local. It was Abhimanyu's first time.

Holding her tight in the circle of his arms, Abhimanyu looked here and there smiling, and then finally said, 'Like being on *Khatron ke Khiladi*.'

Asmita burst out laughing and rested her chin on his chest. He tightened his grip around her. They could smell each other's scents.

The night before, pleased by all the work she'd put into the book, Abhimanyu had messaged her.

'I owe you a big treat for all that you have done for the book.'

'Nothing can be bigger than the treat I had at your place,' she had written back.

'Then how about a smaller one?'

'Okay … if you insist☺.'

'Great, then.'

'When and where?'

'ASAP. Can you take a day off tomorrow?'

'Ax day off?'

'A relaxed long lunch at the Taj and then a matinee movie?'

'Oh boy! That's quite a plan.'

'Game?'

'Do I have the liberty to ask for the kind of treat I want?'

'Of course. Ask.'

'Would you like to spend a non-five-star kind of day with me?'

'Elaborate?'

'Hmmm … let's ditch the Taj and your luxurious car as well. Let's roam around in Mumbai by public transport and eat street food. What say?'

'I am already tired.'

'Hahaha. Come on! What's the use of all that body-building in the gym if you get tired living a day like millions of others?'

'It's just not about that. We'll miss the privacy and the comfort of the car. You know what I mean☺.'

'I do. But I guess you haven't experienced the thrill of holding each other in a Mumbai local.'

'Forget it. I am not going to do that.'

'So, you aren't up for my plan.'

'No! I mean, holding you in front of everyone. Rest, as I said, I owe you. So I am game. But I am not in favour of public displays of affection.'

'We will see☺.'

'Yeah you will.'

'And I will prove you wrong.'

'We will see.'

'Meet me at Churchgate station. 11.30 a.m. tomorrow?'

'Roger that.'

The two were supposed to get down at the Vile Parle station. That was Asmita's plan.

'But hey! This is the best part,' he said.

'What?' Asmita asked looking up at him.

'This! To get to hold you like this! In public!' he said, almost whispering.

'See! I told you!' she said loudly, celebrating the tiny victory.

Joy danced in their eyes as they looked at each other in the moving train. There was no way left for Abhimanyu but to hold Asmita in her arms, in that crowded local. The chatter of passengers, the news broadcast on someone's mobile phone at a distance and the rhythmic sound of the metal wheels sprinting on the rail track, all became a background score to their conversation.

Two stations later, there was not even an inch of space left and yet, somehow, more people entered. Abhimanyu had seen such visuals before, but only on the television or in a movie. To experience this up close was something else. Amazed at how the wave of people kept moving in and out of the train at each station, he kept talking about the adventure of that ride. And while he talked, he made sure that he held Asmita tight in his arms, safeguarding her from the crowd, which had swelled so much that the bogey was bursting at the seams.

As the two stood near the gate, there were moments when they felt the wave of exiting passengers would take them along.

'ABHIMANYU!' Asmita screamed when it happened the first time. Impulsively, she shut her eyes.

Abhimanyu immediately strengthened his grip and held his feet firmly, resisting the push. Blood rushed to his face, as if he had bench-pressed 100 kg. When he succeeded in holding his ground and Asmita as well, she opened her eyes, looked at him and smiled. She was enjoying this.

He couldn't resist and went for her lips. At once, Asmita pulled her face back. Embarrassed, she looked around from the corners of her eyes and then back at him.

'NO!' she whispered loudly, making a worried face.

Abhimanyu kept smiling for a few seconds, after which he said, 'I want it so much.' This! After he was the one who was against the idea of public display of affection.

'You can't have it here,' she whispered.

'You can't have it here,' he mimicked her in a funny voice.

She burst into another big laugh and pulled his nose.

How he wanted to lift her in his arms and take her to the countertop of his kitchen in that very moment!

Something occurred in his mind – an idea to tease her and make her blush in front of everyone. He kept looking into her eyes.

'What?' she asked.

'Were they feeling very cold?' he asked.

'Cold! What?'

'The ice cubes. Beneath you. On the countertop.'

Her eyes grew big, her mouth opened in shock. Then, after ensuring that no one had heard him, she stole her eyes away. Under Abhimanyu's gaze, she looked down at the third button of his shirt, trying to hold back her smile. She pulled her lips in and shut her eyes for a few seconds.

Abhimanyu interrogated her again.

'Or did they make you feel hot?'

She held his waist between her thumbs and forefingers and twitched it hard. 'How does this make you feel?' she asked.

'Oh shit!' Abhimanyu screamed in pain.

People around them looked at the two. Asmita released him.

He looked zapped. 'You are crazy.'

She smiled and said, 'I am. For you.'

Abhimanyu loved how she put it. He kept looking into her eyes and she held her gaze back at him. Recalling that evening in his kitchen, out of a genuine curiosity this time, he asked her, 'I need to know if that evening was fulfilling for you?'

Asmita admired the authenticity with which he asked her. She nodded her chin and said. 'It was.' She meant it.

'I want to experience it again tonight.' He whispered, lest anyone eavesdrop on their conversation.

Asmita wasn't any bit shy to voice her thoughts. 'This time will you make me feel how your stubble feels like in between my legs?' A sense of grave need sailed on her face when she asked him that.

Abhimanyu recalled how the other night over a call, he had virtually made her experience it. That she wanted it for real made him feel ecstatic. That she was demanding, and that their sexual energies overlap so much, made him feel ecstatic.

He tightened the circle of his arms around her back lovingly, making a mental note that he had to satisfy this need of his girl.

The two got down at Vile Parle station. Abhimanyu kept asking her what the plan was. Asmita kept telling him that he would find out soon. They took the staircase and exited from the densely populated station.

Fortunately, the day was pleasant and the sky cloudy, so Abhimanyu didn't miss the private shade of his car at all.

In about fifteen minutes, they arrived at Prithvi Theatre. The moment Asmita stepped towards its entrance, Abhimanyu enquired: 'Hey! Are we going to watch a play?'

She turned towards him, pursed her lips in a funny way and nodded. 'Mmm ... hmmm.'

He smiled.

'What?' she asked.

'It's been a long time since I watched one.'

She kept staring him for a while and then said, 'You are welcome.'

Abhimanyu's smile widened. He ran his hands around her waist to cuddle her.

'What play is it? Have you booked the tickets online?'

'It's based on one of the books I had edited,' she answered, looking at him. '*Three Long Nights.*'

'Ahaaaaan?' Abhimanyu playfully sang, as if taunting her about showing off.

'It's a damn good one. I am sure you'll love it. And no, I didn't book the tickets online. I am old-school. Come! Let's buy them from the counter.' She held his hand and walked him inside.

Little did she know that disappointment was awaiting them at the counter. The play she had wanted them to watch was scheduled for late night.

'OH NO!' Asmita cried the second she heard that from the other side of the ticket counter.

'Old school, haan?' Abhimanyu mocked her planning skills.

She stood there quietly, looking crushed.

He nudged her, trying to make her say something. She remained silent.

'Let me know once you are done grieving,' he said, this time trying to make her laugh. Still, there was no change in her.

Seconds later, she finally said, 'I really wanted to watch it with you.' She seemed heartbroken.

'So we will watch, yaar. Let's watch it tonight.'

'No! I have to go back. Can't be out that late.'

Meanwhile, the ticket counter guy shouted, 'Today is the last show for this play, madam.'

Asmita looked at Abhimanyu's face in despair. She looked like a schoolkid who had failed her exams, was in shock and about to break down.

'Awww!' Abhimanyu uttered and hugged her to console her.

Funny thing was, he was consoling her for the plan she had planned for him but failed to execute. *How surprising was the result of her surprise!*

A while later, they had lunch at an old restaurant in Juhu. It had a unique name – Hotel Majnu. Abhimanyu smiled upon reading the name. The restaurant, which was more like a dhaaba, was again Asmita's plan, though she had lost her appetite by now.

There was nothing fancy about the place; it had plastic fibre chairs and tables. Hygiene was the most doubtful aspect, but certainly not the taste. After all, the restaurant was bustling with people from all walks of life. It was known for its biryani. And, in order to shove away the gloom of not getting to watch the play, Abhimanyu ordered some beer along with the biryani.

The restaurant was the kind that didn't serve pints but big bottles of beer. Asmita was game. Initially, she didn't talk much and only responded in monosyllables. But that changed when Abhimanyu ate the first bite of the biryani.

'Damn! This is delicious, Asmita.'

His reaction lifted Asmita's mood slightly. Finally, he had enjoyed something she had planned. The chicken was tender, the raita refreshing and the aroma of the rice was mouth-watering. After finishing one plate of it, Abhimanyu ordered another. He ate half of it and asked the waiter to pack whatever was left.

With her tummy full of her favourite biryani and her heart happy at seeing Abhimanyu relish it so much too, Asmita was finally feeling upbeat again. Or, perhaps, it was the one and half bottles of beer that had brought her mojo back.

At around 4.30 in the evening, happy and slightly tipsy, they walked out of the restaurant, crossed random roads and found themselves at the Juhu Chowpatty.

The place looked lively. There was some time yet for sunset. However, it being a fantastic day, there were already enough people at the beach.

'What's the plan now?' Abhimanyu asked.

'Hmmm ... we go there and sit,' Asmita said, pointing towards the shore.

Pulling in his lips, Abhimanyu asked, 'Wouldn't Marine Drive be a better place to sit by the shore?'

'You live next door to it. This is a change for you.' Asmita circled her hand around his and dragged him along.

He loved how this slightly drunk Asmita was treating him. It was cute. While being dragged, he felt sand slip inside his shoes. He asked Asmita to give him a second, but she didn't seem to hear him at all.

Passing by the dozens of street food kiosks, he asked. 'How about some pani puri?'

Asmita stopped and looked at him. 'You just had two plates of biryani and now you are again hungry?' she exclaimed.

'Not now, idiot. I meant, before we leave,' he said.

'Oh! That way. Well, we can. But before I head back home, I will take you to a place where they serve amazing vada-pav and bun maska. And we will also have the cutting chai there. That's the last stop of the day,' she said, smiling. Her eyes glittered when she announced her final plan. She didn't want to keep it a secret any more.

Abhimanyu liked how she kept holding him tight and changing the positions of her hands around him. He enjoyed being around drunk Asmita a lot.

'And for the record, I didn't eat two plates of biryani, but one and a half.' He raised his other hand in which he held the takeaway.

'That half-plate you left was out of embarrassment.' She chuckled.

'Embarrassment? What embarrassment?'

'Of me thinking what a bhukkad you are,' she said, letting go off his hand and running away after mocking him. Abhimanyu ran behind her to catch her.

This time, it was he who caught her in the circle of his arms. They wrestled a bit, laughed at the same time and then finally gave up to catch their breaths.

Asmita picked a spot and the two of them sat down to watch the sea.

They chatted for some time. Gradually, the effect of the alcohol wore off. The sound of the waves was music to their ears. The evening was pleasant and the breeze revitalizing. The sun was preparing to deep dive into the far end of the sea.

In this blissful state, Asmita looked at Abhimanyu, who was gazing at the sea. Looking at him, she talked to herself in her head. *It feels perfect. Everything feels perfect. And I know why. It is your company!*

In that moment, she could not have imagined how their world was going to change in next couple of minutes at that very beach. Life! Nothing shocks people like it does.

Seeing a father walking barefoot on the shore, carrying his little boy on his shoulders, Asmita asked Abhimanyu, 'Would you enjoy doing that with your baby?'

Abhimanyu looked in the direction she was pointing at. He smiled. 'Sweet!' he said and then added, 'But no! I don't plan to have babies.'

Asmita turned her head towards him, her smile vanishing. 'You don't like babies?'

'I do, as long as they are other people's. I can't imagine raising kids myself,' he said with a smile and turned his head back to look at the father and his kid.

Asmita wished he would have asked her for her opinion as well. She knew it was too early for them to even talk about marriage, but she also knew that someday she would initiate that subject. She was collecting her thoughts when she heard him speak again.

'Besides, marriage isn't on my radar. So!' He left it
there, his eyes shifting from the father–son duo to the
sea.

The words hit Asmita like a thunderbolt. *What does
he mean?*

'What do you mean *"marriage isn't on my radar"*,
Abhimanyu?'

Abhimanyu looked back at her. Distress had formed
fine lines on her forehead. He wondered what had
happened to her. Her eyes were glued to him, seeking an
answer.

He understood what she was looking for.

'Wait! Asmita! You don't think ... I mean ... us ...
like ... we two ... getting married? You don't, right? I
mean ...'

His words fanned that little spark of newborn fear
within her.

'Abhimanyu!' Asmita began and then paused. She
took a long breath and decided to speak her mind. 'I
know it's quite early for us to even talk about it, but I
am sure there will come a time when I will initiate this
conversation,' she said and stopped again.

She wondered how to put things in perspective, now
that she had an idea of what Abhimanyu didn't want.

Abhimanyu didn't want her to go back home with
questions in her mind.

'I don't mind having that conversation right now,
Asmita.'

'Right!' she immediately agreed. 'It makes sense, because I don't want to find out at a later stage that you don't want to get married.'

He let out a long breath. Taking his time, he nodded his head, letting her know that what she had said was right. 'I don't, Asmita.'

Worried, she pursed her lips and looked at the sand she held in her fist. It was slipping out. All of it.

'Why?' she asked.

He didn't have to think before giving his answer. He knew it so well that it was on the tip of his tongue. 'It demands a lifelong commitment. And I don't want to be in such a committed relationship and lose my freedom.'

For a couple of seconds, Asmita didn't blink.

'What?' he asked when he didn't see any reaction from her.

'You don't see us together in the long run.' It wasn't a question.

Abhimanyu knew he was on the spot. But he didn't want to lie either.

'I want to. But I am not sure about it.'

'What is that supposed to mean?'

'The future is unforeseen, Asmita. And for its sake, I don't want to change my present. I am happy with my present. And I want to live it this way only. Without confining myself to a forever kind of committed relationship.'

'Wait! Do you consider us in a relationship? At this moment?'

'We are dating.'

'And isn't this a committed relationship?'

'Well!' he said and then exhaled loudly, wondering what to say. Asmita kept looking at him worriedly. He finally said, 'I am taking each day as it comes, Asmita. This doesn't mean that in future I cannot date another woman.'

His last words made things very clear for Asmita. And heartbreakingly so! She was stunned.

Trying to find a way to deal with that shock, she finally said. 'Well, then, what am I doing here?'

'What do you mean, Asmita?'

'What do you think this is between us? What do you think I want from this relationship?' she asked in return.

'I don't know, Asmita. You tell me.'

Amazed, she kept looking at him with an empty face. Meanwhile, the sequence of events from when they had met to now began flashing through her mind. It all looked like a dream.

'I want to pick you as that one person with whom I want to spend the rest of my life, Abhimanyu. I want this to be an exclusive relationship. That's how I see us.'

Abhimanyu sighed.

'I appreciate that you think of me that way, Asmita. But I would be lying if, for the sake of making you feel good, I say that I too feel the same way.'

She mustered all her courage so as to not break down in front of him.

He continued to speak. 'I can't pick just one person, like you can. I am sorry, Asmita, but I am only fine with a casual relationship. And there is nothing wrong about it.'

'Aren't you in love with me?' she cut him off and asked.

He pursed his lips and kept quiet.

She spoke again. 'Come on! You said so while we were in your kitchen.'

'Come on, Asmita! We were making out. The context was different. I didn't mean it as an exclusive committed arrangement. I can't do this. Listen, you are a wonderful woman. I am so attracted to you. But love is very different, and it isn't my cup of tea. If any day I commit to a woman some day, most likely I would be lying. I am sorry, but this is the truth and I have to be honest with you.'

Asmita kept listening to him in a state of despair as he went on.

'I write about love but I don't think I can live such a love.' Shaking his head, he added, 'To be with one woman and promise to be with her forever ... I can't do that. I can't love one woman and be hers for the rest of my life. I can't confine myself to such an arrangement. It freaks me out. I am not built to be this way.'

His words crushed her heart mercilessly.

'Asmita,' he said, placing his hand over hers.

She immediately slipped her hand away. 'Don't touch me, please.'

He threw his hands up, wondering where the conversation had gone.

'You should have told this to me before,' Asmita said, looking away from him.

'Oh! So it's my fault now? Did you ever ask me this before?' he retorted.

Tears stung her eyes, but she did her best to hold them back.

'I did ask you if you were in a committed relationship.'

'And I said no. It didn't mean I wanted to be in one.'

She took a deep breath, trying to clear her mind. Abhimanyu was indeed right. They had never spoken about this before. It was she who had impulsively kissed him first. He had only followed her cue.

When she was finally in a state to speak, she said, 'You are right. I should have asked. Instead of assuming things once you had said you were not in a committed relationship.'

Abhimanyu kept quiet. He didn't like at all the way the evening had taken a U-turn. She was in deep pain. He could see that, but he couldn't help her. He didn't want to lie to her either. In his heart, he was doing the right thing by telling her the truth, no matter how brutal it might be for her.

'But now that I know that you aren't going to be in a committed relationship with me, I can't do this any more, Abhimanyu,' Asmita said.

'Do what?'

She looked angrily at him. 'Do I have to tell you this as well? Okay, I will! So that there is nothing left which is not communicated between us from henceforth. I can't be with you this way, as your girlfriend! Oh! I don't even know if you considered me your girlfriend or just a random woman you were f—'

'ASMITA!' He burst out and shut her up before she could go on. 'Why can't we be just the way we are?' he asked patiently.

'I can't do what you are asking me to do. Just like you can't do what I am asking you to do. You see, I am not built to be like this.'

He looked into her eyes for a while and then silently nodded. He knew what was coming next.

That he didn't even try to give her hope that things may change between them was reason enough for Asmita to know she was doing the right thing.

'I am sorry, Abhimanyu. We should break up, whatever you think had been between us,' she said, getting up.

'Asmita, hold on!' He got up with her.

She stood there for a second, still waiting for him to tell her that he needed some time to think things through and come back. Instead, he said something quite the opposite.

'You don't have to rush with this decision. Take your time. Please!'

'I have taken enough time, Abhimanyu,' she said and walked away.

He walked behind her, trying to hold her back, but she was unstoppable. When they arrived on the road, he asked her if he could drop her home.

'Thank you, Abhimanyu. But from here on, I will be on my own.'

They never had those vada-pavs, bun maska and cutting chai.

24.

More than a week passed. Neither Asmita nor Abhimanyu initiated any sort of conversation with each other. Abhimanyu wanted to, but didn't know what to say. All day he would keep thinking about her.

How did my heart never realize the fatigue of missing you? It was a strange realization for him. He had never felt this before. Earlier, a breakup for him would mean moving on to the next available woman; but not this time. This time he was stuck. He hadn't anticipated the aftermath of his splitting up with Asmita would be like this. *What is this crazy feeling of wanting to hold your face and kiss you all the time?*

He knew he would not be able to give her what she wanted. He genuinely cared for her. He thought it was best he let her wounds heal instead of opening them again. At least, he believed that was the best thing to do.

On the other hand, Asmita was slipping into post-break-up trauma. Abhimanyu's words – I don't love you – randomly echoed in her head and took her peace away. A part of her had died when she had heard them the first time; unfortunately not the part that loved him. She had loved Abhimanyu with all her heart. She had loved a man after a long time and this was not what she had wanted. There were times when she would think about him and suddenly she couldn't breathe. There were times she typed a message to him but deleted it before sending, because she knew it was pointless and wouldn't do her any good. She wanted him back, but on her terms.

Thoughts of him were her misery as well as her happy escape. It was chaos. The beautiful world she was trying to build had tumbled down so fast and she didn't know how to deal with it. At nights, her pillow silently consumed all the pain her eyes released. Stains of her tears on it were the validation of how much she missed him. Sleep felt like a distant dream not ready to come to her and when it did, she would dream of Abhimanyu. *How he followed her into her dreams.* The next morning, in those couple of minutes between waking up and getting up, she would wonder if he missed her like she missed him.

One evening, completely unaware of what was going on in between her author and editor, Maaya thought of calling Abhimanyu. She was about to leave her office. She wanted to apprise him of the progress of their plan and had a few questions for him.

He picked up the call. Maaya didn't spend too much time in exchanging pleasantries.

'Abhimanyu, would you have a few Bollywood celebrities in mind for your launches at the literature festivals?'

'Bollywood celebrities? But why?'

'I am trying to make your launches grander. I have spoken to the directors of all the leading festivals. They have all agreed to host your book launch and asked this question. It would be great, no? Besides, there is no other big author who will be holding book launches at this season's lit fests.'

Abhimanyu chuckled and said, 'Two things, Maaya. I don't subscribe to the idea of Bollywood celebs launching my novels. My launches are an affair between my readers and me and I would like to keep it that way.'

Maaya was a bit dejected. She hadn't anticipated that coming. 'Oh … I see.'

There was a temporary silence. Abhimanyu didn't say anything to make her feel better.

'And the second thing?' she asked.

'Every literature festival, every year, has at least a dozen launches. I don't think I will be the only one. It sounds almost impossible. I bet there will many.'

'Oh! I meant from the list of popular authors, baba. Of course there will be book launches. Literature festivals are becoming homes for book launches now, but what I meant was, no other A-lister is doing that. Your launch will be the sole crowd-puller.'

'You are mistaken,' he said in a tone that sounded a bit serious.

'Really?' she was taken aback.

Only a week ago she had made calls and none of the directors at any of the literature festivals had told her this. On the contrary, most of them had themselves mentioned to Maaya that given the lack of any major popular launches, it would be great to have Abhimanyu's work on board. They wanted an assurance from her that PaperInk and Abhimanyu wouldn't back out of it.

'Who else is getting launched?' she asked.

'Rizwan,' he answered.

'Rizwan Siddiqui?'

'Yes.'

Maaya knew Rizwan was a big name and, of course, competition. If he was going to launch his novel at the literature festivals this year, it would certainly mean he would do so with all the glitz and glamour. He would bring celebs on board and paid media and make it all a huge affair. And that meant Abhimanyu's launch would be seen as a lesser event. After believing for a while that it would only be Abhimanyu's novel that would glitter at the literature festivals, the news of Rizwan's launch was a dampener. As it was the print run she was going to put in the market had already been reduced.

Worried, she spoke into the phone. 'But there was no such plan till last week. Who told you? And when did you get to know this?'

Abhimanyu chuckled again. 'I have been in this industry for a while now, Maaya. I have to keep myself abreast of the competition. Besides, Rizwan and my equations have been out in the open ever since our last panel. I know things.'

'Oh, yes!' she said, recalling how she had interestedly consumed the big literature festival gossip about Rizwan and Abhimanyu. At that point in time, the two authors had belonged to rival publishing houses. However, this time one of them was from hers. Their hostility was now going to make things trickier for her.

'I got to know about it this morning,' Abhimanyu informed her.

And with that, Maaya suddenly had a lot on her plate. She hung up and left the office.

25

Asmita was pleasantly shocked to see Abhimanyu's name flashing on her phone's screen. She picked up almost immediately.

'Where are you?' Abhimanyu asked.

No pleasantries were exchanged; just a straightforward question.

It was amazing to hear his voice after so long. In a strange way, once again, she felt connected to him. 'About to leave office. Why?' she asked, slipping her belongings inside her bag.

'I have to see you.'

Hope made her heart skip a beat, but she didn't want to risk assuming anything. 'Is this about the book?' she asked.

'No.'

'Then?' she asked.

'This is about us. I have to see you because I *need* to see you.'

She too was craving to see him. She could sense the underlying desire in his tone. He didn't need to explain or add anything more.

Asmita sighed. 'Oh!' She paused, wondering what to say. She already had some plans for the evening. 'Can this wait? I need to reach—'

Abhimanyu cut her off. 'This can't wait, Asmita. I need you. Right now.'

The sheer force of his need made her excited and nervous at the same time. There was a knot in her stomach. Hope and anxiety both sailed together in her. *Is he coming back to me?*

She wanted to ask that but also feared – what if not. And then it was her heart which wanted to delay any unpleasant confrontation, simply because she was tired of missing him. She needed him. Her knees weakened at the thought of positive possibilities and she sat down on the desk to steady herself.

Asmita loved how candidly he had expressed himself – *I have to see you because I need to see you.* A tiny but a deeply satisfying smile appeared on her lips. Her plans for the evening could wait. She would do anything for this man.

'Don't you want me?' he spoke again.

She took her time before responding, but finally, her heart won over her mind.

'Desperately,' she confessed.

Her words filled his heart with immense joy. After how things had ended with them a week back, he was glad that she still desired him the way she always had.

'I am dying to hold you, Asmita.'

A deep sigh escaped her. 'Ah! Abhimanyu!'

Missing someone this terribly does that to people. It makes them forget, at least for the time being, the reasons why they chose to break up in the first place. The heart has a way of complicating things, and going against its own decisions. And as if that's not enough, hormones turn the world upside down. There is a reason breakups take their sweet time and not happen in one go – couples do call up each other, inspite of telling they would never do so.

'Should I come meet you somewhere?' Asmita asked.

Maneuvering the busy Mumbai traffic, Abhimanyu spoke into his Bluetooth headset. 'Is your office empty?'

Damn! She knew what he meant.

She took a good look around. There were handful of people left in office and they too were about to leave.

'How long will you take to get here?'

'Thirty minutes max,' came the reply.

She nodded to herself and then said, 'Most likely it'll be empty ...' She paused and then finished her sentence, 'by the time you come to me, Abhimanyu.' Her words were loaded as she said them slowly.

Abhimanyu noticed the choice of her words but didn't react. He pushed the accelerator and not for once did his eyes leave the road ahead of him.

Asmita wanted to believe that that after all that had transpired between them, he was coming back to her because he wanted her as the only woman he wanted to be with. He hadn't said so in clear words, but that's what she wanted to *believe because that's what she wanted to believe.*

Humans! How they let feelings overpower logic!

A little after half an hour, Abhimanyu arrived at the PaperInk office. The place was almost empty. He walked straight in. The security guard was nowhere to be seen.

At the other end of the office, Asmita was waiting for him. His eyes caught hers. She wore a white printed top and navy-blue knee length skirt. *God! You look so beautiful.*

Abhimanyu walked fast towards her.

'Everyone left?' he asked. 'I didn't see the guard outside either.' He was still walking towards her.

'I sent him out to buy me some sandwiches,' Asmita said. She smiled guiltily and Abhimanyu knew that she'd done that especially to buy them some moments of complete privacy.

His heart glowed with appreciation. *How well you understand the gravity of the situation, Asmita!*

He came and at once gathered her in his arms. Asmita instantly surrendered herself. Abhimanyu went straight for her lips, as if that was the most natural progression. He kissed her desperately, as if his survival depended on it.

'I have missed you, Asmita,' he murmured in between kisses.

'I have missed you too, Abhimanyu.' She could barely speak. Her kisses reciprocated the same intensity as of his.

They kissed like they'd been starved for each other. As their hands moved hungrily over each other's faces and bodies, Abhimanyu walked her to the Romance Room.

He pushed the glass door of the conference room open behind him with his foot and they went in. On one side of the room was a wall lined with packed bookshelves. Abhimanyu pinned her against it and dug his face in her neck. He smelled her neck and kissed her there. His lips ran up and down on her. His coarse stubble brushed her soft skin.

'Ahh!' Asmita moaned, burning in the ecstasy of this man wanting her so badly, claiming her in the very office where she worked. The moment felt electrical. She didn't want him to stop. All her unanswered questions in her mind were snoozed.

Two books fell off the shelf. Asmita turned her head to look at them through half-open eyes, drunk on desire. Then she closed them again, needing to return to the world Abhimanyu was writing for them in that moment.

Pulling her delicate skin in between his lips, he was marking her with sweet bites of needs. He wanted to embed his presence on her skin.

As he pushed himself against her, more books fell off the shelf.

Abhimanyu looked at them on floor and then back into Asmita's eyes. She made a noise in the back of her throat – a mix of a moan and chuckle.

Abhimanyu turned her by her shoulders and made her sit on the conference table. Her legs hanging, her navy-blue skirt pulled up till her thighs.

He placed both his hands on her thighs and looked right into her eyes. Her lips opened. Abhimanyu's hands swept right inside her skirt and grabbed the waistband of her panties. He pulled them out, kneeled on the floor, and took them off her feet.

He gazed at her white lacy underwear and noticed how wet she already was. The next time he looked up into her eyes, he pushed apart her knees and bent down.

His lips went for her inner left thigh. He kissed her there, still gazing into her eyes as his lips began to crawl up her thigh.

Asmita watched Abhimanyu's head between her legs, desire engulfing her. In that moment she very well knew, he was there to fulfill what she had asked him of, in the Mumbai local. That's when she shut her eyes as she felt Abhimanyu's lips between her legs. The pleasure was divine.

The sweet ache in between her legs found a relief in his mouth. He pulled her in between his lips, nudged her with his tongue and rubbed her hard and fast, setting her on fire. Waves of intense pleasure shot up her. The tension was unbearable. The ache was sweet. She moaned his name. His tongue picked up pace and he invaded her. He tasted her like an animal. With every passing second, she was losing the strength to sit upright, till she finally had no other choice but to lie down on the big table, her legs dangling from its edge, his head partly inside her skirt.

Her moans came loud and fast. She couldn't hold on any longer.

'Come for me baby! Come for me!' Abhimanyu said, grabbing both her thighs in his hands, holding her steady, his mouth still working on his woman.

He had slipped inside Asmita's mind, wreaking havoc with all her senses. *Damn! You want me to come like this on you!*

Her hands reached for his head. She grabbed his hair. He was still busy playing with her. 'Come for me, Asmita.'

His tongue picked pace and brought forth an earthquake in her. Tremors of ecstatic pleasure shot off and shook her body. The tension finally found its release. It was long and an intensely satisfying release.

She opened her eyes and looked at the ceiling. And then Abhimanyu appeared, bending over her. She looked at his face. His mouth was wet.

She pulled him to her and kissed him, tasting herself on his lips.

26

Unfortunately, the office make-out session had brought the two together only temporarily. It failed to bridge their gaps permanently. Once their desires were fulfilled and the longing for each other subsided, they could think clearly, and the differences between them had risen again.

It pained both of them, failing to convince each other of their choices. Asmita realized that she had been wrong about him changing his mind. Her fear had come true. Abhimanyu discovered that her desperation to see him didn't mean that she was going to agree to his terms.

'Don't you see how badly we want each other?' he had said over a call the next morning.

'Not badly enough for you to want only me,' she had retorted.

When he didn't say anything in response, she announced, 'It shall not happen again ... ever ... what we did yesterday.' She didn't blame him. She too was a party to it.

The call had ended. After temporary fireworks, the gloom was back in their lives.

Later that evening, Abhimanyu was at an upscale restro-bar in South Mumbai. He was there to meet an old friend, Sanchita, who also happened to run a big-shot creative consulting agency. She had some exciting collaboration plans for him, which she had wanted to discuss with him. Abhimanyu anyway wanted some distraction in his life. He had readily agreed.

The two were catching up over drinks and snacks. The music was good, the ambience was soothing and the place was bustling with young crowd. Once Sanchita and he were done talking about updates from their respective lives, their common friends and random things, he arrived at the point for which she had wanted to meet him.

'So, tell me about this project you wanted to talk about,' he asked.

'Oh yes!' she began. 'One of our clients is rolling out a platform for which we are bringing a few selected experts on board – names from various creative fields.'

'Okay, go on?'

'These experts will conduct online masterclasses for our audience.'

'I see.'

'And writing is one of these fields.'

'And they want me on board?'

'Well, it's my agency that is going to make the recommendations.'

'Ah! Okay. I get it.'

'So, I thought I should recommend you. You know, if you are open to it.'

Abhimanyu thought for a bit.

'I will send you the proposal later, but we can discuss remuneration right now. So that you will get an idea. Take your time and see if you wish to do this. Given that your book will be out in two months from now, as you mentioned, it may be a good platform to tap into a newer audience and engage with people who are keen about writing.'

Abhimanyu was still thinking. Trying to convince him, Sanchita then said, 'We are not talking about hundreds, but thousands of people here.'

For the rest of the evening, Abhimanyu and Sanchita kept talking about the new app, the client who was rolling it out and the possibilities of Abhimanyu monetizing his presence on it. Sanchita was very keen on enrolling him, while he was keen on upping the ante. He needed to do his research, see what else was available in the market, who the app's competitors were and what would be the right remuneration for him.

Assuring her that he would give it serious thought, he had only gotten up to use the restroom when his eyes landed on someone he abhorred.

Rizwan Siddiqui walked towards him. But ignoring Abhimanyu completely, he greeted Abhimanyu's companion. 'Helloooo, Sanchitaaaaa. What a pleasant surprise.'

Sanchita got up to greet him back. Rizwan hugged her and they air-kissed.

Abhimanyu didn't know that his friend was so close to Rizwan.

'Hi, Abhimanyu,' Rizwan finally addressed him, extending his hand. Abhimanyu took his sweet time to give him his hand for a shake.

'What's up?' Abhimanyu asked.

'Nothing much. Celebrating life!' Rizwan said, raising his hands high, pointing at the people enjoying themselves around them. And then he loudly laughed, as if others were meant to join him.

Sanchita gave him a wide smile back. Abhimanyu's lips didn't stretch even a millimetre.

Rizwan pretended that he didn't notice his competitor not smiling. He kept his focus on Sanchita.

'Anyway, you guys carry on. I have friends to catch up with,' he said and was about to leave when he recalled something.

Looking back at Sanchita, he said. 'Hey Sanch! I will get back to you on that masterclass proposal by this weekend.'

She acknowledged that with a smile and he walked away.

With a fuming heart, Abhimanyu stared at Rizwan's back.

'Looks like you have multiple recommendations for your client,' he told Sanchita, sarcasm clearly evident in his tone.

To some extent, Sanchita knew that these two men didn't see eye to eye. However, it wasn't an important factor, for the masterclasses were going to be a solo project for each expert.

'I am only doing my job here,' she said.

'Sure you are,' Abhimanyu replied.

Sanchita didn't say anything more.

Abhimanyu spoke again. 'But if you need me on board, I will come at a price point more expensive than him. And that's non-negotiable. Your client has to know this. And you have to be transparent with me, because you are my friend.'

Sanchita exhaled. The rivalry that she had earlier considered not that important had suddenly become crucial. She cursed Rizwan's sudden presence on the scene. He might have ruined her plans. Abhimanyu left for the washroom, while Sanchita sat back and went through the menu. She had to place the order for the main course.

Later that night, after Sanchita had left, Abhimanyu stood alone outside the restro-bar. He was awaiting the valet to get his car from the parking lot when Rizwan ran into him again. This time he was drunk.

All the hatred for Abhimanyu he had concealed earlier came tumbling out very quickly.

'Ah! So, we meet again,' Rizwan said loudly.

Abhimanyu acknowledged his arrival by looking the other way.

Rizwan began laughing. 'Hahaha. Heard you are also coming out with your novel this winter?' he said, lighting his cigarette. He offered one to Abhimanyu, but the latter declined.

'Are you not? This winter?' Rizwan persisted, holding the cigarette between his lips.

Abhimanyu avoided indulging in any discussion with him, given that the other author was drunk. He could barely stand on his feet. And yet Rizwan remained. Alcohol had brought out his real self.

'Come on, man. It's okay. I don't mind if you choose the same time when I bring mine out.'

It was a deliberate provocation.

Abhimanyu clenched his jaw. 'What's your problem, Rizwan?' he finally asked.

'Oh my God, anger?' Rizwan mocked him. He stumbled and tried to regain his balance. When he succeeded, he looked at Abhimanyu and laughed shamelessly.

'It's okay, Abhimanyu. It's okay. I understand.' He laughed more and then added, 'Doesn't matter if we bring out our novels around the same time. What matters is that the content should be different. The plot should be different.' He looked at him and exhaled cigarette smoke in his direction.

Abhimanyu smelled something fishy. 'What the hell are you implying? What have you written?'

'Chill, bro! This anger doesn't suite a romance author. You have a reputation to keep.'

Abhimanyu was about to rebut him when the valet called out to him. His car had arrived. He let go of the argument and began walking away. However, Rizwan wasn't done yet.

'An innocent romance between two individuals of different age groups.'

Abhimanyu stopped in his tracks. He turned around and looked at Rizwan.

Rizwan had a mocking smile on his face as he went on.

'The woman is married. The boy is a young adult. That's what I have written.'

The ground beneath Abhimanyu's feet slipped. *What the hell!*

Rizwan spoke his final words, 'And I hope you don't bring out anything similar to that.' He moved his head from left to right while his eyes kept gazing at Abhimanyu.

Abhimanyu froze. He looked the other way, trying to make sense of it. He was in shock. It took him a few seconds before he faced Rizwan again. The latter's eyes were mocking him. Anger exploded in Abhimanyu's chest at once. He jumped at Rizwan, held him by the collar of his blazer and shouted at him, 'What the fuck have you done?'

A drunken Rizwan kept laughing at him. Abhimanyu kept screaming at him. His entire year's labour was at stake. He had to know what this slimeball was up to. He had to know how Rizwan knew about his plot.

The security guards at the bar rushed to separate the two of them. People in the vicinity gathered to look at them.

The guards overpowered Abhimanyu, but before he let Rizwan go, he head-butted Rizwan on his nose. Rizwan fell on the ground, bleeding. For a few seconds, he was knocked out of his senses. Meanwhile, the guards dragged Abhimanyu away.

When Rizwan got back to normal, with watery eyes he saw Abhimanyu being pulled back. He grinned. He was drunk enough not to feel the pain. This time he screamed, 'And you thought she was working on your story, for *you*. Hahaha!'

He laughed through his bloodied teeth. Soaked in anger, Abhimanyu didn't hear what he was blabbering. All he cared about was that his work had been compromised before it could release. The guards made Abhimanyu sit in his car. The windowpane on the driver's side was already rolled down.

Rizwan got up and took a few steps. He stood behind Abhimanyu's car and screamed, 'That whore doesn't belong to you. She doesn't work for you. She works for me. Your new *editor*.'

This time, Abhimanyu heard him crystal clear. His last three words made Abhimanyu look into the rear-view mirror. Like a demon, Rizwan kept repeating himself and laughing through his bloodstained teeth.

27

That entire night, Abhimanyu could not sleep. As if the sudden premature end of his relationship with Asmita hadn't caused enough chaos in his life, he now had Rizwan's bloody face flashing through his mind, telling him that Asmita had stolen his work and given it to his rival.

It can't *be her. She* can't *do this to me.*

His heart didn't want to believe what Rizwan had said. Ever since he had left that bar, all he had wanted was to look into Asmita's eye and ask her to tell him that it was all a lie. And do so loudly and firmly.

Or can *she? What if all this was her way to settle scores with me? For making her surrender to my demand?*

Until an hour ago, he had been missing Asmita terribly, but now he wondered if instead he should hate her.

Abhimanyu's mind found itself at a crossroads, unable to decide which path it needed to take. He could have given her a call in the dead of the night and sought clarity, but he didn't want to take that chance. Not because they had broken up, but because he wanted to see her reaction, read her body language the second he threw that question at her. Till then, he would wait.

That night, Abhimanyu sat at his workstation. Beyond the edge of a brightly lit Mumbai, he gazed at the infinite darkness that had dawned upon the Arabian Sea. Like a handful of stars up above the vast night sky, the tiny jewel-like lights of the faraway ships twinkled in the dark sea. The whole night he kept following those lights, watching them drift further away from him. Meanwhile, he drank an entire bottle of wine. He fell asleep just when the sun was breaking over the horizon.

When he woke up, he had to deal with a terrible headache, along with Rizwan's words, which were still echoing in his head. Abhimanyu drove down to Rizwan's place. He had to know if all that he had said the previous evening was true, or was he just blabbering in his drunken state, and more importantly, how did he get to know of his plot. He had to be sure of things before he spoke to Asmita.

Abhimanyu parked his car outside Rizwan's house. The security guard stationed outside the bungalow walked up to him. At nine in the morning, Abhimanyu was an unexpected visitor.

The guard made a quick call and let him know that he could sit inside the office. Rizwan would take ten minutes to show up. Abhimanyu preferred waiting outside in his car.

A while later, when Rizwan walked out of his bungalow, Abhimanyu stepped out.

'Look who's paid me a visit!' Rizwan smiled as he walked closer. 'Did you catch some sleep?' he asked.

Abhimanyu noticed the swelling around his nose. Rizwan was seasoned enough not to even think of hitting him and levelling the score. He had done him greater damage, something he was very pleased about.

'You mentioned Asmita last night.' Abhimanyu arrived straight to the point.

Well aware that this confrontation was meant to happen, Rizwan chose to invite him inside. 'Come, let's sit and talk.'

Abhimanyu politely refused the offer. 'I am in a hurry. And I am here to ask you only two questions.'

'Shoot, then,' Rizwan said.

'That thing you said last night. Is that true? About Asmita? That she worked for you?'

Rizwan crossed his arms in front of his chest, spread his legs wider and looked into Abhimanyu's eyes.

'Yes,' he said and kept gazing at him.

Abhimanyu shook his head in disbelief. 'I don't believe you,' he murmured.

Rizwan came straight to the point. 'She wanted to trade off your work and I was happy to consider it. Why else you think she annulled her exit and agreed to work on your manuscript?'

Abhimanyu took his time to absorb all the information. The next time he spoke, he asked for evidence.

'Can you prove it?'

Rizwan kept staring into his eyes, making him wait before he finally said, 'Sure.'

He pulled out his phone to show the chat he and Asmita had had a few months back, after she had left his office. For Abhimanyu's sake, Rizwan even tapped

Asmita's name to show him her phone number, so that he could verify it.

Abhimanyu quickly read through Asmita and Rizwan's chats. In it, Rizwan had asked her for her final decision. Abhimanyu could see that on different dates, Rizwan had constantly asked her to rescind her resignation at PaperInk. In her initial few responses, Asmita had written that she was still thinking about it. However, in the end there was a message from her. It read, 'I have rejoined PaperInk.'

In response to it was the smiling devil emoji sent by Rizwan, along with a one-word message – 'Perfect'.

An hour later, Abhimanyu took a shower, changed his clothes, ate some breakfast and left for the PaperInk office. He didn't let Maaya know about his arrival. Instead, while driving, he called Asmita.

Worked up by seeing Abhimanyu's name on her phone again, Asmita wondered the purpose of his call. However, as she was in a meeting, she immediately disconnected his call and texted that she would call him back in an hour.

Abhimanyu couldn't wait any longer and wrote back:

'So, can we meet in an hour?'

She read his message.

'Meet? Where?' She was taken aback at the urgency of his message.

'Anywhere.'

Asmita felt even more positive now.

'I am sorry, but I can't step out of the office today. I have a working lunch with an author here in the office. I have to acquire the publishing rights of her new book.'

'Then let's meet at your office?' he proposed.

'What is this about?' she asked back.

'I will tell you when we meet. I need to see you right away,' he wrote back and kept his phone aside.

These were similar words Asmita had read the last time he had come to meet her in her office. *This can't be happening again. I won't let this happen again.*

'Abhimanyu, I can't do this again. I had told you.' She texted back.

'It is very different from what you are imagining. Trust me.' he wrote back.

Hope sailed into her heart. *Maybe, finally he is going to change his stand. Maybe, he has given it enough thought.* She wanted to step out of the office. She wanted to meet him beyond the scrutiny of her office folks, to make herself available for him completely, if this was about them making up. However, she couldn't. She had to be in office. She began looking forward to his arrival and hoped that her other author, whose publishing rights she was to acquire, would come in late for their lunch.

About an hour later, she stood at the entrance door to receive Abhimanyu. It was a usual affair for any editor to extend this courtesy to their author. There was no awkwardness about it, and Asmita was glad of that. No one thought her waiting there out of the ordinary. The butterflies in her stomach had once again begun to flutter.

Asmita's eyes glittered the second she spotted Abhimanyu. She waved him a hello with a smile from a distance. But there was no equally heart-warming response. Abhimanyu's smile was not only miniscule, it was also short-lived. In that very moment, she realized that he wasn't there for the purpose she had thought.

'Hi,' she said when he arrived next to her.

'Hello,' he answered and then looked towards the direction they were supposed to walk in.

Wondering what the purpose of the meeting was, Asmita escorted him to the meeting room she had booked for them. She politely observed him. Abhimanyu's body language was stiff and angry. She was intimidated.

After they sat at the table across from each other, Abhimanyu told her upfront, 'There is something I need to know. And I hope you will give me an honest answer.'

The manner in which Abhimanyu was talking terrified her.

'What is it, Abhimanyu?'

'Are you working for Rizwan Siddiqui?' He didn't mince any words

Asmita's lips pursed. Thin lines crept across her forehead. Her body slightly sank back in her chair.

The signs were discomforting for Abhimanyu. He held on to his patience and waited for her to respond. His searching eyes kept her under his scrutiny. It was for this very observation that he hadn't spoken to her over a call. He would have missed these signs, which mattered a lot. And now that he was in front of her, he could see his fear coming true.

Asmita inhaled deeply and spoke.

'No,' she said.

That made Abhimanyu's eyebrows rise. Her response was not in sync with her body language.

'Really?' he double-checked.

'Abhimanyu, why are you asking me this?' Her voice was defensive.

'I will answer that question, Asmita, but first I need answers from you. Do you work for Rizwan in any capacity which I am not aware of?'

'What? No! I work here at PaperInk. Now, can you please tell me what this is about?' she demanded.

Abhimanyu ignored her question and moved on to ask another.

'Did you ever work for him in the past?'

She denied that. The seriousness with which he was asking questions one after other bothered her.

Abhimanyu exhaled and crashed back in his chair. He continued to observe her. Asmita's chat with Rizwan, which he had seen on the latter's phone, flashed in his mind. He could almost hear her saying those words.

By now, Asmita had an idea of what Abhimanyu had got to know. And perhaps it was already too late for her to tell him her side of it, she thought.

'All right! Let's start from the basics then,' Abhimanyu said and went on questioning. 'Do you know him? Have you met Rizwan Siddiqui? I mean, have you ever talked to him?'

'Listen, Abhimanyu, I have something to …'

Cutting her in the middle, he shouted, 'JUST ANSWER ME. It's a simple question.'

She didn't like the way he was behaving with her. He had no authority to talk to her like that.

'YES, I DO KNOW HIM. I HAVE MET HIM,' she shouted back.

'I see.' Finally, there was something he could connect with Rizwan's story.

'What do you *see*, Abhimanyu?'

He looked the other way. His face was full of disgust for her. When he looked back at her, he made a scathing accusation.

'You leaked my story to that asshole.'

'WHAT?' Asmita asked in shock. 'NO!'

'Really? Is it not true?'

'It isn't, and on what basis are you accusing me?'

'On the basis of Rizwan Siddiqui telling me so.'

'And what did he tell you?'

'Exactly what I told you.'

'And I told you that's not true.'

Abhimanyu paused for a few seconds and shook his head in disbelief. 'I can't believe I was in love with you.'

'YOU WERE NOT IN LOVE WITH ME,' she reminded him his words.

He was taken aback. 'Ahh! I see ...' he began and on second thoughts said, 'I AM SO GLAD I WASN'T.'

Asmita sighed in anger and looked the other way. Everything about their conversation was heartbreaking.

'HOW ELSE DOES HE KNOW, ASMITA?' He was back to what he was there for.

'WHAT DOES HE KNOW?' Asmita was as pissed off as he was.

'The story! The plot! The characters! He knows every damn thing about my book. He knows it's a love story between a young boy and a married woman. And not only that, he has also written his book with the same plot and I know he is going to bring it out even before mine comes out.'

'WHAT?' Asmita's jaw dropped.

Abhimanyu slow-clapped and said, 'Spare me those theatrics. Please!'

Asmita's mind shuffled between two different disturbing thoughts. First, that Rizwan was doing what Abhimanyu claimed he was. Second, that Abhimanyu believed she was the one responsible for this.

'And you want to know how he knows about the content of my book?' He didn't even wait for her to answer. 'Because he confirmed that you work for him.' He banged his fist on the table.

Asmita was scared of Abhimanyu's behaviour. She wondered if, out of aggression, he would end up hurting her. On top of that, she was also worried about someone seeing him, behaving this way with her, through the glass wall of the conference room.

'I don't know how he knows. And it's not that I am the only one privy to your story.'

'Yes, there are a handful of people who know about it, but why then did he specifically confirm it was you?'

Abhimanyu could have arrived straight to the point and told her that he had seen her chats with Rizwan. But for the moment he wanted Asmita to confess her crime without the mention of any evidence.

To be accused of stealing the very story she had nurtured with all her heart hurt Asmita beyond limits. She sat silent. Her eyes welled up with tears.

'Oh, come on! This won't work with me, Asmita. I am not someone who is moved by tears. If you are thinking of that, then you are wrong. For me, nothing on this planet is more important than my book. Not you. Not Maaya. Not PaperInk. Nobody.'

The brazenness with which he said that broke her. Earlier, he had said he didn't love her and now he was telling her that she wasn't even important. Asmita wondered if all that they had had between them till a few days before had really been so fragile. *Those kisses, those passionate hugs, those intimate chats, those private moments in your flat and in this office – don't they mean anything to you?*

In the backdrop of her thoughts, Abhimanyu continued to shout, 'End this drama right away and confess.'

Tears flowed down her cheeks. She looked at him and said, 'I didn't do it, Abhimanyu.'

'What a pleasant surprise!' Peter screamed, pushing open the door just then. He had seen Abhimanyu and thought he would stop by and say hello. The next second, when he looked at Asmita's face and then back at Abhimanyu, he realized something was terribly wrong. It was too late for Asmita to hide her tears.

When Peter asked what the matter was, Asmita couldn't speak. She needed some time. Shocked, Peter's eyes met Abhimanyu's. He waited for the author to enlighten him.

'There's something you need to know,' Abhimanyu began. 'And, just so that I don't have to repeat this again, it's better if you get Maaya as well.'

The gravity of the situation made Peter summon Maaya immediately. When Maaya learnt Abhimanyu was in the office, she was excited, but once she walked into the scene in the conference room, just like Peter, she was taken aback. To witness Asmita compose herself with deep breaths troubled her.

Abhimanyu didn't waste a second before replying.

'My work has been compromised.'

'What do you mean by that?' an alarmed Maaya asked.

Abhimanyu took his time to tell them all that had transpired. While he did that Peter's and Maaya's gaze went to Asmita a few times. When everything had been said and heard, they all sat down to demand an explanation from Asmita.

Finding out whether Asmita was guilty was Maaya's second worry. Her first worry was that there was a book coming out by another bestselling author, the plot of which was exactly the same as their biggest book of the year; and also, if Abhimanyu's instincts were right, then it was going to come out in the market before theirs. The photo-op launch might happen later at the literature festivals.

She shuddered to imagine what it would mean for PaperInk. It made her blood boil. After all that she had done, she couldn't afford to let this happen. The unplanned meeting now looked like a preview to the catastrophe they were going to witness.

Bringing her focus back to the room, she looked towards Asmita with a scathing gaze for an explanation.

Asmita began talking.

'I didn't do any such thing, Maaya. You have to trust me on this.' The tears in her eyes had dried up. She was finally in a state to talk.

'I can't trust anybody here. I don't know what's true and what's not. And therefore, in order to find out the truth, I am going to ask the questions here. I need to understand this in detail. We will go over this step by step and I want you to come clean,' Maaya said.

And with that began the trial of Asmita by her bosses, in front of the very man she was madly in love with.

This was not the first time the three of them were cornering her. They had done this to her once before as well, when Abhimanyu had signed the contract with PaperInk. At that time too, Maaya and Peter had put pressure on her, on Abhimanyu's instructions. Only, this time they were doing so in his presence, when the equations between her and him had drastically changed.

Asmita felt as if it was the rerun of her life from a few months back. It made her feel sick. It made her feel used and thrown, time and again.

'Did you or did you not meet Rizwan, seeking to work for him?' Maaya asked. She knew Asmita had already confessed this to Abhimanyu, but she had to hear it herself.

Asmita nodded. Maaya looked at Peter while Abhimanyu's eyes were on Asmita.

'And after you met him, did he ask you to work for him?'

'He did.'

Abhimanyu fumed, thinking about how he had held her naked body in his arms in his kitchen. She was a traitor and he had made love to her!

'Then why did you annul your exit?' Maaya asked.

Abhimanyu didn't wait for her to respond. 'So that she could steal my work.'

How he wished he could shout it all out – the level to which his editor had gone, even forging a relationship with him only to keep him in the dark. He believed it was all connected – their intimacy and this theft.

Asmita looked into Abhimanyu's eyes. Those eyes in which she had wanted to find love for herself were now full of disgust for her.

In no time, her eyes were teary again. 'I have nothing to do with all of this.' Her vision blurred and the tears streamed down once again. 'I didn't do it. I didn't steal anyone's work,' she kept repeating.

'Oh really! Abhimanyu smirked. 'Then what was the reason for your resuming your work here, after you had put in your papers out of your own will?'

'I DIDN'T REJOIN PAPERINK TO STEAL YOUR WORK,' Asmita screamed.

Abhimanyu was determined not to fall for her theatrics. He hated the audacity with which she was talking to him in front of the others. Asmita was also tired of taking his anger anymore and didn't care about what he thought of her.

'Yes, I had put in my papers. That's because all of you here had pushed me to that point. You all are responsible for that, for breaking your ethics, for taking advantage of your positions, each one of you. I preferred my integrity and my freedom over working in an atmosphere where my consent didn't hold any value. This, while all of you, in spite of knowing that what you had been doing was wrong, did it anyway.'

Abhimanyu loathed how she was digressing from the main subject and trying to play the victim instead. Not only she was denying her crime, she was accusing him in the bargain.

'So you are trying to justify—' He began to counter her, but she didn't let him and instead continued,

'YES, I HAD PUT IN MY PAPERS AT PAPERINK. YES, I HAD MET RIZWAN. In fact, I went to his home to seek work. What else I could have done? At that time, there was no publisher willing to take me onboard.'

This was enough for Abhimanyu to lose his cool and say what he'd been holding back.

'SO, YOU LAID A HONEYTRAP FOR ME IN THE NAME OF LOVE,' he shouted, shutting her up in the middle of her argument.

There, he had said it. His words stunned everyone in the room. Maaya threw a glance at him and then back at Asmita. There was more on the table than what she'd thought. *Honeytrap? Love?*

'What? That's not true,' Asmita could barely utter the words. Suddenly her voice dropped. Her lips trembled. Her eyes flickered uncomfortably.

Fear crawled into her bones. Her face turned red, then pale. She gently shook her head, looking at Abhimanyu, politely begging him not to say what he was about to in front of her bosses – to keep their private matters separate from their professional. To understand that his interpretation of it wasn't true. That her love for him was pure. She didn't want people to get to know about their relationship in this manner.

She needed him to act mature, but Abhimanyu was already mad with anger. Ignoring her pleading gestures, he rushed to announce to the room things which left everyone else shocked.

'What kind of editor calls her author to the office after working hours and kisses him on account of having finished reading his manuscript?'

Maaya was stunned. Peter was agape. They looked at Asmita, whose eyes now lowered in front of them. A resilient Abhimanyu continued, 'And then arrives at his place to make out on the pretext of "showing him the cover".'

His scathing words pierced Asmita's heart.

There was no need for Maaya to even cross-check anything with her editor. Her red face was a validation of Abhimanyu's statements. She could see the shame and embarrassment on Asmita's face. It all looked like a well-planned scandal which was finally being unearthed; perhaps too late.

The new facts made things a lot more uncomfortable than they had already been. All of this had been happening under Maaya's watch and she had had zero clue about it. At once, she began to think of what else Asmita had been up to. She now felt threatened by her mere presence in her office.

'This is not true ... This ... It's not ... true.' Asmita gasped for breath. She couldn't decide where to begin and how to explain this first to Abhimanyu and then to the others. Her tears continued to fall on the surface of the table.

'Abhimanyu! Please don't talk of my love like this. This is not right,' she was literally shaking and pleading.

'Excuse me?' Maaya interrupted Asmita, who had perhaps forgotten the agenda at hand. It wasn't about her so-called love life, but the book.

However, Asmita's focus didn't change. She kept gazing at Abhimanyu, wanting him to withdraw his words.

'I AM ASKING YOU SOMETHING, ASMITA!' Maaya screamed in anger.

Asmita turned, with her eyes full of tears, towards Maaya. Through her blurred vision, she addressed her boss without even listening to what she was asking. She was still experiencing the shockwaves from the manner in which Abhimanyu had unveiled something so private between them in public.

'I ... I ...' She gasped. 'I loved him. I didn't pass on the story.' She then turned towards Abhimanyu and said, 'Why are you saying this, Abhimanyu?'

She kept repeating that last line. It appeared as if she had momentarily lost control over herself.

Peter could not fathom how Asmita's feelings had changed so dramatically for Abhimanyu. Weeks back, she was willing to quit the company instead of working for him. *What the hell is going on?*

Abhimanyu looked at Peter and shrugged. Peter didn't know how to react to the situation in hand. He was least prepared to handle it. He left it all to Maaya.

'Did you advance a relationship with your author? That you kissed him in this very office?' Maaya asked the uncomfortable question.

'No! No ... I am not denying that, Maaya.' Asmita sobbed. 'We—'

'ENOUGH, ASMITA!' Maaya shut her up. 'It doesn't matter what you say next. I don't care about it any more. What made you think it would be all right for you to have an affair with the author whose work you were editing?'

Asmita went quiet. She would have hidden her love from the world, but she was not going to deny it if and when confronted. And that worked against her.

A lie, jumbled up with some truth, is the most difficult to catch. There was a lot of truth in what Abhimanyu had said, which Asmita couldn't deny. She admitted it all in front of her bosses. After all, she *had* invited him to the office immediately after reading his manuscript. She *did* kiss him at her desk. She *was* at his place the other night. And they *had* made love.

While these were all true, they were also sensational in nature. And if the sensational parts in a story are proved to be true, the rest of the story by default appears true too. People, at times, only see what they want to. The reality, however, may be very different.

'This is a violation of company policy. And it will be dealt with later. Leave aside what else you have been up to,' Peter announced in anger. It was time for him to show his authority now that someone had finally confessed to something.

Asmita had no clue if any such company policy existed. And as if that was not bad enough, she now found out there were repercussions attached to breaching it.

'We will deal with that part later. And we will,' Maaya warned her.

Asmita had had enough. 'And will the repercussions be the same for both the author and the editor? Or will the company policy, like last time, only be applicable to the editor?'

Amazing as it was, both her bosses had ignored raising their fingers at the other individual who was party to this affair. And Asmita reminded them of their mistake.

Abhimanyu had already seen it coming. That by revealing all, he was going to make himself vulnerable too. Peter looked at him and then lowered his eyes.

'We will do what needs to be done,' Maaya announced. 'But for now, I am more interested in you confessing to sharing the plot of Abhimanyu's novel with Rizwan.'

'I didn't do any such thing,' Asmita said firmly.

It was a lot for her to process and react to. She took a few long breaths and prepared herself to respond.

Asmita was clear in her mind that she had done no wrong. And hence, she would defend herself. If her relationship with Abhimanyu was subjected to policies, so be it; she would deal with the consequences. That part didn't matter to her much; not as much as the fact that the person who she had loved had exposed their relationship like this after maligning it. And now that the cat was out of the bag, there was nothing to fear.

'I didn't resume my job at PaperInk because Rizwan wanted me to. I did so because of my mom,' she said.

'What do you mean by that?' Peter asked. *How had her mother come into this?*

'While I was serving the notice period, my mom had fallen sick and required a surgery.' Asmita's voice was soft and slow. 'The need to get her operated on immediately changed everything for me for I needed a lot of money for her treatment. My savings weren't enough. Had I quit, my family health insurance cover, which my job provides me, would have lapsed. On top of it, I wouldn't be earning my monthly salary. I didn't have the means to support my mother's health. So I had to swallow my pride and resume work on the conditions you all had placed in front of me. There was no other way out for me.'

Tears fell down her cheeks. In a way, they were a validation of her statements.

Maaya sighed and reclined in her chair. She looked at Peter, who didn't have anything to say this time. Abhimanyu moved his gaze from Asmita's face. He had not seen that coming. It was a strong reason for anyone to change her mind.

There was a temporary silence in the room. Moments later, Asmita's words dispersed it. This time she didn't speak to answer to anyone, but to make the others listen to her.

'I didn't want to work on your manuscript, Abhimanyu. But I had to, because you desperately wanted it. You had taken it upon your ego to show me my place.'

She paused and, after swallowing the lump in her throat, spoke again.

'And because they let you do this to me,' she said, pointing at both Maaya and Peter. Neither of the two even attempted to counter that.

Abhimanyu finally brought up the evidence. 'Rizwan showed me your chat with him on his phone.'

Ah! Asmita loathed both Rizwan for going to such an extent and Abhimanyu for falling into his trap.

'And what did that chat say? That I stole your work and passed it on to him? Really? Here's my phone. I can open the chat. Find such a line in it.' She pushed her phone towards Abhimanyu.

Abhimanyu at once tried to recall if he had read exactly what Asmita was asking him to verify. He couldn't. All he remembered was a message sent from Asmita's number which said – 'I have rejoined PaperInk.' In response to her confirmation, Rizwan had sent her a smiling devil emoji along with a word – 'Perfect.'

Abhimanyu didn't know how to react to that. Suddenly, he was confused and overwhelmed with the number of thoughts his brain was processing. Asmita's argument was compelling. If all that she had said was true, then he had certainly made a terrible mistake. Not only had he accused her of stealing his work for a rival author, but he had also exposed their short-lived affair, painting a very sordid picture of it and making himself look like a victim.

For once, with her words, the editor had brought the author to a situation where the latter didn't have any words.

Maaya dramatically placed her hand on Asmita's shoulder to show her empathy. She tried to console her. Asmita remained unaffected. She didn't even acknowledge her boss. Her moist eyes were focused on the edge of the table.

She spoke further. 'Rizwan had asked me to do exactly what he claims.'

Maaya lifted her hand. Everyone in the room looked at Asmita, waiting for her to speak further; and she did.

'And to be honest, I was contemplating doing that.' She looked at Abhimanyu while saying it. Then shifting her gaze between all three, she continued, 'It made sense for me to hurt you back. That was his proposal. The truth also is that he was able to leverage the frustrated state of my mind back then, in making me at least give his idea a serious thought. I took my time, only to decide that I was not going to do it. You may not want to believe it, but this is my truth. And if you don't believe it, I am willing to comply with any investigations you want to make.'

It all appeared believable – the rationale behind meeting Rizwan, the reason for her to rejoin PaperInk and her denial of passing on Abhimanyu's plot to Rizwan.

In light of what the three of them had done to her earlier, the urge to hurt them back in order to settle scores would have been a natural human tendency. Abhimanyu now also wondered that if that had been her sole inclination, why would she have worked so hard on his manuscript and taken it to such an impressive level? *Have I made a blunder here?*

He wanted to immediately reach out to Rizwan again and ask him why he'd said what he did.

And as if Asmita had read his thoughts, she further revealed, 'My rejoining PaperInk gave Rizwan hope that I was working as per his plan. And because I didn't, he felt I had betrayed him.'

'And hence he put all the blame on you,' Maaya summarized it for her.

Asmita looked at her and silently nodded.

Abhimanyu had begun to feel terribly sorry about everything. However, he was still puzzled about how Rizwan had copied his plot.

Maaya and Peter had no inclination to quiz Asmita any further. They had already embarrassed themselves by not standing up for their own employee when they should have. While having an affair with an author whose book Asmita was editing was a breach of company policy, which Maaya was supposed to look into, she had a bigger worry to tackle first – their biggest book till date, which was about to go into print any moment now, was compromised.

Only a week earlier, the boat of Asmita and Abhimanyu's relationship had run into rough waters. And now, a ruthless wave had capsized it. Rizwan had unknowingly broken whatever innocence was left between the two. What made the whole thing murkier was the way things ended between them – one accusing the other of betrayal in front of people who knew both of them.

28

In the days that followed, a constant despair occupied Asmita's life. In office, her days would somehow pass in dealing with new edits. She was trying to come out of what looked like the ugliest chapter of her life. It's brutally heartbreaking to witness the most promising event in your life turn into the worst thing that ever happened to you. The happy moments with Abhimanyu would often flash in her head, but they would all end with the visuals of him calling them a part of her honeytrap. It was death by a thousand cuts.

How could you even think this of me, Abhimanyu?

Every time a colleague would ask her anything in reference to Abhimanyu's book, be it the edits or the release, she would respond in limited words and walk away. It was her way of detaching herself emotionally from his book and treating it like yet another project.

Her real struggle, though, was at home in the nights. Images of him accusing her in front of Peter and Maaya would fill her mind. Sleep had distanced itself from her.

And there would be no work or colleagues to distract her. There was a constant heaviness in her heart, which she needed to jettison. On some nights she would cry, trying to vent her pain. On other nights, she felt emptied of tears.

For Abhimanyu, the aftermath was like a walk down the road of guilt. While there was yet some truth left to be unearthed, he realized that he had wronged Asmita, and horribly so – *twice*. At first, it was his vendetta and ego that had brought her to the verge of almost quitting her job and now it was his suspicion. And he had done this to someone who had bared her soul to him.

However, the crisis at hand made him put his remorse on the backburner. His book, the publication of which was now around the corner, was his priority. It needed his immediate attention. As of now, Abhimanyu had two important tasks on his plate. One – to find out who had leaked his story to Rizwan. Two – in the face of the imminent threat from Rizwan, how to prepare his defense and his counter-attack. He had no intention of letting that man win the race by crook. He had to overtake him at any cost now.

Four days after the awful meeting they all had, Maaya called Abhimanyu on his phone.

'Listen, do you want me to push the release date by a few months?' she asked, concerned.

Abhimanyu kept mum. He didn't know what to say. To push the release date would mean conceding to Rizwan. And he wasn't going to do that.

Maaya spoke further, ' … case you think your book and Rizwan's … you know … at the same time …'

Abhimanyu cut her off, saying, 'Nothing changes, Maaya. Nothing.'

'Are you sure?' she double-checked.

Abhimanyu exhaled deeply. 'I am.'

Maaya did not press any further. She had to take him in confidence before she planned her next steps. Amid everything going for a toss now, the last thing she could have afforded was she and her author not being on the same page. There was no room left for any kind of assumptions or communication gaps between them.

'My story is *the* original work,' Abhimanyu continued. 'It's his story which is the stolen one. There is no reason why we should change our plans because of that asshole. In fact, we have all the more reason now to stick to our plan.'

'All right, Abhimanyu. If you insist on this, then I am with you.'

'Just one thing …' he said and paused.

'Tell me.'

'I am going to find out the truth and I am going to sue that bastard. And I want PaperInk to do that as well.'

'That goes unsaid. We will take his publishers down, but for that we need solid evidence in place, which establishes that the idea was indeed copied from your work. And I am not sure if we can dispute this till his book is out. After all, no one has read it.'

Abhimanyu sighed in frustration. When he didn't have anything more to say, Maaya reminded him of something. 'Abhimanyu, please don't mind, but we also need to talk about what you had said the other day.'

'What?' he enquired.

'The ... affair with Asmita,' Maaya said hesitantly.

'Maaya, please, can we do this later?'

Maaya didn't like how Abhimanyu was running away from discussing something he himself had brought to her notice. However, given the situation they were in, she chose to give him the leeway. The book was not just Abhimanyu's priority but hers as well.

'Okay,' she said after a few seconds of silence.

They never spoke about it again.

29

The season changed. Festival time had set in. However, Asmita's world, unlike others, lacked any celebrations. She stepped into this season carrying the gloom from the previous one.

It was going to take her a long time to recover from this. She knew that well. Attachments! They had always been a problem for her. This was not the first time she was dealing with a break-up. She had lived through a long and terrible year after her first relationship had ended, which was why she had decided not to be in one again; but then the heart has its own way of inviting disasters. She wished that she could forget Abhimanyu as fast as she had fallen in love with him, but it seemed impossible. There were moments when she would break down and wonder if there were means to either heal her broken heart or the possibility of a miracle that would make Abhimanyu want her back. Somewhere, deep down, she still needed him.

Contrary to Abhimanyu's earlier assumption, Rizwan's book was still not out in the market. It looked like he was going to launch it first at the Jodhpur Literature festival, which was now only three weeks away.

By now the festival had finalized and published its speakers' list and its programme on its website. Abhimanyu's book launch was due on a Sunday afternoon; a perfect day, because it meant that his younger fans could be there for the release of his new book.

At least, it would have been perfect if Rizwan's launch hadn't been scheduled for the same day, and that too an hour before Abhimanyu's. Abhimanyu wished that he could have gotten a Saturday slot. However, the festival schedule was already frozen, and the flight tickets and the hotel reservations were confirmed.

Maaya had got flights and hotel rooms booked for the PaperInk team. There were a total of eleven employees, including Asmita. At first, Asmita didn't want to go. She wanted to avoid any face-off with Abhimanyu. However, as his editor and an employee of PaperInk, she knew that she'd have to attend the festival. After all, readers and journalists might ask her questions about Abhimanyu's new book – its launch was going to be one of the highlights of the festival.

However, when she found out later that Maaya would be the face of PaperInk for all discussions around Abhimanyu's book, she was relieved. *Of course! How could I think that Maaya would let me have this opportunity?*

Asmita was more than happy to let her boss handle the publicity and chose to focus on her literary fiction list instead, given that all three of her books on the longlist had now made it to the shortlist as well.

Meanwhile, the merchandise and digital creatives for *The Boy in the Neighbourhood* were ready. The book was already up on pre-order and phase-I of the entire social media plan was already activated. However, what was still missing was the real thing – the book itself.

As if the universe was conspiring against it, a backlog at the printer's end had delayed the printing. And then, to make matters worse, all hell had broken loose the day the printing was actually scheduled to begin.

Unprecedented rains had poured over the city of Mumbai. The meteorological department had had a short window to discover this and issue a red alert. Incessant heavy rains for three consecutive days flooded the entire city and brought everything to a standstill.

Monsoons were long over, and the city wasn't prepared for houses and shops to be knee-deep in water in the month of November. The situation turned so bad that trains and flights had to stop plying, for the tracks and airstrips were submerged. #MumbaiFloods trended on social media for three consecutive days. The news channels were flooded with visuals of an inundated Mumbai.

The printing press at which Abhimanyu's book was supposed to be printed reported distressing news too. It was flooded with water. Not only had the heavy machinery been submerged in water, reams of paper were ruined. This only meant one thing – *The Boy in the Neighbourhood* was not going be printed in time for its scheduled launch at the literature festival.

'Shit! How long will it take?' Abhimanyu said into his phone, worried.

'I can't say. Maybe a month … or even more,' Maaya answered from the other end.

'What?!'

'It hasn't rained in the last twenty-four hours. The water has begun to recede. The machines will take a few days to dry up. Even if that happens this week, they don't have the paper. Whatever is left unspoiled isn't enough.' There was a sense of defeat in Maaya's voice.

'FUCKING SHIT!' Abhimanyu screamed and flung the TV remote he held in his hand. 'That means we can't have the launch now.'

Maaya kept mum. She didn't know what to say to him. A part of mind felt relieved that Abhimanyu had reached that conclusion himself and she didn't have to explicitly spell it out for him.

Along with the city, the rains had washed away her dream of unveiling PaperInk's first Abhimanyu Razdan book on the front lawns of the Jodhpur Literature Festival in front of a gathering of thousands of people.

Once the call was over, Abhimanyu thought of his post on social media, in which he had announced the grand launch. He wondered if he should take it down or update it. On second thought, he decided that it was too early for him to update anything and that he would do so a day or two before the festival kicked off.

As if the day couldn't get worse, the very first post he stumbled upon on Instagram was from Rizwan's publishers. They had posted it only a few seconds ago. Featured in it was the printed copy of Rizwan's brand new book, placed on a sleek table. Underneath, the caption read – 'Hot Off the Press'. Unlike PaperInk and its printers, the publishers and printers of Rizwan's book were based in Delhi. There were no rains there to mess with Rizwan's fate.

Seeing his rival's published book before his own felt like someone was now twisting the knife that Rizwan had stabbed into his chest. The number of likes and heart emoji comments under the photo were climbing every second before his very eyes.

Frustrated, Abhimanyu threw his phone on the couch and walked up to his window. He looked out at the Arabian Sea, trying to find a way to vent his anger.

Back in the PaperInk office, for the first time in a long while, Asmita didn't walk away from the discussion on Abhimanyu's book. This took place two days after the water levels had receded and people were back in office. She was done for the day and was about to leave for home when she overheard someone talking, 'So, the book won't be launched at the Jodhpur Literature Festival?'

Following the voice, Asmita looked behind her. There was a tiny gathering. Maaya was apprising the marketing team on the latest update.

'Is he aware of this?' Barging into the conversation, Asmita asked Maaya. The latter knew that by 'he' she meant Abhimanyu.

'Yeah.' Maaya nodded once and then turned around and left, looking dejected.

The team dispersed while Asmita stood there, holding her bag.

Her thoughts were full of Abhimanyu. She wondered how he was taking this news in the light of all that had already happened with his book. She felt sorry for him. In that moment, it didn't matter to her that he had wronged her in more ways than one. After all, she too had poured her heart into his book. Their love story might not have lasted long but that book, which was their labour of love, must succeed!

The novel was a tangible embodiment of her intangible feelings for the man who had written it. In her mind, *The Boy in the Neighbourhood* was going to be a timeless reminder of something beautiful she had once had with Abhimanyu, irrespective of how short-lived it was. It was the only way in which she could see a part of herself seamlessly merge with a part of Abhimanyu. The two had come together to give birth to something so beautiful. Asmita couldn't see it fail at any cost.

She decided that she would not watch silently as the book lost out on all the glory it deserved. Irrespective of what Abhimanyu or Maaya felt about her, she wanted the book to be known as Abhimanyu's best one yet. She decided to take some time to ideate and make some calls, to discuss the things that could still be done to save the book.

But first, she wanted to know the truth.

Staying back in office that evening, she made a call that had been long due. She dialled Rizwan's number.

'Heyyyyyyyy! What took you sooo loooong, dear?' Rizwan sang into his phone as soon as he picked up her call.

On the other end, Asmita was already fuming.

She came straight to the point. 'What did you tell Abhimanyu?'

'Well, well! So no pleasant small talk first?' He chuckled.

'Do I sound like I have got any interest for small talks?'

'Haha. Well, I had been expecting this call much earlier. Anyway, it's never too late, is it?'

Asmita kept quiet, not wanting to indulge in his bullshit. Rizwan changed his tone. It wasn't a pleasant one, but it wasn't sarcastic any longer either.

'I might have said a hundred things. Which one are you interested in?'

'In the part where you told him that I revealed his book's plot to you?'

'You didn't! See, that's where the problem lies.'

'What do you mean?'

'Wasn't that what you were supposed to do when you accepted my offer?'

'I never accepted your offer.'

'You didn't reject it either.'

'Not rejecting something doesn't mean that I accepted it. I had said that I would think about it. I was in a horrible situation back then. I wasn't thinking right. And when I gave it serious thought, I didn't feel it was right.'

'And you realized this after you returned to PaperInk? Which had been my suggestion in the first place, and part of my offer.'

'I DIDN'T GO BACK TO PAPERINK AS PART OF YOUR PLAN!' she screamed into her phone, and then tried to calm herself down. She was tired of explaining the same thing over and over again to everyone. 'I joined it because I needed to take care of my mom's medical needs.'

'You can lie as much as you want. You know what you were up to. And then you ditched me. What happened, Asmita? A change of heart while reading the romance author's manuscript?'

'I am *not* lying.'

'Then why didn't you tell me this before?'

'Tell you what?'

'That you weren't going with my plan.'

'Because I didn't have to.'

'Hahahaha!' Rizwan mocked the confidence with which Asmita spoke to him. He recalled how, only a few months ago, she had been sitting in his office, worried and confused, trying to find a job for herself.

When he was done laughing nastily, Rizwan said, 'And now, *I* don't have to tell you anything either.'

Asmita was left with very little room to play her card now. She tried to calm down. After swallowing her pride, she spoke again.

'If I'd have told you about my mother, you would have again brainwashed me and used me to your advantage. That's why I didn't tell you. That's the truth. I hope I have answered your question. Will you answer mine now?'

'Well, just because you have given me answers doesn't mean I have to believe them.'

'I am not here to make you believe me. Now, *will* you answer me?'

'Asmita, I did what I had to do. You had dropped hints of agreeing to go along with my plans and then you had a change of heart and you kept me in the dark ...'

He wasn't finished yet but Asmita couldn't take it any more. She interrupted him. 'What if I tell the world what you wanted me to do? And that now you have stolen Abhimanyu's work? What will everyone think of you when they get to know the truth?'

Rizwan laughed again, the sound loud and devilish.

'And what proof do you have, Asmita?' he asked. He meant every word he said.

The words stopped her cold. Asmita realized that there indeed might not be any proof. The entire discussion had taken place verbally, in Rizwan's office. There were some messages that had been exchanged between the two, but she would have to revisit them to confirm if they even stated that anything sinister was going on. As far as she could remember, in them he had referred to the whole thing as 'his plan' and it could mean several things.

It left Asmita frustrated. She would check her chats immediately after the call, she thought. In that moment, she felt two different emotions – sick about how Rizwan had played her, and relieved that she had never agreed to help him.

'But then you told Abhimanyu that I leaked the plot to you, which you have used in your novel. That's proof.'

'I never said any such thing.' He laughed again.

Asmita deduced that the conversation between Rizwan and Abhimanyu had been verbal too, and there was no proof of it.

'And if you try telling the world the story I told Abhimanyu, please keep in mind the repercussions – that you will be blamed first, because as part of that story, you stole his plot and gave it to me, while I will claim that I had no clue where you got that story from. I was in the dark about your ill intentions – to level scores against an author you had problems with. Oh! And there *is* written evidence about your hatred of Abhimanyu – our chats. You even confess that you wanted to quit PaperInk because of him. So, think twice before you do anything. I don't respond to threats. I make them. Bye! And never call me back.'

He disconnected the call.

His words shook her. Asmita had not imagined the level to which this guy could stoop. Fear crawled up her spine. In that moment, all she wanted was to confide in Abhimanyu. She felt empty and lonely without him.

She needed him. Anxiety made her find his name in the contact details of her phone, but the very next moment, her self-respect made her pull back. She had made a promise to herself and she wasn't going to break it. She kept the cellphone back in her purse.

On her way back home, the question that Abhimanyu was trying to find an answer for kept haunting Asmita too – how had Rizwan gotten his hands on the plot of Abhimanyu's book?

30

A common crisis brings people together, even ones who have differences between them. That's what Rizwan's actions had landed up doing for Asmita and Maaya.

The two were in Maaya's office, trying to figure out ways in which PaperInk could salvage the launch, which had not been called off – at least not yet. There were no further updates from the printer. But by now, everyone knew that no miracles were going to happen on that front.

'Any thoughts on this from Abhimanyu?' Asmita asked. She also wished to know how he was doing without explicitly asking.

Maaya was the only person who could have given her some updates on him. His Instagram handle had turned gloomy. There was an element of pain and anger in the quotes he put there. It worried Asmita. His indifferent readers loved those as well, as much as they had loved his earlier, happier quotes. Only this time, instead of heart emojis, they lined the comments with broken hearts.

Perhaps they could relate to the grief in his words. On his Instagram stories, he had started posting pictures of himself with an unkempt beard and messy hair. The dark circles around his eyes made him look sleep deprived.

'None,' Maaya answered unhappily. 'He has left it all to us,' she continued, sounding worried. 'The sense I got when I spoke to him yesterday was that he had lost all interest in this book.'

'No! We can't let this happen!' Asmita cried out.

Maaya was glad that Asmita was hopeful and willing to help in spite of all that had happened between them.

'He has been drinking. A lot!' Maaya added, knowing very well that she wasn't just talking to the editor of Abhimanyu's book but also to someone who had been close to him.

Asmita's lips parted. Her concerned eyes immediately caught Maaya's. She wanted to say something but drew a blank.

Maaya took a moment to read her eyes. 'You still love him, don't you?' she asked softly.

Asmita pursed her lips and looked down.

Maaya reached out across the table and put a kind hand on Asmita's. Asmita looked up. From Maaya, this felt like a genuine and positive gesture.

'Listen! I have been a difficult person to deal with. I've been blinded by my ambition and wronged you not once but twice. I regret it and I apologize to you.'

Asmita raised her eyes to face Maaya's. Those words had come out of the blue, and they appeared honest.

'I do,' Maaya repeated and added, 'As your boss, I should have stood up for your rights and instead I let you down. I am so sorry for what I did to you.'

Perhaps it was karma, Maaya felt. The entire project of *The Boy in the Neighbourhood* had begun on a wrong note, by crushing righteousness. Maybe what was happening to PaperInk and Abhimanyu was a result of it. She realized and carried guilt of being a party to this wrongdoing.

Asmita felt Maaya's fingers tightening around her hands, as if her body language was validating her words. She nodded silently.

'I want to fix this,' Maaya said. 'However, given my position in this company, I also cannot ignore that there existed a romantic relationship between an editor and her author.'

Asmita stiffened and tried to pull back her hand, but Maaya held on. 'Hear me out first, Asmita. If I can go to the extent of letting you quit for Abhimanyu's book, I can certainly go to that extent to save your job as well.'

Asmita's immediately looked up, her brows knitting together with worry. 'What do you mean, "save my job"?'

Maaya let out a deep breath before she answered. 'Asmita, our company policies, and for that matter most standard company policies, discourage any sort of romantic liaison between two individuals who are professionally working on the same project.'

'But Abhimanyu is an outsider. Not an employee of PaperInk,' Asmita protested.

'That's true. However, the common project here is his book on which both of you were working while being in a romantic relationship. It leads to undue biases and carelessness, and besides, you had hidden the relationship from us.'

Maaya softened her grip and Asmita pulled back her hand. She stared at the older woman, fear about what was coming in her heart.

'Try to understand. People in this organization have an idea of how much Abhimanyu had insisted that you work on his book. We have an editor who edits commercial fiction and yet this book was handed over to a literary editor.'

Asmita could now see what Maaya was getting at.

Maaya continued. 'Even though I am well aware that you two didn't have anything going on between you back then, and that you vehemently opposed this arrangement, others may not believe it. You see what I am saying?'

If people got to know of their affair, they would all think what Maaya was insinuating; that Asmita had gotten this project because she and Abhimanyu had been in a relationship. However, the truth was so different.

After the two had broken up, the ghost of their short relationship was coming to haunt her in this manner. And once again, she would be guilty until proven innocent in the eyes of strangers! *How ironic this is!*

She hated how often she had recently been finding herself in a spot like this wherein she had to defend herself despite having done nothing wrong.

Asmita pursed her lips again. She nodded in frustration, acknowledging Maaya's point.

Maaya spoke again. 'This kind of thing has never happened at before in our publishing house, but it has happened somewhere else, at least once. And in that situation, the commissioning editor of that publishing house had had to quit. He had hidden his relationship with the author whose book he had commissioned.'

Asmita now understood the full meaning of Maaya's words – *I can save your job.*

'But don't worry,' Maaya said. 'I have wronged you in the past and I want to take this opportunity to fix things for you.'

'But how?' Asmita asked.

'I can keep this silent if you can ensure that no one else in the office gets to know about this affair.'

Asmita sank back in her chair.

'This is the only way I can help you, Asmita. And I want to help you. But if others get to know then I won't be in a position to do anything, because not taking an action on you then would set a dangerous precedence for future. And I don't want to endorse a culture that would go against the company policy. Can you promise me that you'll hide this relationship from others? Forever?'

Asmita took a deep breath. She was being asked to conceal the truth but it was already out to Maaya and Peter.

'Don't worry about Peter, I will handle him,' Maaya offered, as if reading Asmita's mind.

'What about Abhimanyu?' Asmita asked.

'Are you two not on talking terms at all?'

Asmita fell silent. The look in her eyes answered the question.

'Don't worry. I will speak to him and I will try my best. I want you to know that.'

Asmita nodded once, letting her boss know that she wanted to trust her.

'However, my priority is to save this book from sinking. And the way—'

'*It won't*,' Asmita cut her off and said the words with certainty.

Maaya felt bolstered by the positivity with which Asmita spoke. In that difficult time, Asmita's attachment to the book gave her hope.

She smiled and said, 'I hope so, Asmita.'

'I have thought of something,' Asmita said and Maaya sat up, interested.

'What is it?'

Putting her personal as well as professional concerns on the backburner, Asmita laid out the plan she had been toying with since morning.

'How about, instead of waiting for the paperback, we bring out the e-book first?' There was a hint of excitement in her voice.

Maaya narrowed her eyes, trying to absorb what the editor was saying. 'Go on,' she prompted Asmita.

'We launch it with the same pomp and excitement and hold the launch event at the festival, as we had planned to. I am sure that through our common distributors, Rizwan and his publishing house would be well aware that there aren't going to be any copies of Abhimanyu's novel at the festival. However, with an e-book launch, we can catch them off guard.'

Numerous questions popped into Maaya's head. She would ask them when Asmita was done, she thought. For the moment, though, she wanted to hear more from the editor.

'We will keep the entire launch digital. I think this time, instead of partnering with a bookstore, we could partner with EBook app. Till date, at every book launch, every author has launched either a paperback or a hardback, never an e-book—'

'That's because fewer people consume e-books. And don't forget, we might be in a digital era, but paperbacks are still relevant. Paperbacks are love,' Maaya said, cutting Asmita off to make her point.

'You're right. And I am not denying that. However, seeing the situation we are in, we need to look at the positive aspects of this route. It can be a blessing in disguise for us. It makes us independent of our printers.'

'But the money lies in the paperback, Asmita.'

'That's true, Maaya. However, what I am suggesting now is not a solution to make money, but to give this book the chance it deserves. If we wait to bring it out after Rizwan's book, people *will* inevitably call it a rip-off of that, and in their minds, they will position Rizwan's work as the "original". We can't let that happen.'

A hint of a smile appeared on the corner of Maaya's lips. The idea, even though it needed more thinking, had some merit. *Hmm, what are the odds that it'll work?*

'So, what do you think?' Asmita asked when she didn't hear anything from Maaya, despite seeing the smile on her lips widening.

'Nothing, I am trying to play ...' she paused and then continued, '... devil's advocate here and—'

'Find loopholes in this strategy?' Asmita quickly filled in the blanks.

Maaya nodded her head.

'You must,' Asmita added.

'For a moment, even if I assume that Abhimanyu's fans are willing to buy the e-book just because there is no paperback available, e-books are usually one-third the price of a paperback. If his core readership buys his work at that price point, we will end up incurring great losses, given the kind of advance we have paid him.'

'No, his readers will buy the paperback as well!'

'What? Why?' Maaya raised her eyebrows in surprise.

'Because paperback is love. You yourself said this moments ago.'

'I am not sure if I get what you are saying here, Asmita.'

On that note, Asmita spread her hands out and explained the big picture to Maaya.

'This e-book thing is just to stay ahead in the race. With its help, we can overcome our two constraints. One, Rizwan bringing his book out before us. Two, the printers' inability to print the paperbacks for us on time. Our real business will be as usual – the paperback, which will come perhaps a few weeks after. Till then, we run this as Phase 1 of our launch campaign, which is purely digital—'

'But Asmita—'

'Please hear me out first, Maaya,' Asmita requested. Her boss obliged.

'We will not sell the e-book at one-third of the price,' Asmita said.

'Then?'

'We will sell it at the same price as we sell the physical book.'

'And why would people buy it at that price?' Maaya asked, a bit agitated. She thought Asmita was being overenthusiastic and missing the whole sense of business, which was the sales team's domain.

'Because we won't sell it as an e-book.'

Maaya exhaled, frustrated. Suddenly, Asmita was not making any sense to her.

Asmita smiled and asked her not to lose her patience. She was coming to the point.

'What we are selling here is a combo – the e-book as well as the paperback, for the price of the paperback. Only this time, the e-book arrives in their hands immediately, while the paperback will take two to three weeks to arrive at their doorsteps. So instead of giving them one thing for the price, we are now giving them two things.'

Asmita could see the smile returning on Maaya's face. It was a relief to see it.

However, Maaya wasn't done playing devil's advocate yet. 'But won't his fans hate having to wait for the paperback even after they have paid money for it?'

'Not when they are going to receive the e-book with a single click. And definitely not when they are going to receive a signed copy of the paperback from their favourite author,' she said with a big smile.

'Wait? What? *All* copies will be signed?'

'Abhimanyu has never done this before. He has always signed copies of his books at his book events, where his readers have to arrive physically. This will be the first time his readers will receive signed copies in the comfort of their homes. And while they wait for it eagerly, they have the e-book to go through,' Asmita explained.

'Will Abhimanyu be ready to do this?' Maaya immediately asked.

'That's for you to check. I think he will do it. He will do anything for his book. At least I know that much about him.'

'But Asmita, signing thousands of copies?'

'I had thought about it. The book is yet to be printed. I know it's difficult to sign every copy. However, it is a lot easier to sign the stacks of printed title pages.'

Maaya looked at her, trying to visualize what the younger woman was proposing.

'You're right. Before the full book is bound, we can get the stacks of the printed title pages for Abhimanyu. It'll be easier and faster for him to sign these papers.'

'Indeed,' Asmita said with a smile. 'If I ask you to practice your autograph on a blank paper, how many can you do in one minute?'

Maaya thought for a moment and then said, 'Maybe twenty or thirty?'

'Exactly!' Asmita said.

'So, we can take Abhimanyu to the printer and achieve this,' Maaya suggested.

'But, in a way, we are giving the e-book free to the readers,' Maaya concluded, returning to the previous point Asmita had made.

'Yes. But only till the time the paperback isn't available. Once the paperbacks are out, we can uncouple them and sell the two formats separately.'

Maaya rubbed her hands together, smiling and nodding. This could indeed work. It was a brilliant idea and a damn good solution to their current problem.

But Asmita wasn't done yet. She went on. 'Let's get EBook app team on board. Imagine their excitement when they get to know that there will be no paperback of this book for a few weeks. For the first time, they will be getting something exclusive from an author of Abhimanyu's stature. We can do a grand launch at the festival and add digital features to it. Imagine, the moment we unveil the cover on a big electronic screen, the link to buy and download this e-book will go live immediately. Even the people sitting and attending this launch at the festival will be able to download the book in real time, while Abhimanyu would still be on the stage,' Asmita finished.

Out of sheer joy, Maaya couldn't hold herself back. She walked to the other side of the table where Asmita sat and put her hands on the editor's shoulders. 'You've done me proud, Asmita,' she said with real warmth in her voice.

How the tables had turned! This woman, who was once desperate not to work on this book, was now desperate to make the book work. If ever there would be a saying – behind every successful author is a damn good editor – then the story of Asmita and Abhimanyu would be the face of it.

Maaya went back to her chair and asked, 'Do you want to pitch this big idea to Abhimanyu yourself? I am sure he would be excited.' She wanted to give Asmita a reason to reach out and talk to the author. It was a no-brainer for her, seeing how much Asmita loved him and the extent to which she cared for his book.

Asmita's smile disappeared. She gently shook her head. When she didn't say anything, Maaya nodded and said, 'I understand.'

'And when you pitch him this idea, he doesn't have to know who thought of it,' Asmita quickly added.

Maaya kept looking into her eyes for a while. Feeling sorry for her, she silently nodded. Asmita took her leave and walked out of her office.

31

The nights in Jodhpur were freezing. Thankfully, the days were pleasant. The sea of people under the giant shamiyanas at the grand Jodhpur Literature Festival had kept the temperature warm for everyone. People across age groups had all turned up to celebrate books, ideas and opinions.

Under one such huge tent in the front lawns, next to the big stage, stood Abhimanyu. He was in a light blue blazer, with a crisp white shirt, blue denims and white sneakers. He was being mic-ed up when his eyes caught Asmita's. She was jostling with the crowd moving in to fill in the space for Abhimanyu's session.

Seeing him spot her, Asmita froze. It had been a while since the two had set eyes on each other. They had not even spoken on the phone since the blow-up in the conference room. And now, it was as if a raw nerve had been pressed and left her temporarily paralysed. She had prepared herself for seeing him, but not this way, and definitely not for him seeing her too. She had prepared herself to watch him on stage, from a safe distance.

A part of her was delighted to see him in a different avatar from the unkempt version he had been posting on social media. Today, he looked like his old self – refreshingly handsome.

She realized she was smiling and immediately stopped. Then, breaking eye contact, she wanted to say something, but then the mad rush of people carried her away.

However, unbeknownst to her, Abhimanyu's eyes followed her in the crowd. In her pink kurti and white printed dupatta, she looked pretty and relaxed. Abhimanyu followed the pink-and-white figure moving away from him till the time his name was called out from the backstage.

In no time, the emcee on stage announced the start of the session. The crowd primarily comprised youngsters, more women than men. Young women cheered for Abhimanyu when the emcee announced his name.

Abhimanyu walked onto the stage, his gait confident and stylish, waving at the crowd and blowing kisses as the girls screamed his name even louder. He arrived at the centre and joining his hands, bowed down to his audience before taking his seat.

While the emcee spent another minute in reading out Abhimanyu's achievements till date, his eyes were busy scanning the crowd. He was looking for Asmita. He was conscious of her presence. It felt awkward and good at the same time.

But with a packed audience of hundreds in front of him, he failed to find her. However, his eyes did discover something else – the copies of Rizwan's book in a few hands.

He knew that Rizwan's launch had been held an hour before his. And those copies were proof that his rival's book had finally been unveiled. Suddenly, he realized that he would now have to address the same people who might have attended Rizwan's launch, and tell them about the plot of his novel, which was the same as the one in the book they were holding. In a way, it meant that he was going to repeat what Rizwan would have told them just a while ago. He hadn't thought about this earlier. He felt mortified.

At the far end of the shamiyana, Asmita stood in the crowd and noticed the sudden discomfort on Abhimanyu's face on the big LED screens installed for the audience. In those visuals, his eyes were stuck on someone in the front row. The cameraman then rolled the camera and captured the crowd. Asmita could now see a few people in the front row holding Rizwan's book in their hands. They waved at the camera the moment they saw themselves on the big screen. Asmita immediately connected the dots.

The spectacle of people holding Rizwan's book in their hands was bothering Abhimanyu. Hate and discomfort would have bubbled up in his chest – emotions he should not even think about while on stage in front of his fans.

Gosh! I should have told him. She wanted to tell him right away what she had intended to say when the wave of the crowd had taken her along with it. She quickly pulled her mobile out of her handbag, typed a message and sent it to Abhimanyu.

Please please please! See the message!

She saw Abhimanyu slip his hand in his pocket. He pulled out his phone and put it on silent without even looking at it. He then kept it next to the handheld mic on the table in front of him.

Asmita felt deflated. It was important for her to make him see her message before the launch began. Abhimanyu's eyes were back on the crowd in the front row. The uneasiness on his face was still visible. The audience could see it on the screen and Asmita could even read his thoughts. The next second, the announcement of Sonia Sharma's name – the prime-time TV news anchor who he was to be in conversation with – distracted him.

The audience clapped, but not with the same gusto that they had displayed for Abhimanyu. While Sonia shook her hands with the star author and took her seat, the emcee went on to introduce her to the gathering.

Meanwhile, Asmita was in two minds about doing something she thought might help. Finally, she went for it.

She called Abhimanyu on his phone, hoping that he hadn't switched it off for the session, but only put it on silent mode. It rang! She was lucky. The next second, a shrill static disturbance filled the air and all three people on stage immediately checked their phones. It was Abhimanyu's that was vibrating.

He immediately excused himself and picked it up to switch it off, but this time he spotted the name of the caller. Asmita saw him look at his phone and then at the crowd. He was trying to find her, she knew.

Abhimanyu immediately cancelled the incoming call to restore the broadcast audio. The second he did so, he saw the message from Asmita.

'Rizwan lied. His book has nothing to do with your story. I am coming from his session. It's a completely different story. A campus romance! He was bluffing this whole time to mess with us. Your story hasn't been compromised.'

Abhimanyu reread her message and relief flooded his heart. His lips parted into a big, happy smile. Asmita could see all of this on the LED screen. The sudden joy on his face was evident. She was delighted to witness it and to be the reason behind it. It was a far cry from their last exchange, and she felt as if it had erased some of the unpleasantness between them.

'And now, ladies and gentlemen, let's kickstart this highly awaited session! We present to you, the digital launch of *The Boy in the Neighbourhood* by bestselling author Abhimanyu Razdan!' the emcee announced. The crowd cheered. The journalist got up, as did Abhimanyu.

Abhimanyu's eyes were still trying to trace Asmita in the crowd. He couldn't find her, and so resorted to messaging her. 'Thank you,' he typed and then put his phone away.

He walked towards the six-feet-tall rectangular frame wrapped in a red satin cloth. A golden ribbon, which ran across the vertical and horizontal lengths of it, was tied into a bow at the centre. He was joined by Sonia and Maaya, who was there to represent PaperInk.

Right then, an upbeat soundtrack filled the air. It instantly shot up the already excited mood of the gathering to a whole new level. The atmosphere was electric.

Abhimanyu and Sonia together pulled the ribbon in Maaya's presence. Amid thunderous applause, the shinning red satin slid down to the floor, revealing a giant EBook device that had a full-screen display of the cover of *The Boy in the Neighbourhood*.

Taking full advantage of their electronic capabilities, the EBook app team had added a lot of cool features to the launch. Subtle screen filters overlapped the cover and gave it a celebratory effect. The music in the background changed to match the mood on the virtual screen. It was a celebration of romance on-screen. Hearts formed and exploded like fireworks. In a way, the animations summarized the various emotions captured in the book. The crowd was awestruck by it. So was the case with the people on stage, including the author, who hadn't been apprised in detail of this plan for a mega launch. It was very different and far superior to any of his physical book launches.

Somewhere in the crowd, Asmita glowed with happiness on seeing the big launch unfold on stage. In that moment, she was so glad she had pitched this idea to Maaya.

The channel Sonia worked for was covering the festival and had chosen to live-telecast the launch as their weekend highlight feature.

The launch was also being broadcast live on social media. Readers from different parts of the country, glued to the screens, were in for a treat. They felt like they were part of the event, which was happening right in front of their eyes.

The EBook app team had packaged the entire launch very professionally simply because they knew this was an exclusive deal and a first-of-its-kind collaboration with a bestselling author. Knowing that there would be no paperbacks available for a while, they had gone full throttle with it. Hearts continued to pour in on the Instagram live on PaperInk's handle. Thousands were tuning in from across the country.

The soundtrack stopped. Pages began to flip on the big EBook gadget. The audience was in for a surprise yet again.

In no time, the screen was fully taken over by the video trailer of the book.

From somewhere between the pages, a blue sky dotted with fluffy white clouds appears. The background changes. The lens through which the audience is viewing the scene cuts through the white clouds. It zooms in and spans over the densely green hills of Munnar. A voice emerges in the background. It introduces the place and tells everyone that this is where this love story is set. The camera pans across a visual of the tall trees of Munnar, and then the vast tea plantations. It comes to a dead stop in front of a house. 'This is the house where this love story is going to unfold. Between a young boy ...' the narrator pauses and the camera shows a young boy walking towards this house. His clothes are torn and there is dirt all over him. His elbows are bruised. He is holding a flower in his hand. The voice continues. 'And a woman.' The scene changes to a kitchen inside that house. In it, shot from behind, is a middle-aged woman wearing a long dress. She is busy cooking a meal, earphones plugged in her ears.

The camera cuts back to the boy. He must be around eighteen or nineteen. His face is never shown; neither is that of the woman inside. The camera follows his footsteps. From a bright sunlit visual, he enters the slightly dark house. He calls out to her, but she can't hear him. He looks for her in the drawing room, in the puja room, but she is nowhere to be seen. He moves from one room to another till he reaches the extreme end of the house, where the kitchen is.

He lets out a deep breath when he finally sees her. 'Experience one of the most innocent love stories you have ever read,' the narrator says. The camera shows the boy raising the hand in which he is holding the flower. The woman is busy listening to music. He then taps her shoulder. As she starts turning around, the camera freezes. The frozen scene tilts and transforms into the cover. The name of the book, the author and the logo of the publisher appear on it.

The music petered out. The audience went wild, clapping and cheering.

A moment later, the emcee announced, 'Folks, the book is available for purchase right away. There is no need to stand in a queue, as this is a digital copy. All you need to do is send an SMS with TBITN to 52546 and in response we will send you a link to make your payment and download the e-book. And I assure you that you will get your copy within two minutes of the payment being processed. Oh! And please fill in your name and address details on the same link so *that we can send you a signed paperback copy* at your address by next month *at no extra cost!*'

The audience was clearly thrilled. From far behind, Asmita could see heads turning, young women looking at each other, their mouths wide open. Super impressed by the uniqueness of the plot, overwhelmed by the trailer and driven by the sheer excitement of receiving signed copies, they wanted to send that SMS as soon as possible.

Then the emcee played the last card. 'But people! This offer is open only till the end of this month! So, act fast!'

It was a no-brainer now for the readers. They needed to place their orders right away.

On stage, Sonia and Abhimanyu took their seats. The session began. Sonia started the conversation by congratulating Abhimanyu and then took a deep dive into his journey as an author – writing his first book, his initial struggle followed by all the milestones he had achieved to be where he was today.

Abhimanyu dedicated all his achievements to the love he got from his readers. Occasionally, he gave witty responses, to which his crowd cheered. He blushed a bit when Sonia mentioned how she had seen pictures of his female fan base swooning around him. Asmita found that cute.

The discussion then moved on to talking about *The Boy in the Neighbourhood*. The distinctiveness of the story became the talking point.

'How did the idea come to your mind, Abhimanyu?' Sonali asked.

'I wanted to challenge myself. You see, love doesn't understand age differences or whether someone is already taken or not. It just happens. In this case, it happens to a boy who is nineteen years old. It is this age that works so well for this story. Love at this tender age is full of innocence. I understand it may not be a love story that would transform into a relationship, but you can't deny the existence of love here. The heart is so vulnerable at this age. I wanted to write about this rare kind of love.'

'This brings to my next question. Will society approve of this love? Is it right?'

The crowd looked forward to hearing what Abhimanyu had to say on this.

He smiled as soon as he heard the question. On the big screen, people saw him taking a moment to collect his thoughts. Then he began.

'Society's approval?' He smiled again, rubbing his thumb on his chin. 'Tell me a renowned love story which society has approved of?'

The crowd cheered on that note.

Abhimanyu paused for them and then continued, 'Come to think of it, the probability of my love story becoming great increases if society *doesn't* approve of it.' He chuckled. The wave of laughter ran through the crowd along with a second round of claps.

He wasn't finished yet. 'But on a serious note, by writing about it in this book, I am not taking positions. I am only showcasing the innocence of this love story. That yes, love doesn't see age or relationship status. I am not describing the rightness or wrongness of this; it is very subjective.'

'All right! Fair enough. But, Abhimanyu, if you put yourself in your protagonist's shoes, tell us ... would you pursue such a love?'

The crowd held its breath, awaiting his answer. The camera zoomed in to capture his facial reaction. This one had really put him on the spot.

Abhimanyu took a moment and then said, 'Yes! Because like that boy at that age, I would have been madly in love with that woman and I would have wanted to pursue it.'

His response was followed by the longest clapping yet. Sonia smilingly waited for the crowd to settle down. Even those who weren't Abhimanyu's loyal readers were now genuinely interested in reading the love story of this young boy.

The session lasted for another half an hour. In the end, when the moderator asked if the audience had any questions, scores of hands went up. Due to the time factor, only three questions were taken and answered. One of his readers wanted to hug him. He nodded and she ran to him. The crowd collectively aww-ed as Abhimanyu hugged her.

The book launch of *The Boy in the Neighbourhood* turned out to be one of the best sessions at the literature festival. It was already packed when it had started, but by the time it came to an end, there was no space left to even stand. The occasional claps and cheers from the crowd had summoned more people to join in. Abhimanyu was at his best, with his moving and candid answers.

By the time the session ended, the EBook app team was in for a wonderful surprise. Their website had already clocked in over seven thousand orders. Everyone on stage had got up to leave when the team lead from EBook app walked onto the stage to give them this big news. Abhimanyu was thrilled to discover the numbers.

The e-book launch plan was working out way better than he had anticipated. In fact, it had worked even better than a paperback launch.

'Seven thousand in half an hour? Imagine the immense possibilities of scaling this up in the coming days!' he murmured, looking at Maaya, who herself was on cloud nine. Finally, after all the big hurdles, her first Abhimanyu Razdan book at PaperInk had gotten off to a kickass start. There was nothing else she could have asked for.

The audience got up. From the stage, Abhimanyu tracked a woman in pink and white. She was at the far end of the gathering. His eyes were focused on her as he came down. He wanted to reach out to her, but more than a hundred fans stood between them, wanting to take selfies with him and asking for his autograph. Abhimanyu tried to push through but couldn't. He was soon escorted to the book-signing lounge and before he knew it, the figure in pink and white had left the tent.

32

Later that evening, PaperInk had organized a huge party at the City Palace. It was hosted in the vast manicured lawns of the palace. If the week-long literature festival was about books and opinions during the day, it was about parties in the evening. While the festival hosted a party every evening, there were multiple big and small parties thrown by numerous publishers as well. The speakers, delegates and guests were spoilt for choice. These parties were great networking opportunities as well.

It was a perfect evening for PaperInk to host their party. Abhimanyu Razdan was the star of the evening. He walked into the party a bit late. The evening was quite cold. Standing heaters were installed at various points to keep the place warm. The venue was bustling with people; most were crowded around the bar.

'And here is the man of the moment!' Holding a glass of wine in her hand, Maaya welcomed Abhimanyu with open arms. She was in the company of a few other delegates from the festival.

Abhimanyu smiled and gracefully went for a cheek-to-cheek hug with her. 'I had not thought in my wildest dreams that we would be able to save our sinking boat and make it to the shore,' he said.

'Save? We flew over the sea and reached the shore with flying colours!' Maaya quipped.

'We did,' Abhimanyu acknowledged with a big smile. 'Thank you, Maaya.'

'And hey! Did you find out that guy had been bluffing?' Maaya said, without naming Rizwan. There were others around them after all.

Abhimanyu shook his head and smiled ruefully. 'What a crazy man.' But he felt relieved too. It was all over, and it was time for him to put the ugliness behind him.

Maaya smiled and introduced him to the people she had been standing with.

'So, did you get mobbed by fans today?' one of the guests asked.

Abhimanyu smiled. 'Something interesting happened,' he said. Maaya was all ears. 'After the session, I was taken to the book-signing lounge. Of course, there were no books, but I had agreed to take selfies with my readers—'

'They love you! You must have taken thousands of those!' Maaya said.

Abhimanyu smiled at her and continued, 'So, a few readers came up with an innovative idea. They clicked their pictures with me on their Instagram stories and then made me sign my initials with my finger on their touchscreen phones.'

'Oh, boy!' Maaya said, genuinely impressed.

'Yeah!' Abhimanyu said and added further, 'They tagged my handle and then posted those stories with my autograph on it. It became a trend. So I had to oblige everyone.' He laughed.

'This has been a truly digital launch for you guys, hasn't it?' one of the delegates said, looking at Maaya.

A brief conversation later, Abhimanyu excused himself to get a drink. Maaya walked with him, hoping to introduce him to more people.

On their way to the bar, Abhimanyu kept looking around, as if searching for someone. When he couldn't trace the person anywhere, he asked Maaya, 'Is Asmita not around?'

She didn't reply but stiffened. Abhimanyu noticed the sudden awkwardness in her body language and stopped in his tracks.

'What's wrong?' he asked.

Maaya let out a deep breath and said, 'Today is Asmita's last day at PaperInk.'

'*What? Why?*' He was shell-shocked. The creases on his forehead revealed his concern.

Maaya looked at him for a few seconds before replying. 'Did you two ever talk after that meeting?' she asked.

He looked away. The next time he faced Maaya, he shook his head. 'But today, she dropped me a text when I was onstage.'

'What was it about?'

'That Rizwan's book has a totally different plot.'

Maaya chuckled sarcastically. 'And do you know how that asshole got to know about your plot?'

'No! Do you?'

Maaya finally solved the puzzle.

'Interestingly, the photographer who shot the cover of your book happens to be friends with Anirban, Rizwan's assistant.'

Abhimanyu kept listening.

'The photographer – I even forgot his name,' Maaya said and continued, 'He was briefed on the plot of *The Boy in the Neighbourhood* before he shot the kitchen scene for the cover. It was during one random conversation between Anirban and this photographer that Anirban got to know about your plot. That's how the information travelled to Rizwan.'

'And how do you know all this?' Abhimanyu asked.

'Asmita told me. She happened to see this photographer and Anirban hanging out together at the festival.'

'And what is this photographer doing here?'

'He does cover shoots for quite a few publishers. And he is one of the speakers at the session on book covers.'

'I see!'

While Abhimanyu was curious to get more details, his mind was also full of the news of Asmita quitting PaperInk. In the last few weeks, he had missed her, terribly so on some occasions. And now, when his professional life suddenly seemed to be back on track, Asmita's absence strongly pierced his heart. He was already dealing with the guilt of mistreating her at various junctures, personally and professionally. He had doubted her intentions, judged her character. And now, even the last missing piece of the puzzle was resolved. She had been blameless, and he had accused her in front of her bosses.

Meanwhile, Maaya continued, 'She chatted with this photographer when he was alone. She had had her suspicions and during the chat, she discovered that he had indeed mentioned the cover shoot to Anirban. Later, when she ran into Anirban and confronted him, he first stammered and then made an excuse and walked away.' Maaya chuckled.

It was all crystal clear. Abhimanyu was embarrassed that he had fallen into Rizwan's trap. *That bastard played me!*

Not only had Rizwan played him, he had also unintentionally ruined whatever was left between Abhimanyu and Asmita after their break-up.

'Abhimanyu, I don't know how things are between you and Asmita now. But it is her last day with us, and I think you should reach out to her and thank her.'

He looked at Maaya, trying to interpret her words.

'I want to tell you something that you don't know,' she said.

Abhimanyu waited, silent.

'You think this digital launch was my idea,' she said.

He kept gazing at her.

'It was not,' she confessed. 'It was Asmita's.'

'*What?*'

'The entire thing! The whole idea – making it an e-book-only launch, the combo deal of signed paperback copies at a later stage – it was Asmita who conceptualized it and choreographed everything that unfolded on stage today.'

Abhimanyu was too shocked to speak.

'In all honesty, if it wasn't for her, we wouldn't have been able to fly our sinking ship today.'

'Why didn't you tell me this before?'

'Your ex-girlfriend made me promise not to.'

It hit him hard, the way Maaya referred to Asmita. She had overlooked the fact that she was his editor and instead chosen to underline the relationship Abhimanyu had had with her for a brief period. Perhaps she wanted to tell him that it was his mistake to let a woman like Asmita walk out of his life. That he should hold her back if it was still in his hands to make things right.

Like a volcano, his suppressed emotion of wanting her back finally erupted.

'Where is she? Please, tell me where she is!' he said, desperation on his face.

Maaya was strangely happy to see Abhimanyu react with this kind of urgency.

'Moments before you walked in, she told me she wasn't feeling well and was about to leave. Check the hotel reception. She has an early morning flight back to Mumbai. Her new job is in Delhi. She is moving there with her mother.'

Without a word, Abhimanyu turned around and rushed straight to the reception area.

Away from the hustle-bustle of the party gathering, Asmita was waiting for her cab at the reception. She was alone. Abhimanyu's run came to a halt the second he saw her. Asmita heard the approaching footsteps. She turned around.

Abhimanyu stopped for a moment to catch his breath. His eyes didn't leave her face for a single second.

Asmita's heartbeat quickened. She wasn't prepared for a confrontation with him. She had not answered the text message Abhimanyu had sent her after the session – *I need to see you.*

There was no need for her to meet him. Seeing him would make her weak, and the pain of loving and losing him would come rushing back. It would revive terrible memories of being wronged time and again by him, something she was trying to put behind her. This was the main reason she hadn't wanted to attend the party in the first place. But, Maaya had asked her to be there as her last request before Asmita left PaperInk. She had agreed to show up as a formality and chosen to leave before Abhimanyu arrived

She didn't want to be rude and tell Abhimanyu on a message that she didn't want to meet him. Instead, she chose not to respond. And now, caught by him with nowhere to hide, she hesitantly watched him come closer to her.

The fear in her heart was the same as what she had felt months ago, outside the washroom at the PaperInk office, when he had finally caught her after that first meeting. She had tried to escape his eyes then and she was trying to escape them now. This time the reason was very different, though.

'Hi,' Abhimanyu said as he walked up to her.

'Hello,' she said, trying to gather all her strength to face this moment.

'Heard you are quitting PaperInk.'

She nodded.

'Why?'

She took a couple of seconds to speak. 'I have been offered a better job. So ...' She trailed off.

How could two people who, not too long ago, had been so intimate, have moved so far away from each other! There was discomfort and awkwardness in the air between them, so much so that even a simple conversation felt difficult.

'Is that the real reason?' he pressed.

A vehicle arrived outside the reception area. Asmita looked towards the gate and said, 'My cab has arrived. I have to go.' She had just turned towards it when Abhimanyu stretched out his arm and held her wrist. 'Wait.'

A current ran underneath her skin. That touch! It was familiar, even though it had been a while since she'd felt it. She turned back to slip her wrist out of Abhimanyu's grip, but he held on tighter, not letting her take her hand back.

'Abhimanyu!' she said and then looked at the busy reception. 'Don't make a scene.'

'I need to talk to you,' he said in a firm voice.

Swallowing the lump at the back of her throat, she took a moment and said, 'Please let go of my hand and I will talk.'

'Come out, then.' He pointed to the exit on the other side. It was an open, secluded space. Asmita obliged and walked with him.

Once out, Abhimanyu didn't mince any words.

'Asmita, I am sorry. I made a terrible mistake.'

She felt those words touch the surface of her wounds. She didn't say anything in return and stood there like a living statue, willing to absorb all that he had in his mind.

'I was so wrong, Asmita. So wrong!'

His face had a look of immense remorse. He wanted Asmita to react to that, say something, anything. But she remained silent.

When he didn't hear anything from her, he asked her with folded hands, 'Do you think you can forgive me? I am not sure if I even have the right to ask this question—'

'I forgive you,' Asmita finally spoke, cutting him off, but not really looking at him. The sooner she said that the quicker she could leave.

He immediately paused and looked at her, trying to verify if what he had just heard was indeed what she meant.

'I forgive you,' Asmita repeated herself. There was neither a smile on her lips, nor the creases of concern on her forehead. There was one thing for sure – empathy. And it looked genuine.

Abhimanyu gave a big sigh of relief. His lips stretched into a smile, but then the next second that smile vanished when he observed the quietness with which Asmita stood and continued to look at him.

'What's wrong?' he asked, concerned.

His words brought her out of the spell of holding his gaze. She forced a smile and shook her head, telling him that everything was fine. It was a lie.

Relief found its way on Abhimanyu's face again. His eyes lit up. 'And I have to thank you,' he said.

'For what?'

'For what?!' He chuckled. He was much more relaxed now. 'Maaya told me everything. This entire launch was your big idea. How did you ...' He paused and looked at the sky above and then back at her to finish what he was saying. 'How did you even think of this brilliant, brilliant idea?'

She kept staring at him for a few minutes. *How soon you got back to your book!*

'I am glad it worked out well for you,' she said.

'I guess it worked out well for all of us, Asmita,' he said softly and stepped forward to hug her. He wanted to feel that she had genuinely forgiven him and that things between them were going to be like before.

At once, Asmita stepped back and blocked him with her hands. 'No, Abhimanyu!'

His body froze. His arms were left clutching empty air. The next moment he backed off, but his eyes didn't. They tried to read her mind. His hands turned upside down as if asking her – *what just happened?*

'We should maintain a distance, Abhimanyu.'

'Haven't you forgiven me?' he asked, worry on his face.

'I have,' she said looking into his eyes. 'But if you think you and I can get back to being who we were before, then I am sorry. This forgiveness isn't about that. Besides, there is no question of forgiveness in that case.'

'Don't say that,' he said. 'I *need* you, Asmita. I want you back.'

'No, Abhimanyu. I cannot give you that.'

'Why not?'

There was discomfort on Asmita's face. She looked away, trying to collect her thoughts and frame them into words for him.

'Because you don't love me—'

'But I have missed you.'

'Missing someone isn't loving them.'

'But it is a part of it.'

'Yes, it is. But there is lot more to love than just missing someone.'

'Listen, Asmita,' he said, reaching out for her hand and trying to make her understand how much he meant what he was saying. Asmita let him hold it.

'I do love you.'

'No, Abhimanyu. You don't. Please understand! You think you do. But it's only for this moment. This feeling is temporary. It will go away.'

'That's not true.'

'You had said this yourself, in crystal-clear words – you don't love me,' Asmita said and at once that moment she was referring to flashed through his head. It left him blank for a while.

'Then what is this thing that I am feeling for you? Why am I missing you like this? What is it, if not love? This ... I don't know ... all this ...' Dejected, he mostly blabbered to himself.

She could feel what he meant. She could understand what he was going through. A part of her felt content knowing that he too had missed her, like she had him. That he had missed her so much that he felt the need to confide in her and wanted her back.

The next time he caught her gaze, Asmita consoled him. She told him she understood how he was feeling and what he was going through. 'Give yourself some time. And it will be fine,' she said.

Abhimanyu continued to hold her wrist in his grip. A part of him wanted to feel that she still belonged to his life and only his life. And that he wouldn't let her go away.

'All this time that I had given myself ... it made me realize how much I love you.'

'Abhimanyu, please stop saying that. You *think* you love me, but you don't. And that's the reality.'

'No, it is not.'

'Yes, it is.'

'Don't talk this way, please. I care about you.'

'You don't, Abhimanyu. *You don't.* And you *can't* care about me. That's the whole point. You can never love me the way I loved you. I will never be your priority, but you will always be mine. Even if you break my heart more than once.'

Every single word of her last statement was brutally true. And she was glad she spoke them out loud. Abhimanyu could clearly understand now what she was hinting at.

She continued, 'I will continue to care about fixing things for you, even when you won't trust me and bulldoze your way and crush my feelings. And for the record, I am not proud of myself for doing this. I am emotional, and not practical like you. That's my problem and I have to fix it. So please don't put me on some higher pedestal for this, because in my heart I hate myself for being so attached to you.'

He let her talk and vent it all out. And so she did.

'I had never fallen for anyone the way I fell for you. I had never done such crazy things with anyone, the things I did with you. I mean, I couldn't even hold myself back from kissing you in the office. That is not the usual me, Abhimanyu. It was something so different that I felt for you. And all this happened to me after I had begun to hate you for what you did to me back then. Can you believe that? Do you realize how insane the love has to be for someone to … to … to fall in love with someone she hates?' She sarcastically chuckled at herself. 'And realize that the other person doesn't even love her. God! This is … this is so confusing for anyone else to understand. But I do … I do, Abhimanyu. Your words had possessed me. I am in love with them and I will always be. But you are different. You are different from your words.

You are different from the kind of love you talk about in your books.' She furiously nodded while talking, as if validating how much she meant her words.

'I shouldn't have fallen for the author just because I had fallen for his words. I was stupid.' She smiled. 'How silly that being an editor, I missed this ... this basic point.'

'Asmita! Don't say this! Come back to me. Please! I care for you.'

'Abhimanyu, you think so, but that's not true. You didn't and wouldn't care for me the way you care for your work, your words. You will never craft our relationship the way you craft them and I will always feel the lack of it. There will always be women throwing themselves at you and you will entertain the ones you like, and I will lose my importance. *If I commit to you, I would be lying* – remember? Those are your words. You had said them back then to make me remember them tonight.'

She had made him eat his own words. And now the man of words was left speechless.

'Love demands reciprocity, Abhimanyu. I wasn't there to be one of the many women in your life. I wanted to be *the* one. And I knew you didn't want it, and I didn't even want to push my way to make you want what I wanted. I set you free. And by doing that, I have been trying to set myself free from this expectation. Let's just respect that.'

Tears swam in Abhimanyu's eyes.

'All that you are saying, Asmita ... is true. I used to be that person. But not any more. I have realized this, and I feel differently about you today. Don't you see it?'

'You are feeling this today because you are overwhelmed. Because all the hurdles on the road of your priority have been cleared now. You care about nothing else the way you care about your book.'

'That's not true, Asmita. Don't say that.'

'Then ask yourself why you are feeling this today and not before? Did you feel this way while you were worried about your book launch?'

He again ran out of words.

'Were you as worried as much about trying to save our relationship as you were about trying to save your book?'

He attempted to say something, anything, but failed. Her scrutinizing eyes watched him break down and she did nothing about it. A part of her wanted to envelop him in her arms, for she couldn't see him crumble like this. And yet she held herself back, for his and her good.

'How could I have, Asmita? When I didn't trust you? I thought you were the one—'

'How can I be with someone who doesn't trust me, after doing all that you did to me in the past? This wasn't the first time you had humiliated me and shown me my place. I would lose all my self-respect if I let you do this to me for the third time. I can't give you that right. I am sorry!'

Abhimanyu's grip around her wrist softened. She took her hand back. Tears ran down her face as he held her in her blurred vision. In that moment, he knew that he had lost her, perhaps forever.

In that moment, trying to comfort him, Asmita softly spoke, 'You have changed my perception of the genre you write in. And I am so glad you did. You will remain my favourite author forever, for no one can move me with words like you did.'

He continued to stare at her, completely silent, tears in his eyes.

'Goodbye, Abhimanyu,' she said, turned around and walked away.

It was only when she was safely inside the cab that she finally let her tears flow.

Three months later…

The bestselling author who was celebrated for his fictitious sad endings had landed in one in real life. It was the first time he experienced what heartbreak feels like and it broke him – completely!

In order to find closure and move on, he decided to pen down the love story between him and his editor in a book. He chose to name it *Write Me a Love Story*.

Acknowledgements

My sincere thanks to the following people, without whom this book would not have turned out to be ... well ... what it has turned out to be.

To Richa S Mukherjee, once a debut author who I published at my publishing venture Black Ink and now my friend, a fellow author and co-author for my e-singles. For being the very first reader of *Write Me A Love Story*, helping me with your valuable feedback and keeping a check on the progress. Richa, you know how much I love discussing creative ideas with you. You are a darling.

To my editor Swati Daftuar for wonderfully cleaning the mess I had made in the manuscript. For coming up with the very title of this book. And above all, for taking the risk of editing a love story in which an editor has fallen in love with the romance author whose work she is editing. I am sorry you were not given a choice on whether you would want to edit such a book or not. And I am glad you were not, because the book reads so well to me. ☺

To Amit Malhotra, for designing this fabulous, fabulous cover. God! I am in love with it. It's like seeing the idea in my head come true and wrap my love story. Thank you, Amit.

To Shabnam Srivastava, for being always a text away and executing the marketing and promotion activities for this book. I admire how fast you respond and the zeal with which you work.

To the rest of the team at HarperCollins India. I hope this will make you all feel proud.

About the Author

Ravinder Singh is a bestselling author. *Write Me A Love Story* is his eighth novel. He has edited and compiled three crowd-sourced anthologies as well. His work has sold more than 3.5 million copies. After having spent most of his life in Burla, a very small town in western Odisha, Ravinder is currently based in Gurgaon. He has an MBA from the renowned Indian School of Business. His eight-year-long IT career started with Infosys and came to a happy ending at Microsoft where he worked as a senior program manager. One fine day, he had an epiphany that writing books is more interesting than writing project plans. He called it a day at work and took to full-time writing. He has also started a publishing venture called Black Ink (www.BlackInkBooks.in), to publish debut authors. Beyond his love for words, Ravinder is a fitness freak. You can reach out to him at his Instagram handle @ThisIsRavinder or write to him at itoohadalovestory@gmail.com